Booth Moffett
Tulsa, Okla
10/15/87

CATALOGUE

A Novel

GEORGE MILBURN

DAVENPORT PRESS LTD.

NEW YORK

Library of Congress Cataloging-in-Publication Data

Milburn, George, 1906-1966.
  Catalogue.

Originally published: New York : Harcourt, Brace, 1936.
  Bibliography: p.
  I, Title.
PS3525.I46C38   1987   813'.52   87-5432
ISBN 0-940827-00-X (alk. paper)

Also by Geoge Milburn

OKLAHOMA TOWN

NO MORE TRUMPETS

JULIE

THE HOBO'S HORNBOOK (ed.)

FLANNIGAN'S FOLLY

HOBOES AND HARLOTS

George Milburn
1906-1966

INTRODUCTION

C ATALOGUE, considered by most critics to be the best of the three novels written by Oklahoma native, George Faries Milburn (1906-1966), was originally published 50 years ago by Harcourt, Brace and Co., Inc. The novel generally met with a good critical reception, though some critics who knew his short stories well were somewhat disappointed. CATALOGUE sold 3,000 copies in hard cover, a respectable sale in 1936-37.

The work chronicles the events in a small Oklahoma town following the arrival on the same train one hot August day (1930?) of both the Sears Roebuck and Montgomery Ward "Fall - Winter" catalogues. "It's a hard, raucous, accurate series of tales and sketches held together by a few strands of plot," wrote F. T. Marsh in his review in *The New York Times* of September 20, 1936. Noting that the book gave "the strong flavor of the town and country and its people," Marsh said, "It doesn't take Milburn many words, or, apparently, much laboring to knock off these people to perfection or to knock together a story about any one of them."

And some 70 characters find their place in CATALOGUE, with a score of these receiving deft characterizations as the primary actors in this small town drama. Postmaster Shannon ["He stood in front of the plate-glass doors, fumbling with his keys. His image looked out at him: a straight, stocky old man with pleasant gray eyes and a firm jaw. His panama hat, colored like old meershaum, was pushed back on his moist crinkled fore head, showing his tough mop of white hair. He had on black sateen sleeve guards, elbow-length, in place of a coat, but even in August he wore a clean starched wing collar knotted with a black string tie.] is the central, and the most appealing adult character, about whom much of the action revolves and who many believe was modeled on the author's father. Hollywood once optioned CATALOGUE as a vehicle to star Bing Crosby as Postmaster Shannon but the movie was never made.

Then one finds the wide array of characters who abound in any small town, particularly an Oklahoma town viewed by one as perceptive as Milburn (who quickly dropped his middle name): W. S. Winston, the paunchy town banker, who cares not one whit about sickness among the poor so long as he can defeat a sanitary sewer bond issue which will raise his property taxes; Eagle Catoosa, the oil wealthy Indian who drives a red Packard and exerts his sexual powess on the Widow Holcomb and the teen-age daughter of Ira Pirkle, the filling station owner; "Swede" Ledbetter, the weekly newspaper editor, who rallies the local merchants in a futile attempt to stop the locals from making catalogue purchases; young Ledbetter, whose time payment purchase of Montgomery Ward's Hawthorne Speed Model Cherry Red bicycle, provides some of the best action and writing in the book; and Sylvester Merrick, the black porter in "Double S." Winston's bank, who is poignantly evoked in one of the novel's darker threads.

A successful young short story writer before the publication of CATALOGUE, Milburn may have had the success of his first novel diminished by his reputation. Writing in the *New Republic,* October 7, 1936, Hamilton Basso said, "CATALOGUE falls short of its most excellent intentions. It contains a number of interesting episodes, and a few very funny ones, but as a novel, coming from a writer of Mr. Milburn's talent, it is extremely disappointing."

Yet CATALOGUE is more than a series of short stories. It is, indeed, "a fictitious prose tale of considerable length, in which characters and actions professing to represent real life are portrayed in a plot." (*Webster's Dictionary*). Perhaps had

Milburn burst on the literary scene first with CATALOGUE, Basso and other critics who were of similar opinion may have been able to view the work as a novel-not as a series of short stories strung together by the device of mail order catalogues.

Some two years before the publication of CATALOGUE, H. L. Mencken, who was first to introduce Milburn's talents to the national scene, wrote to a friend: "What has become of George Milburn I don't know. I agree with you thoroughly that he has a very genuine talent. Moreover, he is not only good at fiction, but also the writing of articles. I used to print him in *The American Mercury* whenever I could get hold of any of his stuff. Unfortunately, he is somewhat eccentric. Once he showed up in New York with a wife, a baby and a goatee. The wife and baby seemed lawful and reasonable, but the goatee gave me such a shock that I persuaded him to chop it off. He then seemed to be in some danger of falling into the Greenwich Village orbit. What has become of him since I don't know. His book of short sketches, *Oklahoma Town,* is one of the best things of this sort ever done. [*The New Mencken Letters,* pp. 313-314, The Dial Press, 1977.]

Mencken first published Milburn's "Tales from Oklahoma" in the 1929 November issue of *The American Mercury* and continued to publish his stories there until August, 1933, shortly before Mencken retired from the magazine.

Born at Coweta, then in the Indian Territory of Oklahoma, on April 27, 1906, George Milburn was to etch in humor and in acid comment the sharp contrasts and inconsistencies of American life as he observed it in small towns of Oklahoma. Although he lived at times in Chicago, New York City, New Orleans and Hollywood, he wrote almost nothing about these places or their inhabitants. Neither did he write of his experiences while living in Majorca or England on a Guggenheim fellowship.

The son of a lawyer, Downey Milburn, who later became

a postmaster, and Etta Faries, a native of Pilot Mountain, North Carolina, where her father kept a general store, George Milburn was of Irish, Spanish, Scotch and German ancestry. He had one sister, Mary, and one brother, Sam, who was three years younger than George. One other child of the Milburns had died at the age of ten. George early showed a bent for writing, beginning to write stories at the age of five when he entered school. He showed his early interest in journalism by working as a printer's devil for the *Coweta Times Star* at the age of 11. He remained at home, where he was greatly influenced by his father who read to him regularly from *Gulliver's Travels, Robinson Crusoe, Don Quixote* and other classics, until he finished high school at the age of sixteen. He had left home for one school year, to live with his "Aunt Pink" and "Uncle Jack" in Linneus, Missouri, where the school was considered to be better. "Aunt Pink" was Florence Nightingale Milburn, the sister of his father. "Uncle Jack," Clarence St. Elmo Swinney, had married "Aunt Pink's" sister. After the sister's death, "Aunt Pink" and "Uncle Jack" continued to live in the Milburn family home. They never married.

Just out of high school, George was fired from his job as a messenger and obtained his first newspaper assignment, covering National Guard exercises in 1922 at Fort Sill for the *Pawhuska Daily Capital.* Milburn's 500-word story of the troop train to Fort Sill, its "plastered" citizen soldiers and their visceral disturbances astounded the editor and the piece gained recognition as a local classic. The keen observation and reporting skills exhibited in this first assignment helped to get Milburn a reporter's job at *The Tulsa Daily Tribune,* a paper for which he also had written as local correspondent during his senior year at high school.

However, at seventeen he enrolled at the University of Tulsa, the first of several colleges he was to attend over the next several years, with time out for newspaper jobs and travels around the country, studying as an English, journalism or anthropology major or as a general studies student. In his early teens, Milburn had first succumbed to the wanderlust that was to mark most of his creative life, riding first in the caboose of a cattle train to Kansas City and a hog train to St. Louis. He was fascinated by trains. In a letter to "Aunt Pink" written December 8, 1936, in which he told her that CATALOGUE was scheduled for adaptation as a Broadway play and that he hoped to visit in Linneus on his way to New York, he wrote "Of course we are all eager to see you and Uncle Jack again – but I am made doubly eager by your telling me that Mr. Hoffman has arranged for me to ride an engine cab to Kansas City. It would be an extraordinary experience for me and I wouldn't miss it for anything."

After two years at the University of Tulsa, Milburn transferred to Oklahoma A. & M. at Stillwater in September, 1925, where he was editor of the college humor magazine, *The Aggievator*. But growing restless again and also being short of funds required for school, he made his way to Chicago where for two years he supported himself by writing and compiling 20 or more "Little Blue Books" for Haldeman-Julius. He also put together the material for *The Hobo's Hornbook*, his first published book. From Chicago he bummed his way to New York City where he first saw Greenwich Village and knew real hunger even while his imagination was fired by the heady atmosphere of the 20's Village life.

Leaving New York, he passed a few months at Commonwealth College where he both wrote and earned money by helping to lay stones for the library fireplace, and then, free as a migratory bird, rode into New Orleans on Thanksgiving Day, 1927, on the blinds of an Illinois Central train.

His appetite for the life of a literary bohemian whetted by his stay in Chicago and Greenwich Village, Milburn spent almost a year in New Orleans, where, as he felt was proper, he lived in an attic in the French Quarter, loaded bananas, sold racing forms at Fairgrounds Park, wrote and sold fillers to the pulps and utilized his skills as a typist for William Slavins McNutt and James Hopper, popular novelists of the day, among others. He also worked briefly on the *New Orleans Item-Tribune.* He met Roark Bradford and Oliver La Farge and other members of the New Orleans literary set. A member of this group, John McClure, a fellow-Oklahoman and the book review editor of the *Times-Picayune* knew Mencken and was to provide the introduction which led to Milburn's work first appearing in *The American Mercury.*

In 1928, upon learning of his father's serious illness, Milburn gave up the pleasures and struggles of life in New Orleans and returned to Oklahoma. His father recovered, Milburn resumed his education at the University of Oklahoma in Norman.

A fellow student there remembered Milburn as "a small, slightly freckled-faced young man dressed in white linens, who, given a job on *The Oklahoma Daily* as a general utility worker, turned out "features and news stories of much wit and vigor." [Savoie Lottinville, *The Sooner Magazine,* Vol. VI, No. 9, June 1934, pp. 206-207]. When the position of humor columnist became available, Milburn began his column "Hear and Their" to the delight of the students who termed it the "morning bomb."

Pursuing his studies as an unclassified student, Milburn also wrote his daily humor column, at night read galley proofs in the composing room of *The Oklahoma Daily,* stoked the furnace and in odd moments continued to work on the short stories he had begun in New Orleans. He was sending the stories out to publications, receiving rejection slips that were encouraging to him in their critical comments.

In the Spring of 1929, having married Vivien Custard that January, "the prettiest co-ed I could find," he took over the job putting out the student supplement which appeared weekly in the *Cleveland County Democrat News,* receiving more pay and quickly building a large readership for his "Hear and Their" column in the supplement. At the end of the Spring semester, he accepted a job as proof reader for the University of Oklahoma Press, re-wrote stories at hand and wrote new tales. That Autumn his efforts were rewarded when Mencken bought three of the stories for *The American Mercury.*

Some six years later, Lottinville wrote of Milburn: "To those who knew him in his student days, he was an enigma. The fault was more theirs than his, perhaps. In those days of Hoover prosperity, few young people brought up in the 'rugged individualism' could understand one of their own years who complained of the injustices of poverty, the folly of war, and the smugness of respectability. Milburn was, perhaps, what one of his friends called him, a vindicative sentimentalist. The assertion is partly true and partly false—if anything it errs on the side of severity. Milburn was simply, deeply and consistenly humanitarian." [*The Sooner Magazine,* supra.]

Three stories, "Pete Williams," "Beulah Huber," and "The Holy Roller Elders," appeared in *Folk-Say,* I, a collection of regional miscellany edited by B. A. Botkin, then a young English instructor at the University of Oklahoma. These and other stories amounting to nearly two dozen in all appeared in *The American Mercury* over an 8-month span. Most of these, together with other stories, made up OKLAHOMA TOWN, published in 1931.

Other major magazines of the day, including, *Vanity Fair, Harper's, The Saturday Evening Post, Scribner's, Collier's Equire* and *The New Yorker* published Milburn's short stories.

Botkin has written, "It must not be thought that because, on occasion, he flayed Babbittry and Rotary, George was simply a hick baiter. His stories and articles (including 'Poesy in the Jungle' and 'The Sage of Tishomingo') stood on their own merits as Americana, in the American language. . . . . By

the age of twenty three then, he had definitely arrived. With
the publication of his second collection of stories, *No More
Trumpets,* in 1933, he had considerably widened his range
and his market, (and from his first stage of uncovering 'bright
episodes' he had passed to his second stage of setting them
'into an interesting tale.' In spite of a certain slickness that
began to appear along with the suppling of his technique, the
best stories in *No More Trumpets and Other Stories* were still
sufficently close to his earlier material and manner to prove
that George would never be entirely happy or successful very
far from them. In three of these stories — 'A Pretty Cute Little
Stunt,' 'The Fight at Hendryx's,' and 'Heel, Toe a 1, 2, 3, 4'
— all employing the device of a narrator and the methods of
oral narration, he showed himself equally at home in the
common speech (for the rhythm as well as the idiom of which
his ear is as perfect as Ring Lardner's), folk speech (as tall as
the tale itself), and hobo parlance. In his own style he is always
freely, naturally and inoffensively colloquial; and it is his art
of casual narrative in the oral tradition as well as his use of folk
and popular materials that for me constitutes his real importance as a short-story writer." (*The Saga of George Milburn,*
unpublished manuscript 4/3/1938)

Milburn's stories were (and continue to be) printed in
anthologies. Translations appeared in French and German
journals and his stories were printed in English magazines.

He spent the summer of 1932 at Yaddo, the summer of 1933
at Triuna Island, Lake George, the guest both years of the Trask
Foundation. Following two years in the East, with winters in
Provincetown and in Connecticut, he and Vivien and their
daughter Janet made a brief visit in the fall of 1934 to
Oklahoma before sailing for Spain and Majorca, Milburn
having won a coveted Guggenheim fellowship. His stories had
appeared in the annual collections of best short stories com-
piled by E. J. O'Brien in 1931, and 1932 and 1933. *No More*

Trumpets, consisting of 18 stories, was published in September 1933. The Guggenheim grant came as a result of his growing fame as a short story writer.

The Milburns stay in Majorca was cut short by Vivien's illness. She and Janet returned to her parents in Oklahoma where George joined them in the spring of 1935 after a brief sojourn in England. Milburn's beloved father also died while he was abroad on the fellowship. For whatever reason, Milburn wrote nothing that drew on his experiences while in Majorca and England — neither fiction nor non-fiction.

After spending some months with his wife's family, George and Vivien decided to settle on a farm in the Ozarks. They selected a 25-acre place on Big Sugar Creek, near Pineville, Missouri. Here George worked on the final pages of CATA-LOGUE in a one-room cabin near the main house. These were happy days for the Milburns, with their own house and garden and their own wood and water. In a letter of June 18, 1936, to "Aunt Pink" and "Uncle Jack," Milburn wrote:

> . . . I am so eager to have you both see what a pretty place we have here and for you to enjoy it. Of course we don't have it anything like we want it yet - that will take time and money - but we have made some improvements - have 16 fine fruit trees set out and have done about $200 worth of painting and repairing this Spring.
>
> . . . A person could almost live on nothing a week down here there is so much game and fish and wild fruit. As a matter of fact some of these natives do live right off the land.
>
> . . . I got my novel called CATALOGUE off to the publishers May 15 and it's to be published in September. I have fantastic hopes of the movies buying it for $15,000 and our having some money

at last. This being a poor man is getting mighty old with me I can tell you. If we had say $10,000 to put out on this place we could make it a paradise.

Some extra money was earned from parts of CATALOGUE which had been sold to *Harper's, Southern Review, Collier's* and *Esquire.* George was to continue this practice, as Malcolm Cowley noted a few years later:

> . . . The essay had lengthened to the point where no magazine of general circulation would be willing, at the time, to print the whole of it. Accepting the fact, I did the best I could. I beefed it.
>
> The term is one that I first heard from George Milburn, the author of CATALOGUE, an entertaining first novel about an Oklahoma town. His friends waited for a second novel, but it didn't appear. When I asked him about it, he looked unhappy.
>
> "I was spending the winter on Cape Cod,' he said, 'and I had the book pretty near finished. Then I wanted a pair of riding boots, so I cut off a chunk of it and sold it to *The New Yorker.* There was a bill I owed at the store, and I cut off another chunk. Whenever I needed cash I sold a piece of that novel. It was like I had a steer hanging in the woodshed and was always cutting off steaks. By the end of winter, Jesus, I'd beefed the whole novel.' [*The Faulkner-Cowley File* by Malcolm Cowley, New York: The Viking Press, 1966, pp. 20-21]

While living on the farm, Milburn wrote "The Road To Calamity,'' mainly autobiographical, which appeared in the *Southern Review* in 1936. Royalties from CATALOGUE and his other fiction being insufficient to support him and his family — Hollywood electing not to buy CATALOGUE for a movie — Milburn accepted an offer to collaborate with Allan Seager in the writing of "Scattergood Baines," a radio show that was broadcast five days a week. He continued to write for this show until June, 1941, and probably earned more money from this work that he did from his other writings combined. Also in the early 1940's, Milburn travelled between Hollywood and Pineville, writing scripts for Paramount, Warner Bros., and Twentieth Century Fox. He moved with his family to Hollywood in 1942. After the outbreak of World War II, he also wrote for the Office of War Information.

His novel *Flannigan's Folly* was published in 1947 and his only other novel, *Julie,* loosely based on Chaucer's "The Miller's Tale," was published in 1956. His creative days essentially were over by the advent of World War II. Milburn moved from Hollywood, where his wife had filed for divorce, to New York in December, 1948. The divorce became final in 1949, his wife Vivien retaining custody of their two children, Janet and Steve.

Milburn worked for a short period in 1949 for *The New York World-Telegram.* He also worked as a receptionist in the emergency room of St. Vincent's Hospital in Greenwich Village. Paramount about this time took an option on CATALOGUE, with the expectation of having Bing Crosby play the role of Postmaster Shannon but the movie was not made. Also that year he married Mary Sullivan and they lived for a time in Allentown, Pennsylvania, where they both worked for Rodale Press, publisher of *The Organic Farmer.*

Returning to New York and Greenwich Village, Milburn wrote articles and taught creative writing at a division of New York University. Late in 1958, he took a job as a file clerk with the Motor Vehicle Bureau of the State of New York. Later, he transferred to the Workmen's Compensation Board. In 1960 he was first diagnosed as having arteriosclerotic heart disease.

While at work in October, 1963, he suffered a heart attack. The following June he underwent heart surgery. In early September, 1966, he complained of severe abdominal pains and was admitted to St. Vincent's Hospital where he died September 22, 1966.

Richard Gehman, writing shortly after Milburn's death in 1966, said, "George never was well-known, except to other writers. To the ones who did know him, he was something of a legend.

". . . By 1946-1947, when he and I first met, he seemed to all us younger fellows a disillusioned man. We had been told by older men that he had been spendidly full of spirit. He had been told that he would be a major talent, but when his things were published and were esteemed by critics, they did not sell enough to support him and his family. It must have been terrible for George to face the realization that his trivial efforts, on radio, brought him more than the stories and books into which he put his main strength and his soul.

"Too many writers are recognized for what they were after they are gone. I hope that one of these days someone recognizes George Milburn for the excellent talent that was his—the way-down country talent, the talent that gravitated toward derelicts, the talent for understanding human beings no matter what their misfortunes had brought them to. One of these days there will be a George Milburn revival, just as there was one for a friend of his, Nathanael West. It is a shame that George will not be around to see it." [*Chicago Tribune* Books-Today, Oct. 23, 1966.]

It is hoped that this new edition of CATALOGUE, the novel having been out of print for many years, will in a modest way initiate such a revival.

November 1986   Louis Davenport Bailey

CONTENTS

CONTENTS

CATALOGUE

Six thousand tons of paper . . . whirling through great power presses . . . using seven hundred and fifty pounds of ink an hour. More than a thousand printers . . . working night and day. Machines with great mechanical fingers sorting, gathering, and binding papers into books. . . . Four hundred artists and camera men making thousands of illustrations. . . . A great battery of two hundred typewriters clicking out the true story of value. . . . And behind these facts other things you cannot see. . . .

THE CATALOGUES came in one August afternoon on the 5:45. The 5:45 stayed at the depot twelve minutes, eleven minutes longer than usual. The railway postal clerk had all the mail bags ricked up in front of the mail-coach door, but it took eleven minutes to load the catalogues on Fivefinger Earp's truck. The conductor stood by with a big gold watch in his hand, timing them.

The catalogues did not come in without forewarning. A month or so earlier Postmaster Shannon had been sent the mail order companies' long, purple-stenciled rolls of names and addresses for correction. There had been a time when they had made him gifts —such things as 845B6455, the self-filling fountain pen, or 18K1822½, the genuine steerhide billfold,

3

each with his name handsomely embossed in gold—for his courtesy. But nowadays they simply paid him sixty-five cents for the hour he spent in going over their mailing lists. It was a favor Postmaster Shannon was glad to do anyway. It saved time and work to have few duplications or returns among the heavy catalogues.

Although Postmaster Shannon knew that the Fall-and-Winter catalogues were to be expected any day, and the R.F.D. carriers knew that there was no getting round the catalogue delivery, and everybody had a notion that it was getting about time for the new catalogues, their coming was as surprising and exciting as it would have been if the catalogues had not been expected at all.

That much mail came only once a year. The Christmas rush was nothing to compare with it. The Spring-and-Summer catalogues were thinner and lighter. That year the Sears Roebuck and the Montgomery Ward catalogues all came in on the same mail. That was extraordinary. It made an even bigger load than usual.

When the mail clerk heaved the last squared bag out on the gray stack in Fivefinger Earp's truck, the grumpy little conductor stopped chewing his white mustache, snapped his watch lid to, and threw up his gold-braided arm to give the high ball. The throbbing locomotive let off two long blasts, spewed a low fog of steam, and the three-coach train began moving out at once. The conductor swung himself up on the steps of the Jim Crow car. The railway postal clerk tossed out two thin lock pouches that held the first-class mail. Fivefinger Earp caught them neatly by their leather-strapped necks.

Fivefinger Earp, who hauled the mail between the depot and the post office half a mile away, had only one hand. The right sleeve of his hickory shirt was pinned back to his shoulder in a double flap folded at his elbow. He stood holding the two thin mail pouches in his one hand, with the sweat stain under his left arm twice as large as the sweat stain under his other arm, watching the last coach ball the jack toward Muskogee. The sun, far down, made a hot glint on the long bright rails.

A thick farm boy in blue overalls scuffed across the splintery freight platform. He jumped down beside the ironpipe hitch-rack where two drowsy mules stood whisking flies.

A pock-faced man buttoning his pants stepped from behind a board wall marked *Gents* and limped over to a Dodge sedan that had lettered in red chalk on its windshield: *Jitney to Town, 25c.*

The farm boy spoke to him as he walked by: "Hidy, Spike!"

"Hi, Homer," he mumbled, going on toward the car.

5

Homer called after him, "How's the new baby over to you' all's house, Spike?"

"Died last night," Spike Callahan said without turning his thin bitter face.

"Gosh, that's too bad!" Homer said blankly to himself as he untied the mules. He climbed into the gray wagon and began jerking on the lines, bawling as he turned the mules away from the station, "Haw! You, Nig! Haw! Git outa that, Dude!"

Fivefinger Earp, a nimbus round his blond-stubbled jaws, kept squinting down the track at the last coach growing small. The wobbling, rust-framed end of it raised a faint dust cloud from the white chat roadbed.

Spike Callahan, the jitney driver, stepped on the starter of his Dodge sedan and roared off with his cut-out open, scattering gravel. Not a single passenger had got off the 5:45. Everyone was traveling by bus these days.

The truck driver woke up when he heard the jitney drive off. His weight-sagged truck stood ended to the empty track. He walked round to the cab and tossed the two lock pouches in on the ruptured oil-cloth seat.

Fivefinger reached into the pocket of his hickory shirt and got out a sack of Bull Durham. He flicked a cigarette paper off the pad, creased it with his thumb and forefinger, and opened the sack with his teeth. Holding the tobacco sack in the crotch of his

6

half-arm, he jiggled it, filling the paper trough with dry flakes. He rolled a cigarette with a snapping motion of his thumb and forefinger, licked it, and held it straight up while he caught the round paste-board tab on the yellow drawstring between his lips. He pulled the tobacco sack shut and tucked his chin to drop it down into his shirt pocket. He felt along his hat band for a match.

Harry Conklin, the Katy depot agent, a chunky little man with a stringhalt step, came out of the sanded, green-painted depot carrying a telegram. He slid the door of the freight house to, snapped on the padlock, and started off down the cinder platform.

"That ort to be a big enough mail to suit you, Fivefinger!" he said loudly, pausing by the truck.

Fivefinger Earp bent his neck and lighted his cigarette. "Yeowp, I'll say it is," he said. "It's the catalogues come in."

"Well, that's a load of 'em all right. But it still ain't nothing like it was before they put in these here hardsurface roads. Why, I recollect, when Old Pete Dunn was hauling mail in the hotel bus, he used to have to make two or three trips to get 'em over to town."

"Nawp, I don't guess they're putting out as many of the big ones as they used to. Mr. Shannon tells me that they're putting out more of these here little special catalogues ever' so often. But it sure looks

7

like these here would be enough to keep ever'body in strikin' paper for a while, don't it?"

Fivefinger Earp grinned slowly and Harry Conklin tittered.

"How many you estimate you got on there, Fivefinger?"

"Better than a ton, I reckon."

"I mean, how many catalogues?"

"Well, let's see. I'd have to do some figuring to tell you, Harry. Them Number 2 slip pouches will hold twenty catalogues each. I counted twenty-six Number 2's. That'd be twenty times twenty-six is—"

"Four hunderd and— No! Forgot to carry my one. *Five* hunderd and twenty, 'y goddie!"

"And nine Number 3 pouches. Them holds ten each. Ten times nine is ninety. That's dang nigh a thousand catalogues, Harry."

"Six hunderd and ten, I make it."

"Yeowp. I guess that's right. You headed for town? Git in and I'll carry you over."

The depot agent climbed into the truck cab. Fivefinger leaned in and turned on the switch.

"I got a telegram going over to Double S Winston's," Harry Conklin said. "That ornery Tom of his is wiring home for money again."

Fivefinger Earp said, "Well, I guess Old Double S has got it to put out," as he reached down and twirled the Ford crank.

8

"When it's anything for him or his family, he has," Harry Conklin said. The engine gave three phlegmy pants. Fivefinger came round and put it on the magneto. "Goose her for me," he said.

Harry Conklin pulled out the choker wire and Fivefinger spun the crank and the engine banged. Black smoke rose up about the quivering mound of dingy, ridged mail sacks as the Ford truck churned out of the graveled depot yard in low.

HOW TO SAVE SALES TAX

State Sales Taxes do not apply to merchandise shipped from one state to another. The sale and shipment of such merchandise is Interstate Commerce. If your state has a Sales Tax, you pay no tax on goods ordered from another state. If our mail order house to which you send your order is in a different state from yours, omit any State Sales Tax.

THE Conchartee County *Democrat*, as usual, was a day late in going to press. R. W. E. ("Swede") Ledbetter, its energetic editor, was helping Red Currie, the linotyper, bolt forms in the flatbed press. Hot August sunlight was striking in through two grimy back windows and the rear of the *Democrat* shop was like an oven. Editor Ledbetter, holding his blackened hands spread away, dabbing with his elbows, kept trying to push his rope-colored forelock up from over his sweat-sticky spectacles. Red Currie had just pied the Whipple Mercantile Company's quarter-page ad, and R. W. E. Ledbetter had almost reached the end of his patience.

Waldo Ledbetter, Junior, came dashing in at the front door, waggling a red gasoline can, his short bare legs thumping against the oversize, ink-stiffened canvas apron he had on. Gasoline was sloshing out of the spout as he ran. A black smear streaked one side of Waldo's startled, wide-eyed face.

"Gosh, papa!" he shrilled as soon as he was in the door. "You ought to come look!"

R. W. E. Ledbetter jumped and dropped the key with which he had been tightening a form. "Don't holler at your papa like that!" he cried. "You ort to have better sense!"

"But, gee whiz, papa, just go take a look at the load of mail they're bringing over from the depot. About a million bags of mail. They got such a big load they're stalled out in front here."

Red Currie went on tightening a lug. Editor Ledbetter poked at his pale forelock with an elbow and yelled, "You git on back yonder and finish cleaning that job press like I told you to."

Waldo moved off slowly. "Yes, but, papa, a whole truck *load*, filled up with mail. It'd make a piece for the paper."

"If you don't quit running in here storying to me, I aim to cut me a hickory and wear you out! I'll break you of that lying habit if it's the last thing ever I do!" the editor said angrily, stamping his feet toward his small son.

Waldo hurried on back to the job press, his smudged face puckering. "Papa, I'm telling the truth this time, honest I am," he whimpered. "If you don't believe there's about a thousand sacks of mail coming in today, just go look out front there and you'll see."

11

Editor Ledbetter turned and looked toward the front windows. He could see the truck standing there in the street. A dozen men were clustered round it. He sauntered up to the front door, stretching his neck to get a better look. Then he went outside.

"What you'd ort to do, Fivefinger," an onlooker was saying, "is turn 'er around and back 'er up. She'll take that grade in reverse easy."

"If he'd coast back a piece and get a little start on it, he could make it all right. This here Broadway grade ain't sich a steep grade," another loafer put in.

"What's going on, boys?" R. W. E. Ledbetter called pleasantly.

"The catalogues have come in!" one man shouted.

"A whole truckload of Monkey Ward catalogues!"

"Sears-Sawbuck catalogues, too! Earp's truck cain't make the grade, he's got on sich a heavy load."

"Swede, you better give this here a write-up in *The Weekly Struggle*."

"Yeowp, I guess we'll have to!" the editor said, scowling at the load of mail sacks. Back in the shop he heard Red Currie starting the gasoline engine. Above the explosions came the wheeze of the flat-bed press. He turned and hurried back into the shop.

"Hold it, Red, hold it!" he bawled above the noise. "We gotta rip out that front page! Stop the press and tear 'er out! I've got a Page One Must editorial to stick in there. Two column width, 14-point type, spread right down the center of the front page. I'll start shooting you back takes in just a minute."

"Good God, we ain't never going to get this rag out," Red Currie said sullenly as he shut off the engine.

Before the flatbed press had stopped gasping, Editor Ledbetter was hunched at his desk, rigid fore-fingers stabbing the keyboard of his dusty green Oliver. The pyramidal typebars clattered down on the ragged purple ribbon—

TO THE GOOD PEOPLE OF CONCHARTEE'S
TRADE TERRITORY:
Once more there has arrived at the Conchartee Post Office a whole truck load of mail order catalogues. This constitutes the Kansas City and Chicago mail order concerns' bid for your Fall and Winter trade.

He ripped the page out of the typewriter and called, "All right, Red! First paragraph. Take it away!"

Red boosted the heavy, type-filled form on the stone table and came up to the desk. The editor had twisted another sheet of paper into the typewriter and had started jabbing the keys at high speed again. Red picked the copy from the cluttered desk.

"Better leave that top line for me to hand-set, Red," R. W. E. Ledbetter said without looking up. "I want that in stud-horse type."

13

"What am I supposed to kill on the front page?" Red asked.

R. W. E. Ledbetter raised his long, sweat-streaked face.

"Kill?" he asked hazily.

"Yeah. We got to make room somehow."

"Oh, yes. Well, let's see. How about taking out that two-column box?—the one headed 'Can Conchartee Go Forward Without a Sewer System?' "

"That's the follow-up on that big editorial you had in last week's paper," Red said doubtfully.

"Yes, I know. I know," R. W. E. Ledbetter said, plucking his lower lip. "I hate to have that crowded out, too. Well, tie a string around it and maybe we can run it next week. If the city council passes a sewer bond resolution Monday night, it'll be just as timely next week as it is this, if not more so. But you hump yourself and set this piece I'm writing now. It's more important. I'll take care of the make-over on that front page when I get through here."

He bent to the typewriter again:

. . . only safe place to get Quality Goods at Honest Prices is from your Home Town Merchant.

Before you send off one red cent to these foreign concerns, the Conchartee County *Democrat* wants to ask you a few questions. Then if you feel like you can go ahead and send your money off without being a traitor

14

to your home community, GO TO IT! Now just ask yourself:

Who helps to support your ministers of the Gospel, helps to keep up your churches, lodges, etc.? Who does their part in paying taxes to support your roads, schools, law enforcement, etc.? Who hires Conchartee County labor?

Who has worked and slaved to build up this town so as you would have a place to come for amusement and a market for your produce, etc.? Who pays cash for your cotton, corn, cattle, hogs, poultry, etc.? Who pays highest cash prices cash or trade for your butter, hides, eggs, etc., and all country produce? Who extends you credit for food and clothing when you are waiting for a crop to come in and do not have the cash to buy with? Is it a K. C. mail order co.?

USE YOUR THINK TANK! Your HOME TOWN MERCHANT is the only one that does all these things for you. Why not honor HIM with your entire patronage by patronizing HOME INDUSTRY? Did your HOME TOWN MERCHANT ever show you a faked-up picture and make you read a mess of fancy description and then ask you to buy a "pig in the poke" the way these mail order companys do?

If you feel like you can answer these questions honestly by sending your money off to the millionaires of KANSAS CITY and CHICAGO, go right ahead. Don't let "ye ed" stop you. But then do not come bellyaching around about hard times here in Conchartee County when you have helped cripple the FAIREST, FRIENDLIEST little community in the U. S. A. by mailing off your money to fill the larders of some rich man 1000 miles away.

DON'T BE A DAMPHOOL!

KEEP HOME TOWN MONEY AT HOME!

"Nuf Sed!"

"I wish we could do a red-ink job on it, that's what I wish we could do," R. W. E. Ledbetter muttered as he pulled the last page out of his typewriter. "But we ain't got time for the extra run."

□ UNCLAIMED   □ UNKNOWN
□ FOR BETTER ADDRESS   □ DECEASED
□ MOVED—LEFT NO ADDRESS □ REFUSED
□ RETURNED PER MAILER'S REQUEST
□ NO SUCH POSTOFFICE IN STATE NAMED

POSTMASTER—*If not delivered in* 15 *days, please check reason for non-delivery and return to us.* RETURN POSTAGE GUARANTEED. *If Change of Address on File, notify us on* FORM 3547 *postage for which is guaranteed. In case of removal to another post-office, do not notify the addressee but hold the matter and state on* FORM 3547 *amount of forwarding postage required, which we will promptly furnish.*

A TOWN can have two or three of everything else. It can have two or three general stores, two or three filling stations, two or three hardwares, two or three meat markets, two or three barber shops, two or three drug stores, two or three chilli joints, two or three cotton gins. But they don't make a town big enough to have more than one post office.

"What kind of price you all got on one-cent stamps today, Mr. Shannon?" they ask, slapping a coin down at the stamp window.

"Five for a nickel today, Harve."

" 'Y goddie, if I don't reckon I'm going to have

to start me another post office in this town yit! What this here post office needs is a little competition!"

Then they both laugh, because it is a joke that nobody ever gets tired of. They know that there could not be more than one post office in town. And only one man at a time can be postmaster.

Most people think that as soon as a man gets to be postmaster all he has to do is settle his rump down in a swivel chair and watch the town come to him. He hires a couple of girls who have been off to Draughns' Business College in Muskogee, and they do the little work there is to be done. No one has any idea of how many things a postmaster has to see after back of the varnished oak partition with its pebbled-glass windows and its tiers of glass-paneled, gunmetal lock boxes. They all believe that a postmaster's work is done as soon as the post office windows are closed for the day.

When anyone tried to josh him about the way postmasters are supposed to spend their spare time, Postmaster Shannon always said mildly, "Why, we don't have time to read half the postal cards, much less the letters."

That afternoon he sat at his desk beside the broad front window, waiting for the 5:45 mail to come over from the station. It was after six o'clock and the stamp window, the general delivery window, the money order window, the parcel post window, all were closed. The two clerks were counting stamps and coins, marking numbers on the daily inventory form. Postmaster Shannon was running up the money order receipts on his desk adding machine.

The 5:45 had whistled out thirty minutes ago.

"Earp certainly is late tonight," Gladys Ferguson said at the stamp drawer. "He must of had a breakdown with that old truck of his."

Then Postmaster Shannon heard the noise. He looked out the plate-glass window and saw the loaded truck laboring toward the alley that led to the back door of the post office.

"Yonder come the catalogues," he said calmly to the clerks.

Gladys Ferguson stopped counting stamps. Elvira Draper dropped the tweezers with which she had started to change the date in the wooden-handled steel canceler. They both came running to the big front window just in time to see the swaying gray hill of mail sacks heave past and out of sight into the alleyway.

Gladys looked at Elvira and Elvira looked at Gladys. Their mouths gaped for a moment and their faces went blank with surprise. "Ah-o-o-uh!" they groaned together in elaborate dismay. Then they began shrieking with laughter and fell into each other's arms.

"I just had a feeling in my bones that that was what was keeping Earp—that the catalogues had

19

come in," Postmaster Shannon said gleefully. "But I didn't say anything."

Fivefinger Earp clanged open the steelbarred back door and walked in dragging a half-filled slipcord sack and carrying the two letter pouches. He slapped the lock pouches down on the smooth-worn separating table and grinned sheepishly.

"I sure enough brought you some mail tonight," he said. "My truck stalled on that grade whur you turn onto Broadway. This here is the Telsy *Tribune* sack. Three packages of parcel post. All the rest is catalogues."

Fivefinger went on out and unfastened the endgate on his truck. He hoisted one sack up on his right shoulder and pulled off another sack with his hand. Carrying one and dragging one, he went back and forth, and the gray stack grew in the rear of the post office.

"I suppose we had better stay and separate them tonight," Postmaster Shannon said. "But we won't put the notices in the boxes until tomorrow. That'll keep them from pestering us in the morning while we're separating the first-class mail and getting the newspapers up. Get the rural routes separated tonight, too, and the carriers can start taking them out right away."

Gladys Ferguson reached in the locks drawer and pulled out the master key at the end of its long brass

20

chain. She quickly unlocked the two pouches. She shook out about a dozen letter ties.

Elvira Draper slipped the cord on the other sack and dumped out two bundles of Tulsa *Tribunes*. She tossed one bundle into a lock bin for Cripple Lund, the newsagent. She ripped the wrapping off the other bundle and held the opened roll curving in one arm while she walked along the honey-combed inner side of the partition, mechanically stuffing newspapers into lock boxes.

"I wish Slemmons had been here to watch them come in," Gladys Ferguson said. "Won't he howl, though! He claims that Route Four gets twice as many catalogues as any of the others."

"Last year he took two weeks getting shut of his," Elvira said.

"Well, he'll have to get 'em out quicker this year," the postmaster said crisply. "Nothing causes patrons to complain like having their catalogues delayed. They'd rather miss their newspaper."

Postmaster Shannon sat on a stool sorting the first-class mail. He flipped the R.F.D. letters up into five pigeonholes and the town letters into a larger box. The clerks kept taking away handfuls, dealing them expertly without looking at the names on the boxes.

"Slemmons 'll have to have a truck," Elvira Draper said.

"Oh, no," Postmaster Shannon said. "He can get

21

a lot of catalogues in the back of that flivver of his. It shouldn't take him more than two trips to clean up his pile."

"Ah, Mr. Shannon, why don't we just leave them in the sacks until tomorrow? Me and Gladys can get them separated tomorrow when things is slack."

"No, sir-ee! You and Gladys go on to supper if you want to. I'll stay and separate the catalogues. The *Democrats* 'll be coming in tomorrow and we'll have plenty to do to get them up. Meanwhile the patrons will be here faunching for their Fall-and-Winter catalogues, and I don't propose to have the patrons disappointed."

He did not talk loudly enough for the townspeople, milling outside in the lobby, to hear. The three voices, muffled by the blank-windowed partition, came as the mysterious murmuring of an oracle.

Shoes scuffed on the cement floor, tobacco spit rustled in wastepaper barrels, throats were cleared, fingers drummed on the wooden window shelves, but there was little talk. People were too nervous with expectation.

Now and then, when a bit of white flicked into a lock box, one of them would stop pacing and step up to twiddle a combination, take out a letter, and clack the small door to. Or another would stop reading the afternoon paper and stoop to peer through a glass panel in an empty lock box with the door left ajar.

Cripple Lund poled his toy wagon up to the post office door with a sawed-off billiard cue. Two or three men stepped forward to lift him over the step. His steel wagon wheels rumbled through the lobby. He tilted open a lock bin and got his bundle of newspapers and handed out a few to those of his customers who were waiting in the postoffice lobby. He joined them.

A fat Indian wearing a broad white Stetson drove up out in front in a Packard roadster. He eased himself out of the cherry-colored car and came into the post office. He waited stolidly for a little while. Then he bent down to the letter drop. Talking through the slot in a husky barytone, he asked, "Mist' Shannon, have you got a gov'munt restricted lettuh foh Eagle Catoosa, hunh?"

"Not yet, Eagle. One here for Jackson Wacochee, though. You tell him to call for it if you see him."

Eagle Catoosa went out, but this exchange of words with the secret place emboldened the others. Throats were cleared, lips were wetted, people got ready to speak.

Meanwhile, at the back of the post office, in and out, in and out, went Fivefinger Earp. One sack gritting across the concrete floor, one sack thudding down from his shoulder, the gray pile growing.

"Mr. Shannon, you got ary a Mon'gom'ry Wahd catalogue there for me?"

"Not yet, Mrs. Tinsley. Won't be distributed till morning."

"Mr. Shannon, I was aimin' to go to Telsy first thing tomorrow morning, and I was wonderin' if I couldn't git my catalogue tonight?"

"Catalogues 're still in the sacks, Ira. It'll take us some while to get them unsacked, let alone sorted."

Wilbur S. Winston, the richest man in town, came into the postoffice lobby behind his paunch, walking with great dignity as if his belly were not a part of him at all. He turned the dial on Number 18, the Conchartee National Bank's lock drawer, and took out a large sheaf of mail.

The crowd in the lobby watched him in silence, but Cripple Lund was too simple to be awed. He wedged his thick shoulders forward and rolled up to hand the banker his afternoon paper.

"Mr. Winston," he said in a low voice, "I'm still waitin' to get some word on that little matter I was speakin' to you about the other day."

"Hmmm. That so, Lund?" W. S. Winston said absently, glancing at the headlines. He took out his watch.

"Mail all up, Mr. Shannon?" he asked in a gruff voice.

"All up, Mr. Winston."

Double S Winston followed his belly out of the post office. One by one the other townspeople followed Banker Winston. It was a ritual. Every night,

24

as soon as it was apparent that the mail was all up, when there was no longer any sound of letters clicking into lock boxes, W. S. Winston, on the outside, asked, "Mail all up, Mr. Shannon?" And Postmaster Shannon, on the inside, said, "All up, Mr. Winston." Then, filing out slowly, one by one, everyone followed Double S Winston out of the post office.

Only the dogged Ira Pirtle stayed on that night, waiting for his catalogue. He could hear the sounds back there, the zip of the metal catches on the slip-pouch cords, the pellmell thumps of the catalogues falling out of the sacks on the separating table, the swish and sough of empty canvas sacks flapping down. He could hear the voices droning:

"All this sack for Route Five."

"All this sack for Route Three."

"All this sack for town."

"Is C. R. Butts still on Route One?"

"C. R. Butts gets his general delivery now."

"James R. Sloat; what become of him?"

"Moved to Yellville, Arkansas, two weeks ago."

Thin dust floated up back of the partition, softening the electric glare, turning the unshaded light bulbs into milky little moons.

About nine o'clock Postmaster Shannon walked up to the front and snapped back the Yale lock on the partition door.

"Here's your Sears' catalogue, Ira," he said dryly, "and here's your Ward's."

CATALOGUE

Ira Pirtle, looking beyond the postmaster's shoulder, saw five brown pillars at the R.F.D. carriers' high desks. On the floor near the separating table lay a long rank of hard-packed edges, colored inserts striping the broad layers of gray with yellow and orange and green and pink. The catalogues looked nice, all tightly bound in their manila paper slipcovers.

APPROVED BY U. S. POSTMASTER GENERAL

The only type box approved for R.F.D. Routes. Required by United States Post Office Regulations. Heavy galvanized sheet steel construction through-out. Rustproofed aluminum finish for greater pro-tection. Weather-proof—snug-fitting, water-tight door. Top and sides strongly reinforced for greater strength. Double bottom with corrugated top—keeps packages dry in bad weather. About 23³⁄₁₆ in. long, 11 in. wide, 13⅜ in. high, inside measure. When requested we stencil your name on both sides and send you stencil—free of charge. Print Name Plainly. Shpg. wt. 28 lbs.

99F9449 .... $1.89

P OSTMASTER SHANNON came walking up the quiet street brushing his teeth with an elm twig. A fringe of tall ragweeds along the sidewalk grazed his baggy pantlegs damply as he passed. The road dust was still laden with dew. Not far ahead the naked August sun was rising out of the M. K. & T. railway cut. Its rays glinted on the nickel bows of his spectacles.

He had left home a little earlier than usual, be-cause he had the biggest day of the year before him.

27

He had worked late at the separating table the night before, but he was eager to get back and see the catalogues out that morning. He stepped lively for all his slight rheumatic limp.

A short way up the street the low brick post office stood shadowed by two-storied buildings that faced eastward on the courthouse square. Each end of its corrugated-iron front awning carried a modest tin sign:

UNITED STATES POST OFFICE #62571
THIRD CLASS
CONCHARTEE, OKLAHOMA

Postmaster Shannon paused at the edge of the shade and looked up at the sign nearest him. A patch of paint was missing. There was a large bright dent where the last two figures of the office number should have been.

"Now what do you reckon could have possessed the son-of-a-gun who did that?" he muttered to himself, stretching his leathery neck. "Throwing rocks at the United States Post Office sign just like it was an old patent medicine ad out on a barn some place! They'll be shootin' at it next; I wouldn't be surprised. It's a downright insult to the U. S. gov'ment, that's what it is. These toughs around here are going to learn to respect the gov'ment, if I have to teach 'em myself."

He moved on, muttering and clicking his tongue.

28

He stood in front of the plate-glass doors, fumbling with his keys. His image looked out at him: a straight, stocky old man with pleasant gray eyes and a firm jaw. His panama hat, colored like old meershaum, was pushed back on his moist crinkled forehead, showing his tough mop of white hair. He had on black sateen sleeve guards, elbow-length, in place of a coat, but even in August he wore a clean starched wing collar knotted with a black string tie.

He gazed into the dark glass and ran his fingers over a corner of his jaw, feeling a grizzled patch he had missed with his razor that morning in his haste. There was a scurrying noise in the gravel round the corner. He started and turned to see a lumpish young man in a Boy Scout uniform hurry out of the alley alongside the postoffice building.

"Hi, there, Bill Huggins!" the postmaster called. "What're you up to, boy scoutin' around this time of morning?"

Huggins plunged to a halt. His beefy face went so pale that the pimples on it stuck out like gooseberries. He was about seventeen years old. His uniform was tight on him, but there was an odd bulge in his shirt front. It gave him a napoleonic look. He jerked his faded khaki coat together and glanced furtively at the postmaster.

"Howdy, Mr. Shannon, howdy!" he blurted. The next moment he wheeled and fled.

Postmaster Shannon stared after the running boy.

Then he chuckled softly and turned to unlock the lobby doors.

"That lad needs to wear boxing gloves at night," he remarked sagely to his image in the glass. "That's what's ailing him."

He pushed open the doors, gathered up a small bunch of mail from the night letter-drop, and peered over his crescent-lensed glasses at the disordered lobby.

It was one of the duties of Art Smiley, the town marshal, to lock the lobby doors every night at ten o'clock. It seemed that wasn't early enough.

Someone, the evening before, had tipped over the wastepaper barrel in the center of the lobby. A clutter of wadded wrappers, torn newspapers, lavender smithereens of a love letter, slick red-printed folders with one-cent stamp seals unbroken, all darkly splotched with tobacco juice, lay strewn across the cement floor. Over at the wall desk an entire pad of money order application blanks had been painstakingly torn into paper lace. There had been scuffling or lounging against the big bulletin board. Its outer layer of onionskin legal notice manifolds was wildly rumpled, and though all the stout black government announcements were still in place, a lithographed recruiting poster, brilliant tropic background with army officers looking resolute in white linen uniforms, dangled by a single thumbtack.

30

Postmaster Shannon gazed at this slovenly scene with as much startled disapproval as he would have had if he had never seen it before.

"Downright disrespectful to the United States Gov'ment, that's what it is," he said aloud as he set the wastepaper barrel upright. " 'Y gunny, I'm going to have the patrons of this office understand that this post office represents the Federal Gov'ment in this town, and that it's got to be treated with the respect beholden to such, or else I'm going to know the reason why!"

Waggling his head, he let himself in through the varnished partition door. Back of the partition everything was neat and orderly. The manila-wrapped mail order catalogues, all ready to be delivered, stood in snug brown stacks. Early light fell gray through the translucent stamp windows and through a dingy, iron-barred clerestory above the long separating table.

The postmaster, his footsteps soft on the rubber matting runner, walked back to the steel entry cage where the midnight and five o'clock mail bags were already piled. He unlocked the iron door. An open flivver came chugging into the deserted alley and Earl Plunk, the Route One carrier, came in the back door just in time to help drag the mail sacks up to the separating table.

"Well, I wisht you'd look at what Santy Claus

31

brung us last night!" Earl said when he saw the stacks of catalogues.

"Yep, and all ready to go out again, Earl," the postmaster said proudly. "The girls and I worked until nearly nine o'clock last night getting them sorted."

The snaplock on the partition door clicked and Elvira Draper came in, yawning and sleepy-eyed. Gladys Ferguson got there a few minutes later. One by one the R.F.D. carriers' automobiles came clattering into the back alley. As each man straggled through the back door he had some exclamation to make about the catalogues.

"Lordy! Lordy! Lookie what the cats drug up and the kittens wouldn't eat."

"Well, sir, Mr. Shannon, if this here's the best you can do fer us, dogged if I ain't goin' to go right on back home and not drive my route today a-*tall!*"

Slemmons, the Route Four carrier, stopped in his tracks and scratched the hank of coarse black hair combed over on one side of his long peaked head. He had a pained look.

"Dag gunned if I don't get twict as many catalogues on my route as ary a one of you other fellers," he said sourly.

Up at the main separating table there was a whisper of shuffled letters and the tock of envelopes flicking into lock boxes. Everyone worked in silence for a while. The rural carriers stood dealing mail into the wire-bail slots of their tall route desks.

Slemmons came walking up to the front where Postmaster Shannon sat on his stool sorting the first-class mail. He had a catalogue with him.

"Mr. Shannon, here's this Birdie Hollinsworth. That's Orin Hollinsworth's womern."

"Well, isn't that right? Haven't you got Hollinsworth on Four?"

"Yes, in a way I have. Didn't I tell you about it, Mr. Shannon? See, Orin and Birdie set up housekeeping, right after they was married last Spring, out there on Winston's south forty, two mile west, and Orin put him up one of them old-style little nine-by-seventeen-inch boxes. I told him right then it wouldn't do. I says, 'Orin, that there size of a box is agin the P. L. & R.,' and I cited him to the part where it says we're not required to deliver mail to them little small-sized boxes no more if they've been put up since the new ruling. So I says to him that he'd have to get him a regulation-size box and put it up.' "

"That's right, Slemmons," Postmaster Shannon said briskly, quoting from memory, "Section 1058, P. L. & R.: 'Persons wishing to become patrons of rural routes shall provide and erect, at their own expense, standard boxes of the number two size, the manufacture of which has been approved by the Department. Standard box size is 23 and $\frac{5}{16}$ inches

33

long, 11 inches wide, and 13 and ⅜ inches high.'
So what did Hollinsworth say about it?"

"Well, Orin, he got hard with me, and said that box he had up was plenty big for all the mail he got. I told him it wasn't a question of that, but of obeying the postal laws and regulations. And, fact of the matter is, Mr. Shannon, Orin's womern, Birdie, seems like she's been doing a sight of ordering from the mail order houses lately. Sometimes she gets two or three packages a week. Course that box he's got up now won't take much of a package and most generally she comes down to the road to meet me. That's what's got me worried. Orin—seems like he's such a crazy-jealous man—I guess you heerd about, right after him and Birdie got married, him carving up on that oldest Tompkins boy one night at a pie supper out to Sunny Glade, just for—"

"You haven't been dragging your wings around Birdie, have you, Slemmons? Come clean now!"

"No, sir, Mr. Shannon, I ain't. That's just it. I'm scared she's stuck on me, though, because she's always down to the box to meet me. And I will say one thing, I never have give her no encouragement, and it worries me to have her always comin' to meet me like that, which she will do so long as she's got the excuse that that little old box Orin put up ain't big enough to take the packages she gits."

"All right, Slemmons. Leave Hollinsworth a notice that mail will be held at the post office until an approved R.F.D. box has been put up. Form Number 4233: Notice to Rural Patron."

"Well, I sort of hate to do that, Mr. Shannon. I hate to cause any ill feelings with Orin, because, like I say, he's a mean customer if ever he gits it in for anybody, and—"

"Slemmons, you're carrying the U. S. mail! Don't you realize what that means? You're under the protection of the Federal Gov'ment. As long as you're in your line of duty, nobody dare interfere with you. You heard what they did with those two country toughs that beat up an R.F.D. carrier over at Bull Wallow last Winter when he was driving his route. Sent 'em both to Leavenworth for a good long stretch."

"Yes, but, Mr. Shannon, how did that he'p the rural carrier after he'd done got beat up?"

"Don't argue with me about it, Slemmons," the postmaster snapped. "Send Orin Hollinsworth in here to me. I'll tell him that he's got to put up an approved box if he expects to keep on getting R.F.D. service. You tell Orin I want to see him the next time he comes to town."

"All right, Mr. Shannon. I'll tell Orin you said so. But I guess I might as well take Birdie's catalogue out today, because she'll most likely be down at the box asking about it. She got another package today, too. All I don't like about it is, Orin Hollinsworth being such a crazy-jealous man, and ever'body knows

35

what a flighty girl Birdie Keefer was before she got married and all."

"Never you mind Birdie. You get that Orin in here for me to talk to. We'll see what the U. S. Gov'ment amounts to around here. The way some of these patrons are beginning to act, you'd think it was just a one-horse business. I aim to put a stop to that kind of attitude toward the U. S. postal service in this town."

When the morning mail was all sorted, the carriers began packing out. The fronts of their high desks bristled white with newspapers, farm weeklies, and letters. The carriers worked hand over hand, taking down the mail they had put up a few minutes before, last boxes first, packing their big square leather pouches. They carried out armloads of catalogues.

Promptly at eight o'clock they shouldered their heavy pouches and trailed out to their cars. Their motors popped and sputtered in the yard back of the post office. One by one they rolled out of the alley, headed in five directions on their long daily rounds through the countryside.

Postmaster Shannon went over to the big steel safe to get the United States flag. He ran it up every morning at opening time. Each night at closing time the flag was folded methodically into a small blue triangle and was placed on top of the safe. But this morning the top of the safe was bare.

"Now I wonder where that flag has been put!" he said testily. "Have either of you girls seen the flag?"

"No, I haven't seen it, Mr. Shannon," Gladys and Elvira both said at the same time. Giggling, they hooked little fingers and pulled, making wishes.

"Lord, what a morning!" the postmaster groaned. "Which one of you brought the flag in last night?"

"Oh, Mr. Shannon!" Elvira gasped. "We forgot to bring in that flag last night. On account of us working so late, sorting the catalogues."

"The flag must've been out all night," Gladys said in an awed voice.

Postmaster Shannon hurried out the back door to see whether the flag was still up. The flagpole was bolted to the brick wall on the alley side of the building. He saw the halyard dangling loose from the pulley at the peak of the staff. He turned and went back into the office, white in the face.

"Someone has stolen the flag!" he announced.

"No!" cried Gladys and Elvira.

"It's an insult to the U. S. Post Office and it's an insult to the U. S. flag," he said grimly, "and nobody can get away with anything like that while I'm postmaster."

Gladys and Elvira stood stock-still with their mouths agape. They were all silent for a moment.

37

"Well, let's get these windows up," Postmaster Shannon said. "It's already five minutes after eight and the patrons are out there waiting for us to open."

They moved into their usual places. Elvira Draper stood at the money order window. Gladys Ferguson stood at the general delivery window. Postmaster Shannon stood at the parcel post window.

When they were all stationed, he gave a nod, and the three pebble-glass windows shot up as one.

CHARRED OAK KEGS

Made of tough white mountain oak. Close-fitting staves kiln dried and carefully shaped. Non-porous. Riveted hoops of heavy blue steel. Kegs with a ship. wt. of 35 lbs. or more are Not Mailable. Smaller sizes mailable. State size.

11F05740..*Cap. Gal.* 10..*Shpg.wt.* 21 *lbs.* $2.10

SLEMMONS, hunched at the wheel of his crumpled Ford, went jouncing out of town at a good speed. Route Four led west on the hardsurfaced section line, an oozy black strip lapping out across the sandhills.

His first stop was at the Widow Holcomb's box on the other side of the railway underpass at the outskirts of town. Slemmons let his engine idle in front of the neat white cottage while he reached down to his full mail pouch.

"Did you bring me my catalogue?" the Widow Holcomb called from the honeysuckle bower at one end of the front porch.

She lay in a gaudy hammock, taking her morning's ease. A screen door banged at the side of the house as a colored girl came to throw out dishwater on the parched grass. The widow was still living on the life insurance money she collected when

39

Charlie Holcomb, in haying season the year before, jumped out of a barn loft onto a pitchfork handle.

"I sure did bring your catalogue, Mrs. Holcomb —two of 'em!" Slemmons called back as he slipped two fancy envelopes, one addressed in Eagle Catoosa's feathery ornate hand, the other in Ira Pirtle's crabbed scrawl, into the fat crease made by the folded bulk of the two catalogues.

The Widow Holcomb came down the walk, her pink kimono parting at her plump bare ankles, a lacey boudoir cap pulled down over her ears. Slemmons eyed her covertly: a large handsome woman with ample flesh curving smooth and warm under a silken sheath. The unkind morning light traced fine wrinkles at the corners of her dark, heavy-browed eyes and a pad sagged under her chin. But when she let go the top of her kimono to unlatch the front gate, Slemmons caught a glimpse of her fine big bosom, and his hand was jittery as he gave her the mail. He jammed in his clutch and sped away, hardly acknowledging the widow's gold-flecked smile of thanks.

From there on his route was a thirty-mile circuit of stop and go: now at a bright, loaf-shaped box with neatly stenciled name; now at a rusty flat box at the end of a peeled hickory pole spanning the roadside ditch; now at a crossroads where a varied cluster of mail boxes, fixed with baling wire to an old buggy wheel, turned on an upright axle.

The heat waves flickered out ahead of the car like glass portières. Sudden spurts of hot air twirled little funnels of dust across the road and sent them rustling among scorched cornstalks beyond the barbwire fences. It was the eleventh week of the drouth.

All along the road broad cotton fields were beginning to be dabbed with white. The stunted bolls were opening rapidly, and families of sharecroppers, men, women, and children, white and black, were crawling down the hard-baked rows. They hitched at their long gray pick sacks and straightened up, one by one, to watch the mail carrier pass.

Two miles west of town Slemmons saw ahead a buckboard drawn up at a mail box waiting. He recognized Herman Gutterman's gray mare, and, coming near, the blowsy face of the old whiskey-maker, placid in the shade of a tattered black felt hat set jauntily.

Slemmons stopped his car and shut off the engine. Boiling water growled in the radiator.

"Mornin', Herman. What can I do you fer?"

"Howdy, Mr. Slemmons. I was wantin' a money order to Sears Roebuck this morning, Mr. Slemmons. I could take it to the post office jist as well, being as I'm headed fer town anyhow, but I seen you comin' and I 'lowed I'd jist pull up here and hand it to you. Seems like so much slips my mind now'days when I ain't got the old womern around to jog my mem'ry. And I shore want to git this order off today."

Slemmons opened his tin box and took out a carrier's receipt book and a pad of money order application blanks. Herman Gutterman handed over a brown, print-addressed envelope, unsealed.

"How much for, Herman?" Slemmons asked, scribbling on the money order application blank.

"It's wrote right there on the outside the envelope, Mr. Slemmons. Eight twenty-seven, ain't it? I'm orderin' me some more charred kags. The shiruff took him an ax and turned in and busted up ever' empty charred kag I had on my place that day last Spring when they took my old womern away. I aim to run me off a little batch next week and I'm short a couple of exter kags."

"That comes to $8.38, Herman. Eleven cents money order fee. And three cents more for the stamp makes it $8.41."

Herman peeled a $10 bill off a thin roll and handed it to the mail carrier. "Bessie is comin' home next week, Mr. Slemmons," he said proudly. "That's what part of this here order is—some little oddments I'm gettin' to surprise her with. And besides that I'm goin' to th'ow a real celebration fer her the evenin' she gits out. We're goin' to have a big square dance at our place."

"Is that so, Herman?" the mail carrier said, count-ing out change. "Is Bessie's sentence up a'ready? Why it don't seem like no more'n yestiddy that you was tellin' me about the shiruff ketching her."

"It shore don't seem like yestiddy to me, Mr. Slemmons. It seems like six year to me since the shiruff ketched Bessie. Six long months in the county jail, Mr. Slemmons. I kept tellin' Bessie she'd better be more particular about who she sold to, but she wouldn't mind. Then the shiruff got that middle Tompkins boy to come over here that afternoon last March when I was off from home, and they nabbed Bessie jist as she set him out a quart. Old Judge Throgmorton give her six months and a $50 fine. Course Bessie took it calm like she always does. She has crocheted her a counterpin since she's been in this time, and Mrs. Ferguson, the shiruff's wife, has been mighty nice to her. And I've did ever'thing I could to make her comf'table in there and to keep things up at home. Bessie has always been a good wife to me, but I jist never could learn her who to trust and who to suspicion."

"Yeah. Bessie's shore a big-hearted womern all right."

"Yes, sir, she shore is, Mr. Slemmons, and she has always been one to like a good time. Me and her both. So I aim to put on a real party fer her when she gits out next Friday and invite ever'body that keers to come. I thought I'd see about roundin' up

43

the dance music while I'm in town today. I want to git old Matt Keefer to do the fiddlin'—old Matt's the best dang fiddler that ever went a-fishin'—and maybe one of them Earp boys to play the guit-tar. But what I actually want is somethin' a little exter. What I want to git is a good accordeen player. You don't know of a good accordeen player I could git, do you, Mr. Slemmons?"

"Why, Tony LaFarge in there at the Sanitary Barber Shop—don't he play on the accordeen pretty good?"

"Well, now that you mention it, Mr. Slemmons, I guess maybe he does. I'll go see him about it. Now you and your wife be shore and come out next Friday night! We're goin' to have a high old time at my place."

"No, Herman, thank you jist the same. My old womern is a Hard-shell Baptist and we ain't been to a dance since the year we was married. The only way I could come would be to slip off and come."

"Shucks, cain't you change your old womern's mind? Anyhow, you all could come and par-take of the re-fresh-ments, couldn't you? It'll be a big time fer all."

Slemmons stepped on the starter and said above the motor's roar, "I'll think about it, Herman, but I reckon not. Like I said, my wife's dead set agin' dancin' of any kind. But, w' up, here, w' up. I got

44

to talkin' with you and I was about to drive off without handin' you your catalogue."

"Gosh, don't let me git your mind off your business that much, Mr. Slemmons," Herman cackled. "I was wonderin' if that wasn't the catalogues I seen in the back seat there."

Slemmons leaned over the front seat and picked out one of the thicker, more square catalogues. "Here's a Sears, Herman. I don't think I noticed any Ward's fer you."

"No, jist a Sears is all I git, I reckon," Herman said, taking it. "Well, I'll be seein' you, Mr. Slemmons."

"Good-by, Herman."

Slemmons rattled off in a cloud of dust. Whiskery old Herman Gutterman sat looking after the car for a moment. It went out of sight beyond the low hills. He picked the worn leather reins off the dashboard and slapped them gently on his mare's fat rump.

"Giddap, Omega," he said.

YOUTH TONE

The Perfect Hair Colorator. Used in exclusive beauty salons. Brings back Youthful Beauty to Dull, Faded, and Gray Hair. True in shade! Hair stays soft, lustrous. Does not alter structure of hair—you can get a successful permanent, marcel or water wave over Youth Tone. The result of scientific research. Colors: Black, darkest brown, dark brown, medium brown, light brown, light warm brown, auburn, ash blonde, blonde, light blonde. State Color.

8F3882..*Four treatments*..*Shpg wt.* 1 *lb.* 12 *oz*...
$2.29

THE GREEN and gold hammock was molded smooth under the Widow Holcomb's ample backside. She lay with the heavy catalogues unopened on her middle while she read the two letters she had got in the morning mail. The hammock creaked on its metal hangers. A humming bird beat its veiled wings among the honeysuckles.

Across the rough tablet paper the pale pinched pencil marks crawled:

DEAR DELLA:
Called up at your house last nite to ask you where you wouldent like to go to the piture show. But you

46

was not at home and the nigger girl did not say where you was. Guess I know where you was all rite cause a Certain Party seen you drive off with Eagle Catoosa.

Della you aint treaten me fare. now do you think it rite to advice me I ort to forbid my own daughter going out with that onery indian which I done and now soon as I forbid my daughter going anywheres with him you turn rite around and take up with him your ownsef is this fare to me?

honey, I jist can not see how you figgure your treaten me fare after you told me yoursef that he was jist out for all he could git and it was as good as a girls repatation was worth to go out with him. warned me again letten him go with my little girl and now you go let him cut me out with you. You no his aint no true love like my love I hold for you. it make my hart acke to see that indian jist playen you for all he can git out of you. It is not pure intentions on his part like it is on mine, dont come from the hart. Big old fat greasy thing.

Now Della honey you do not never come past the station no more like you always use to and you aint never home no more when I phone you. Now why is this is it fare? So I was thinking maybe if you say the word maybe we could go together somewheres next Fri. nite it's a week maybe eat supper in Tulsa and go to show I ain't got no big car like his but you use to think it was alrite. Pleas let me no baby as will

47

CATALOGUE

have to hire man to keep the station. Now I am not
stalling and my intentions is of the best.

I am, Sincerely,

IRA

She stuffed the letter back into its jagged envelope.

The other letter was written with violet ink on a
pink page edged in crinkled silver. She took up one
of the yellow tassels at the edge of the hammock
pillow and stroked her nose, smiling softly as she
read:

HELLO DELLA!

Come in to-nite & could not sleep so thot would
drop you a line & let you know I sure had a swell time
tonite. Wish it could be the same ever nite Do not
blame you for holden out on me lak you done as I
always know you was not no tramp. But a perfec lady.
Sweetheart this is the real thing so far as I am cun-
serned I mean I sure do love you & no kidding. Like
you said I was when I say the same to you last nite.
Do not know why you & me never stepped out together
before your jist my tipe Baby. Guess I been picking
them to young not that you are not plenty Young
enough but what I mean is h.s. girl etc. What I mean
is I sure do go for you in a Big Way woman How
about tomorro nite (Sat?) Will call you up or drive
by tomorra but thot would drop you a line to-nite &
put it in p.o. so you get it first thing tomorro a.m.

48

Well Baby must ring of for this time. Hopping you
Dreem about same Thing I do.

as ever from a Friend,

EAGLE

The Widow Holcomb folded the letter slowly.
She closed her eyes and put her arms over her head
and sighed and writhed and made a grab for the
two catalogues as they started slipping. She sat up
and swung her shapely legs over the fringed hammock side, groping with bare toes for her lavender,
feather-fringed slippers.

She clumped across the porch and let the screen
door slam behind her. The living room was shadowy
with velvet drapes and half-drawn shades. It was
furnished with an overstuffed velours davenport
matched by two fat rocking chairs, a carved radio
cabinet with a tapestry runner and a bowl of wax
oranges and bananas on it, and a Maxfield Parrish
print, hung from the wall by a silky tasseled pink
cord, showing in a polychromed frame two naked
blue women perched on a marble rail over the Grand
Canyon. The widow's feet thudded across the nas-
turtium bouquets on the Brussels carpet.

She went on into her bedroom and carefully closed
the door. A long-legged doll fluffed up with pink
organdie lay among fancy crêpe paper pillows on
the big brass bed. She dumped the catalogues on the
bed. Over at the bird's-eye maple dresser she pulled

49

off her lace cap and parted her thick black hair with her fingers, peering anxiously into the mirror. A dingy line of gray was beginning to show near the roots and a greenish purple hue merged into the black.

She opened the top dresser drawer and took the top off a pasteboard box filled with six small bottles. She unscrewed the cap on one and stuck in a stained cotton swab. The swab rattled in the bottle. When she held the bottle up to the light she saw the dry black flakes at the bottom.

"Heck!" she said.

She walked over to the bed and tore the wrapper off the Sears catalogue. Her forefinger trailed down the H's in the pink index and her wetted thumb flicked quickly through the thin gray pages to a place. She sat on the bed reading. Her large black purse lay on top of the cluttered bureau. She got up and rummaged through the purse and found a lint-fringed stamp and a pencil stub and her check book.

"Let's see," she said aloud to herself. "Today is a Saturday. Sunday. They'll get my order first thing Monday and send it out that same day. Should be here Monday afternoon on the 5:45 or Tuesday morning at the latest."

She tore an order blank out of the catalogue and on it began copying:

8F3882 *Four treatments Youth Tone Black* $2.29.

After she had flipped over to the table of parcel post rates in the back of the catalogue, she made out a check for the total. She sealed the letter and stamped it. Then she put on her boudoir cap and opened the bedroom door.

"Blanche!" she called.

A black girl in a thin gingham dress that did not cover her knock-knees came slowly out of the kitchen. The rag-bound tufts that stuck out from her head in all directions gave her a frightened look. She was about fourteen.

"Blanche, you know how to mail a letter, don't you?" the widow asked.

"Yas sum, Miss Della. I been to the post office many a time wid my mammy," Blanche said solemnly.

"Well, you take this letter to the post office and mail it. Hurry, now, because I want to get it off on the noon train. I'd take it myself if I was dressed to go to town. The stamp's already on it and it's ready to go. Soon as you mail it, you get right on back here. There's plenty to keep you busy around here today."

"Yas sum, Miss Della. It won't take me long."

Blanche went padding off toward town with the order in her hand.

The telephone jangled in the kitchen. Widow Holcomb went to answer it.

"Oh, hello, Eagle," she said, puckering her mouth

to make her voice thin and sweet. "How's my boy? I got that cute note of yours. Sure give me a thrill . . . Not much of anything . . . No, hon, you better not today. I'm not feeling very well. . . . Just a little headache, mostly . . . Oh, I guess Monday night. Maybe Tuesday . . . Huh-unh, not before then . . . Ah, don't you be anxious, now . . . I tell you, call me Monday evening and I'll let you know then . . . No, it's not that, Eagle, honest it's not . . . Oh, I've got certain reasons. Have you seen Irene today? . . . Well, you better not! . . ."

RUBBER COLLARS

Rubber composition collar with a dull, linen-like finish. Has the appearance of a starched collar. Easily cleaned with a damp cloth. Front about 2 inches; back, about 1½ inches high. Sizes 14 to 18. Half sizes. State size. Shipping weight of three, 6 oz.

33F8244 . . . . 3 *for* 60¢

P IRTLE'S filling station was the brightest spot on Broadway. It was garish with yellow and red paint by day. It was festooned with colored electric bulbs by night. The glass barrels of its three tall pumps showed for sale red (ethyl), white (untreated), and blue (low-test) gasoline.

Ira Pirtle sat at his dusty roll-top desk in the stucco office. A mail order catalogue open at the men's apparel section lay on the desk before him. He wiped his watery eyes with black-creased fingers and his withered brown lips moved slowly as he read the fine print. He licked his pencil point and began writing on an order blank.

A long red roadster drove into the station and stopped at the pumps. It blew a trumpet blast. The driver was an Indian with a face like polished mahogany.

Ira Pirtle closed his catalogue, leaving his pencil

53

in it to mark the place, and got up slowly to go out front.

"Fill 'er up," Eagle Catoosa grunted from the wheel without looking at Ira.

"You want the ethyl or the white?" Ira Pirtle asked in a surly voice.

"Want what I always take—best you got."

Ira lifted the ethyl hose nozzle off its hook. Before he moved round behind the car to unscrew the cap on the gas tank, he took a faltering step toward the front seat.

"Eagle," he said in a changed, wheedling tone, "I was wonderin' if maybe you couldn't pay me a little something on your bill this mornin'."

"It ain't the first yet, is it?" Eagle asked darkly.

"No, it ain't the first yet, but it's pret' near the first, and this here bill of yourn has been running since July without nothing paid on it."

"I'll pay you whenever I get my gov'munt check."

"How soon you goin' to git your check?"

"Doan know. Might be at the post office now."

"All right, Eagle. I ain't got no objections to sellin' you gas on time—it ain't that I doubt but what you're good for it—only I jist wish you'd keep me paid up more regular."

Ira went round to the back of the car and let gasoline in the tank until the level in the glass barrel fell to nine gallons on the measure. He hung the hose back up without draining it. He turned to go back into his office, but Eagle Catoosa called to him.

"What you been tellin' Irene about me, hunh?" Eagle asked when Ira came back to the car.

"Why, I ain't told her nothing about you!" Ira said pertly.

"She claims you won't let her go with me no more."

"Oh, is that what you meant? Well, yeow, Eagle, I did tell Irene that she was goin' to have to quit this here runnin' the streets of a Saturday night and climbin' in cars with boys and so on. That child ain't got no mother to look after her now, Eagle, and I aim to be exter strict with her."

"What you got against me, Ira?"

"Oh, I ain't got nothing again' you person'ly, Eagle. It's jist that you ain't been divorced from your last wife only a few months. My daughter is too young a girl to be runnin' around with an ex-married man. Irene ain't out of high school yet and she's already tryin' to act like she was a full-grown womern."

"Hunh, Ira, how about you? Your wife ain't been dead six months yet and you're already makin' a play for the Widow Holcomb."

"You ain't seen me makin' no play for her lately, have you?" Ira asked glumly.

"Yeah, but that ain't because you're not still tryin' to. It don't look to me like you got much call to keep

55

Irene from havin' a good time after the way you
been makin' a fool of yourse'f over Della Holcomb."

Ira spat tobacco juice on the concrete floor. "I
don't know as I made a fool of myse'f over her yit,"
he said sharply. "And besides it ain't nobody's business but mine if I did. And furthermore I reckon it's
my privilege to say who Irene can go with and who
she can't. I'm her father and she ain't of age yit and
till she is I'm going to keep that young lady strictly
to home."

"Yeah?" Eagle said insolently. "O.K., Ira. It
don't make me no difference. I guess I can git me
another womern easy enough."

"I heerd you already had got you another one."

"I sure have, Ira. I've got the Widow Holcomb
clean away from you, all right. You act so smart
about Irene, I'll show you. I was out with the widow
last night and I'm goin' to be out with her ever' night
from now on. How you like that?"

Eagle's fat lips curled back for an evil chuckle.
He stepped on the gas and the Packard roared out
of the station. Ira stared after the blue haze of the
exhaust. He stood scratching his scrawny neck.

"Who was that just drove out?" a voice said behind him.

"What do you want to know for?" he asked
savagely when he turned and saw the doll-like
blonde. She was about seventeen.

"It was Eagle Catoosa, wasn't it?"

"It ain't no business of yours if it was. I guess you come sneakin' up to take it all in, didn't you?"

"No, I didn't, papa! Honest, I didn't. I walked up jist as the car drove off."

"What did you mean by runnin' straight and tellin' him that I had forbid you to go with him for?"

"Well, papa, how was I going to git around it? He asked me for a date, and I jist told him that I couldn't go with him no more because you said you was going to whip me if I did. And besides he's been dating that old slut of a Widow Holcomb, and I wouldn't be seen with him after that. It would be as much as a girl's reppatation is worth to be seen with a man after he's took that old Widow Holcomb out."

"Listen here, young womern! You mind your mouth, or I'll take me a corn cob and some soft soap and warsh it out fer you. What do you know about the Widow Holcomb, anyhow?"

"Shucks, I don't know nothing about her," Irene said, sniffing and shrugging her small shoulders. "All I know is what people say."

"You jist pay a little better attention to the way you act your ownse'f, young lady, and a little less to what these scandalmongers say."

"All right, papa. I guess you ought to know plenty about the Widow Holcomb. You've been around her enough to, haven't you?"

57

"And another thing, you better watch out how you talk to your father, you disrestpecful little snippet, you. I'm not going to have you sassing me. You're not so big yet but what I can't turn you right up and tan your hide. What're you doin' uptown this morning, anyhow? Didn't I tell you I wasn't going to have you switchin' around up here on the streets at all hours of the day and night?"

"Aw, I jist come to the post office, papa. Mr. Shannon told me you got the new catalogues last night. Would you let me take them home with me to look at?"

"No, I won't!" Ira snapped. "I'm not through with them catalogues yit. You got plenty to keep you busy at the house without you studyin' no mail order catalogue."

"Papa, I wish you'd anyway let me take the new Ward catalogue. I'm needing me some things."

"What're you needin'?"

"Oh, some clothes."

"Looky here, little missy! Didn't I spend $5.67 on you for clothes when I ordered last week?"

"Yes, but you got me them old black sateen bloomers, and I'm going to send 'em back. Girls don't wear nothing like that these days."

"You'll wear what I buy you, or I'll wear you out. I guess I know where the money comes from to pay for all these silk stockings and things you think you've got to have. If you had to git out and earn the money, you wouldn't be so free with the way you spend it."

"Why, papa," Irene said, turning her wide blue eyes up at him, "you don't want me going around here *nekkid*, do you?"

"No, sir-ee, I don't," Ira Pirtle said soberly.

MAE WEST PERFUME

"You've got to be feminine to attract anything masculine," says *Mae West. And this is her secret of allure—a perfume she has been using for years, created by Mme Gabilla of Paris. It is offered to you now—delightfully feminine and expressive—at a small price. Ship. wt.* 1 *oz.*

53D3130 *Dram Size Bottle*................59¢

A GIRL in crisp beach pajamas stood waiting at the next mail box. The mail box was new and bright, but it was much smaller than any of the other new mail boxes along the route.

The girl was pretty. Her sleepy brown eyes were set wide apart, her mouth was small and red, and there was a faint dust of freckles across her pert little nose. The points of her breasts stood firm beneath the red-and-blue plaid of her low-cut pajamas. The cotton cloth stretched tight over her pear-shaped bottom.

"Hi, there, sugar," she called cheerfully. "It's about time you was coming along."

Slemmons stopped his car, but he let the motor idle.

"Where's Orin?" he asked warily.

"Oh, Orin's way back up in the field pickin' cotton. Don't you let Orin worry your mind, hon," she said, leaning against the side of the car.

"It's a wonder to me that Orin would let you get this fur away from the house so early in the mornin'. You look purty as a speckled pup in them things you got on."

"Listen at the man! Ain't he a sweet-talking man!"

"Did you jist put them things on to come down and see me in, Birdie?" Slemmons asked, leering at her.

"Heck, no! I got to come down here after the mail, ain't I? You claim you cain't, or anyway ain't supposed to, leave it in the kind of box Orin put up. And I guess I've got jist as much right to dress up and look nice as them town girls has, ain't I?"

The engine skipped and almost died, but Slemmons caught it with more gas in time.

"You shore have, Birdie. And you got ary one of them ever I seen beat four ways to Sunday fer good looks. But to tell you the truth, it sceers me. I cain't he'p thinkin' what Orin's goin' to do when he finds out you're down here at the box to meet me ever' mornin'."

"Well, if you aim to be an old grouch about it and start that again, hand me my mail and I'll be gittin' back. What did you bring me this mornin'?"

"I brung you a couple of mail order catalogues,"

Slemmons said, turning round to reach over in the back seat.

"Oh, goody! the new catalogues has come. Hurry up and give me mine!"

Slemmons pawed among the catalogues and got out two. He handed them out to her.

"They's a little old package of some kind here for you, too," he said, bending over the mail pouch beside him on the front seat.

"Hot dog! I guess that must be my per-fume I ordered."

"You must jist about keep Orin busted, orderin' all the time."

"Thunder, I don't spend near as much orderin' as Orin does on his drinkin' liquor," she said, tearing into the package. "Besides it's my own chicken and egg money and he ain't got no right to tell me how I can spend it." She held up a small vial of perfume and said, "Cute?"

"Yeah," Slemmons said, racing his motor nervously. "Well, I got to be gettin' on. I'm already late this mornin'."

"How come you was so late? I waited and waited for you. I thought you never was comin'."

"I had to stop down the road a piece there and write a money order fer old Herman Gutterman. He got to talkin' to me and helt me up I reckon ten minutes."

"Oh, did you see Herman? Did he say anything

about th'owin' a square dance for Bessie when she gits out next Friday? I seen him in town last Saturday and told him he'd ort to."

"Yeah, he mentioned it to me."

"Are you comin'?"

"Shucks, no. I don't keer nothing about a square dance. Never did."

"It ain't cause your wife is saved and won't let you git away, is it?"

"Humf. My wife bein' saved ain't got nothing to do with it. She wouldn't have nothing to say about it. If I wanted to come to Gutterman's square dance, I guess I'd come all right. But they wouldn't be nothing there to intrust me."

"Oh, I don't know! If you was to come, I might make it intrustin' enough fer you."

"Yeah, you!" Slemmons said, getting red in the face. "I know you. Even if you was to be at the square dance, Orin wouldn't let you dance with nobody but him. Not without he started a fight."

Her eyes narrowed and she burst out in fury, "That's jist it, the mean old hog! I'm gitting t'ard of settin' home without never gittin' to go nowheres. Orin stays drunk half the time and he ain't no fun fer me. His old pappy makes it and Orin ain't drawed a sober breath since we was married last Spring. Drunk as a bear ever' Saturday and Sunday, jist when I want to go somewheres. Well, don't you never worry—I'm going to see to it that he gits so

63

drunk the night of Gutterman's square dance that he won't be able to stir a limb away from home. He figgers he's got ever'body sceered off from me, but I'm going to step out by myse'f Friday night and have myse'f a good time."

Slemmons moved his neck from side to side, not looking at her, peering at the road and at the cotton field. He raced his motor again.

She caught his shirt sleeve. "Don't rush off," she said. "Stay and talk awhile. Nobody ever comes round me any more, Orin is so crazy-jealous."

"I know that," Slemmons said in a trembly voice. "And I keep tellin' you, Birdie, I don't like it, you comin' down to the box to meet me all the time. One of these days somebody is going to come along the road and ketch us talkin' like this and go tell Orin. Besides, even if you was to come to that square dance, they wouldn't be nobody dance with you— they'd all be so sceered of Orin findin' out about it after he sobered up."

She made an indecent sound with her tongue. "Listen, Mr. Man, it ain't dancin' I'm comin' to that square dance for." She let the long lashes droop down over her left eye. "Now you git me?"

Slemmons gulped and licked his lips. "I guess so," he mumbled in a tight voice.

"You goin' to be there now?"

"I might," Slemmons said hoarsely.

She leaned forward and brushed his blue-shaven

64

jaw with her lips. Slemmons was so startled that he jammed in the clutch and the car bucked away. She fell back and watched it gather speed.

"Remember what I told you!" she called.

He was lost in a cloud of dust.

She turned and followed the clay wagon ruts back to the windowless gray shack in the center of the cotton field.

THE AMOUNT OF PAPER USED

if spread out in a single sheet, would pave a high-way from New York to San Francisco—12,000 tons of paper or twenty trainloads of thirty cars each. Into it went enough printer's ink to fill two standard 60-foot-long swimming tanks. If the entire edition of catalogues were stacked up, they would make a column 142 miles high, or 946 times higher than the Woolworth building.

POSTMASTER SHANNON finished lettering the strip of paper with red ink. The general delivery line had thinned out and the lobby was almost deserted.

Art Smiley, the town marshal, was standing back in a corner reading the descriptions of stolen cars and escaped convicts he had got in the morning mail. The postmaster looked up from his lettering job and saw him there.

He called quietly, "Oh, Art! I want to speak with you a minute."

The gaunt law moseyed over, pausing to spit at the wastepaper barrel. The postmaster didn't say anything, but he frowned. The town marshal hunched down at the parcel post window with his elbows on the shelf.

"Art, somebody stole the postoffice flag last night or early this morning."

"No!" Art said, straightening up in amazement.

"Yes. We forgot and left it out last night, account of being so busy with the catalogues; first time that's happened since I got my appointment. And it wasn't there this morning."

"Why, Mr. Shannon, what ornery scalawag would pull a low-down trick like that—swipe the flag offen the post office?"

"Well, of course, I can't name him for sure, Art. But I'll say this: there's a growing disrespect for the U. S. Gover'ment around here, and I'm going to put a stop to it. Now you take those cardboard signs I've got up out there in the lobby. Gover'ment issues them to me. 'No Spitting' printed on them in great big box-car letters. Well, sir, you'd be surprised if I was to name you people who'll go right ahead and spit in the lobby wastepaper barrel. And the street door not three steps away. I've just finished making me a sign here to put on that wastepaper barrel, asking people to use it instead of littering up the floor. But it looks like they'd know better than to spit in a wastepaper barrel."

"Sure, sure, Mr. Shannon," Art said hastily. "But what about that flag? Ain't you got no clues as to who might of stole it?"

"Yes, I've got a clue, Art, only it ain't enough of a clue to say positively. But when I do find out who

67

stole that flag, I mean to have some action. Be dogged if I'm not fed up on the way people think they can sneak around and get away with anything. This post office represents the dignity of the United States Gover'ment just as much as the National Capitol does—well, maybe not *just* as much, but pret' near as much."

"I reckon it does at that, Mr. Shannon," the town marshal said thoughtfully. "When you come to think about it, I guess you're absolutely right about that, Mr. Shannon."

"And stealing a U. S. flag from a U. S. post office is a pretty serious offense. It wasn't a brand-new flag, but it had to do for another three months at least."

"Well, you give me that clue, Mr. Shannon, and I'll sure run it down. Tell me who you suspicion and I'll sure bring him in, I don't keer who it is."

"Good for you, Art! I want you to go find Bill Huggins and bring him in here. I've got some questions to ask that lad."

The town marshal was suddenly aghast. "Bill Huggins? Bill Huggins, Mr. Shannon? Oh, you're off on the wrong trail there. You don't mean Bill Huggins. Bill Huggins wouldn't steal no flag. Why, Bill teaches the junior boys' Sunday school class at the Baptist church. I know, because I go to the Baptist church myse'f. Besides Bill is a strong worker in the Boy Scouts, and you know them Boy Scouts— they're not supposed to steal."

68

"Yeah? Well, mind you I didn't say he was the thief, Art. All I know is that just as I was opening up this morning I met Bill Huggins coming out of the alley with a big bulge in his shirt. I didn't think anything about it at the time. But a few minutes ago, while I was printing this sign to paste on the lobby wastepaper barrel, it just flashed through my head—that bulge *might* have been the postoffice flag. If it was, I'll have Bill jailed just as I would anybody else, Sunday school teacher or no Sunday school teacher, Boy Scout or no Boy Scout. You bring Bill Huggins in here and let me talk to him."

"O.K., Mr. Shannon," Art Smiley said in a doubtful tone, "but I'm scared you're after the wrong party. I'll go try and find Bill, though."

Postmaster Shannon reached for the stickum pot and began smearing mucilage on the back of his red-lettered sign. Art Smiley went out of the post office.

Postmaster Shannon picked up the sticky strip of paper and, holding it by one corner out in front of him, went out into the lobby through the partition door. He was squatted at the wastepaper barrel, pasting the sign on it, when Art Smiley came back into the post office.

"Oh, Mr. Shannon," Art began haltingly. "I jist got to thinkin'—wouldn't it be better, instid of jist goin' right out and nabbin' Bill Huggins—wouldn't it be better if I was to kindly keep him under surveillance for a few days? Then if you had made a

69

mistake and suspicioned the wrong person we wouldn't—"

Postmaster Shannon finished pasting the sign on the wastepaper barrel and stood back to survey his handiwork.

"Do as you like, Art," he said dryly. "If he comes in the post office here, I'll question him myself. But if you think you'd have a better chance to catch him with the goods on him by watching him for a few days, go to it."

"Yes, that was my idea, Mr. Shannon. And if he ain't the thief, I could mighty soon find out by shaddering him a little. I wish you'd let me handle it, Mr. Shannon. Ketching criminals is my business, you know."

Postmaster Shannon looked out the window and saw R. W. E. Ledbetter stalking up the alley with two bundles of newspapers.

"All right, Art. You go ahead and see what you can find out. I won't say anything to him for a few days. Here comes Swede Ledbetter with this week's *Democrats*. He's two days late this week instead of one. I'll have to go through to the back door and let him in."

Art Smiley went out a second time. The postmaster tapped at the partition door and Elvira Draper put down her magazine to turn the lock. He walked back to the cage and opened the iron-barred door for the newspaper editor.

"You missed the routes this week, Swede," he said with a hint of reproof. "*Democrats* won't get out on the routes now until Monday. But we'll put the town papers up right away."

"Yes, sir, Mr. Shannon, I sure was sorry about missing the routes this week, but it couldn't be he'ped. Right at the last minute I had to shove in a hot editorial and that throwed us another day late."

"That was a good editorial you had in last week's paper all right—that one on how bad this town needs a sewer system. That's just the kind of thing this town needs to sort of wake it up. When you publish something constructive like that in your paper, the *Democrat* is serving its highest purpose in the community."

Editor Ledbetter toed the floor and said modestly, "Well, thank you, Mr. Shannon. It's mighty nice of you to say so, but I guess you was the one that put the idea in my head—that talk we had last week."

"Oh, I don't know," the postmaster said, wagging his head. "There was a lot of original thought in that editorial. And I'm not the only one that says so. I've heard plenty of favorable comment on it right here in the office."

He took one of the thin, six-column papers from the top of the bundle and unfolded it. "Whereabouts is that follow-up piece on the sewer bonds you was tellin' me about having for this week's issue?" he asked.

71

"Well, sir, Mr. Shannon, I was jist going to tell you about that. I had that piece all in type and bolted in the form, front page two-column editorial, but it got crowded out right at the last minute by that piece you see there on the front page about the mail order catalogues."

"Does that mean you're dropping the sewer bond question?" Postmaster Shannon asked sharply.

"Oh, no! Oh, no! Not at all, Mr. Shannon. We'll run that follow-up piece in next week's paper. It'll be just as timely then as it is now."

"But I understood that you men on the city council were going to vote on the sewer bond resolution next Monday night."

"Oh, yes! Yes. We're going ahead and vote on the resolution Monday night jist the same. But don't you see, Mr. Shannon, after we vote the resolution to call a bond election, then will be the time to open up with both barrels in the *Democrat*."

"I see," Postmaster Shannon said, carrying the two bundles of papers over to the flat beam scales. "You didn't bring the zone bundles, did you?"

"No, Mr. Shannon, we're still wrapping the out-of-county papers. Red Currie will bring them jist as soon as we git them wrapped. But I thought I'd better come ahead with the town papers and the bundle for the routes, being as we're so late this week."

"All right, Mr. Ledbetter! Girls! Here are the

Democrats. Come on. Let's get them in the boxes before we have to make out that noon mail."

Elvira laid down her magazine. Gladys closed the Sears catalogue she was leafing through. They got down from their high stools at the windows and came back to distribute the Conchartee County *Democrats,* two days late.

A bony Negro girl with rag-plaited hair came slipping into the post office lobby carrying a brown letter. Her bare gray feet hissed across the concrete floor. She gave a shy glance about and saw no one. The barred windows were empty. Her rolling white eyes were caught by the new red-lettered sign on the wastepaper barrel.

She stood spelling out the words in a whisper.

PLEASE PLACE LITTER IN THIS BARREL

She reached into the empty barrel and carefully laid the letter on the bottom. She turned and glided out of the post office lobby.

Sylvester Merrick, the bank porter, came driving up in a shiny old flivver. He got out with a bunch of bank letters for the noon mail.

"Hi do, Blanche," he said to the knock-kneed Negro girl.

"Hi do, Mr. Merrick," she said before she started hurrying right back.

73

EASY PAYMENTS

All Wards Hawthornes costing $20 or more may be bought on Wards Budget Plan—See Page 593, and the monthly payments amount to around 14¢ to 17¢ a day—less than the cost of renting a bicycle for an hour.

SUNDAY morning, Waldo Ledbetter, Jr., sank deeper in crime. He held back the nickel his father had given him for the Presbyterian Sunday school collection. After Sunday school he was just going into Danziger's Pharmacy to buy an ice cream cone when the sheriff caught him.

He had long felt the shadow of the reform school hovering over him. All his Summer days—those bright vacation days he had looked forward to so eagerly back in the sixth grade last Winter—were clouded with fear. Sometimes he would forget for a few minutes, simply by not trying to forget, but the guilt was always with him to twist him sick and sad again. There was no one to whom he could turn for mercy, least of all his own parents.

"Lord God, boy! that's a penitentiary offense," his father cried that terrible noon in May when the deed first came to light. "To think that I'd raise a son up, and work with him, and try and teach him to do right, and then—then to have him sneak off

74

and pull a crooked trick like this. The law would put a man back of the bars for doing such a thing. But you're a minor. They'll just ship you down to Pauls Valley to the reform school. That's the place for young crooks!"

Waldo glanced toward his mother for sympathy, but she sat cold and silent, her lips pressed in a straight line. She had not mentioned his crime, one way or the other, from that moment on. Her silence was even more terrifying than the things his father said, and his father said some awful things.

"I'm not going to whip you this time. I've tried whipping you, but whipping don't do any good. This time I'll just let the law take care of you in its own proper fashion. Don't come whining to me when the long arm of the law finally catches up with you."

"Papa, I didn't know it was a penitentiary offense," Waldo quavered. A moment later he flung himself at his father's feet, wailing, "Honest, papa, I didn't know it was against the law."

"Ignorance of the law excuses nobody. And don't try and fib out of it now. If you didn't know you was doing wrong, how come you didn't ask me first? If you'd ask me, like any honest boy would, I might of bought you a bicycle. But, no! you had to sneak off like a thief in the night without saying a word to anyone. Well, I wash my hands of you. The judge can ship you off to reform school for all I care. I'm

75

through trying to do anything with you. Absolutely through!"

All this had been said back in May, the day after the bicycle came. It had been repeated many times since. But in May there had been a glimmer of hope. Waldo had supposed then that if he could only avoid the sheriff through the Summer he could pull himself out of danger before September. Now, Summer was gone and there was nothing but blank despair. Every ominous prediction his father had made was rapidly coming true.

Sometimes he would wake up in the morning feeling free, and he would whisper to himself that the whole thing was nothing but a bad dream. He had dreamed in the night that he was about to be sent to the reform school. Now that it was morning again he could laugh and forget that nightmare. But as soon as he was fully awake dread settled on him again, and he knew that it was not a dream. It was real. Another day of cringing fear had begun. Dreaming could be used to make unreal things real, but it would not work the other way.

Dreaming, in fact, had led Waldo into forgery and using the mails to defraud. He would have explained that to his father if his father had been an ordinary man instead of R. W. E. Ledbetter, editor of the weekly *Democrat*. He could have explained enough, at least, to prove that he was not a real crook. He might deserve a whipping, but not the reform school. How, though, could a man who wrote what the whole town read be expected to waste time on nonsense?

Waldo remembered clearly how it started. It had started as a made-up game. It was a strange game, because there was no one to beat and there was no way to lose and it had to be played in secret. He played it first with his geography, looking at the animal maps. Little pictures of animals native to each continent were on the maps.

He would hurry home from school every afternoon and go into his bedroom and thumb-latch the door. Then he would lie prone on the matting-covered floor, his elbows propped on his open geography. He would continue the long lists in a special pencil tablet:

AUSTRALIA

4 kangaroos
2 duckbills
6 dingos . . .

Africa was more exciting:

24 lions
6 giraffes
120 elephants (African)
100 zebras
4 gnus

77

CATALOGUE

4 rhinocerouses
4 gorillas
100 monkeys
2 hippopotamuses . . .

Here was the part, though, that Waldo didn't know how he could explain to his father. Here was the crazy part. While he was making those lists he was R. W. Emerson Ledbetter, the millionaire circus owner. Ledbetter's six-ring circus and wild animal menagerie, the greatest show in the world, the most complete aggregation of wild animals ever gathered together under one canvas from the jungles of seven continents. Even Ringling Brothers had only one hippopotamus. Ledbetter's Circus had two hippopotamuses. The lists on pencil tablet paper were the animals in Ledbetter's Circus. Making those lists was not merely as much fun as owning a circus. Those lists *were* Ledbetter's Circus.

Waldo knew that he would have to tell his father about the circus before he could so much as explain about the steamship booklets. His father had never fully understood about the steamship booklets. The steamship incident had given his father the fixed idea that Waldo was a liar with criminal tendencies.

His circus lists were almost complete when travel advertisements suddenly interested Waldo. "Send for free illustrated travel brochure!" Waldo cleaned

78

out the medicine chest, washed up a bunch of old prescription bottles, scalded them bright, and sold them to Danziger's Pharmacy for a dime. He found three empty tow sacks out in the barn, and sold them at Gresham's Grist Mill for fifteen cents. He wrote on twenty-five one-cent postal cards:

GENTLEMEN:

Will you kindly send me your free illustrated literature, as I am interested in making a trip around the world.

Yours truly,

R. WALDO E. LEDBETTER, JR.

He addressed the cards to all the steamship and railroad companies he could find advertised.

Later his father said that what Waldo wrote on those postal cards was a bare-faced lie. That proved that his father did not understand. Waldo did not even attempt to explain that when he was writing those cards he was R. Waldo E. Ledbetter, Jr., the famous millionaire globe-trotter.

The steamship companies did not question it. Large brown envelopes, fat and heavy with free illustrated literature, began coming in. Usually Waldo would be right there at the post office waiting, but his father happened to get two or three envelopes full of steamship booklets from the post office. He didn't scold Waldo at the time. He seemed approving. He thumbed through some of

79

the pamphlets, looking at the pictures, and he passed the free illustrated literature on to his anxious son with the mild comment that it certainly was educational. Many were beautiful booklets, sumptuously printed on heavy slick paper, run through and tied with flossy cords that held on the embossed cardboard covers, all with pictures of foreign lands more exciting than any in the geography. Waldo spent hours over the steamship booklets, planning a world tour.

A day or two before a big envelope came in there would be a personal letter to Waldo from the general passenger agent, saying that the free illustrated literature he had requested was being forwarded under separate cover. The general passenger agent always wrote as courteously as if Waldo really were a millionaire globe-trotter. The letter would say also that Waldo's request was being referred to the company's district representative. Such letters made Waldo feel important, but they made him feel a little uneasy, too. As soon as he read them he would tear them up and toss them into a postoffice wastepaper barrel. He was having too much fun with scenes of far-off lands to bother with letters.

One noon his father sat down to dinner and said, "Well, Waldo, a man came in at the *Democrat* office this morning to see you. Said he had come all the way from Kansas City to see you about a steamship ticket around the world, for that trip you're going to take."

Waldo felt sick. He didn't know whether to believe it. His father seemed in good humor. His father and mother both laughed and teased him that day. They took it as a great joke at first.

"Well, son, when do you expect to start around the world?"

That was before the steamship company men began arriving thick and fast. There seemed to be an impression among them that R. Waldo E. Ledbetter, Jr., was a farmer who had struck oil. Scarcely a day passed for a week without a stranger getting off the train and inquiring for Mr. Ledbetter. Even after they could see it was a hopeless quest, they would hang round the *Democrat* office, trying out their sales talks on Waldo's father. One Thursday two steamship men arrived, both on the same train, and Thursday was the day the *Democrat* went to press. That day Waldo's father came home and unhooked the razor strap.

"I'm going to break you of this lying," he said grimly after he had led Waldo out back of the house. People living over in the next block heard the heavy thwacks punctuating Waldo's squalls.

That whipping should have warned Waldo in time to abandon his mail order catalogues. He realized that later. But it was not until he was about to go to reform school that he saw clearly the circus lists, the steamship booklets, the catalogues, as links in his crime.

He kept the Sears Roebuck catalogue and the Montgomery Ward catalogue in a big pasteboard box in his room under his bed. Everything that was valuable to him was in that box: his stamp collection, his steamship booklets, his marbles, his pencil tablets full of lists, and his mail order catalogues. He made believe that the pasteboard box was an iron-bound chest. When he put the lid on, everything in that box was as safe as if it were locked in an iron-bound chest. It had never occurred to Waldo that anyone else could lift the lid.

One afternoon early in November he was stretched out on the floor with his mail order catalogues. He had been so eager to get back to them after school he had forgotten to thumb-latch his door. He was, at that moment, Rafe Ledbetter, the North Woods trapper, fitting out an expedition. He was jotting down a list of supplies:

    1 Cantleek canvas canoe
    1 pneumatic mattress
    1 waterproof wall tent
    1 lamb's wool sleeping bag
    2 ponchos
    1 46-pc aluminum camp set
    1 pr moccasin boots
    1 Winchester .32 repeating rifle

He heard his father's step on the front porch. A moment later the door to his room opened and his father looked in. Waldo quickly flipped the catalogues shut and covered his list with one arm.

His father stood over him, asking, "What're you doing, always laying around after school with your nose stuck in some catalogue?"

Waldo said, "Nothing much, papa. I'm just playing."

"That's no way to play. Why don't you get out in the open air and play like other boys do? Or else get out and do a little work around the yard. You'll never earn a nickel with your nose stuck in some old mail order catalogue all the time."

Waldo wondered how long his father was going to keep on standing there talking. What did he want to earn a nickel for? What was a nickel when you could be a millionaire and could have anything you wanted simply by putting it on a list? His father talked on.

"If you don't cut out this crazy fool business of laying around on your stomach all the time with your face in those old catalogues, I'm going to do something about it. You see if I don't! A person would think you had softening of the brain. I've got a notion to take those catalogues out in the alley and set fire to 'em. It's a shame and a disgrace to have them in the house anyway."

His father didn't understand about the catalogues.

His father never would know how much fun a person can have with mail order catalogues, making believe he is a rancher fitting himself out with everything from branding irons to angora chaps; or a farmer equipping a model farm; or simply a father ordering toys for his son. The toy list was the most fun of all.

"You'll never make a nickel. You won't be able to lay around on your stomach like that all your life. You're going to have to get out and hustle for yourself one of these days. There'll come a day when you'll be wanting a crust of bread for your stomach, and you won't find it in any mail order catalogue, neither."

Waldo studied the red and green straws running through the tan matting weave. His father finally turned and walked out. Waldo began to see what his father meant, though. If he ever expected to have any of those things actually, instead of making believe he had them, he must make money to buy them. But it still seemed better to imagine he had a million dollars and everything that could be found in the big catalogues than it was to have a few real dollars and nothing more than those few dollars would buy.

Tom Draper, next door, had a bicycle. He was stingy with it, but sometimes in a trade he would let Waldo ride it. It wasn't much of a bicycle compared with the bicycles in the catalogues. Waldo had never had as much fun riding Tom's bike as he had had in making believe that he owned the best bicycle in the catalogue.

He opened the catalogues again now that he was alone. Each thick book fell open easily at the slick paper section of bicycle pictures in colors. There in Sears' catalogue, large and bright, were the Cardinal and the Bluebird and the expensive Silver Eagle. And in Ward's, the Super Flyer, black-and-ivory-enameled and chromium-plated; the De Luxe, cherry red or Royal Packard blue; and the lower-priced Speed Model. Waldo read the descriptions over slowly, relishing them for the hundredth time.

But now, for the first time, he pondered whether it was better to buy one bicycle and have it to ride than it was to make believe that any bicycle in the catalogue—even to the Road King bike motor which changes an ordinary bicycle into a motorcycle—was his when he put it on his list.

Suddenly the prices in the catalogues seemed very large. There was the Silver Eagle, completely equipped with electric horn and headlight, $32.90 cash; even more on easy payments. That would be 329 dimes. Could he hope ever to have that much money? It made a difference, looking at a catalogue with prudent thoughts of buying. It gave him a sad, lost feeling to know that he was small and penniless after so much had been his. Never after that was he able to recapture the old pleasure he had taken in the catalogue game.

Once Waldo got started, making money became as exciting as the catalogue game ever had been. The next day, a Saturday, he went out to the barn to see how many empty gunny sacks had accumulated since the last time he had needed postage money. He searched through the heap of dusty jute sacks and found two that had no holes. The rats had got to some, and the grist mill wouldn't buy torn sacks. Then he found the gunny sack that would make three others.

It was the biggest tow sack Waldo had ever seen. He remembered the night his father had carried home groceries in it from Whipple's store. It was lined with fiber paper and a faint aroma came from it as he held it up to read, printed in large red letters across its coarse brown weave: "100 lbs Fancy Roasted Rio Coffee." Waldo calculated happily: if an ordinary cornchops sack would bring a nickel, this sack should be worth at least fifteen cents.

"Gosh, no, son," Mr. Gresham said at the mill, fingering his bedraggled, flourdusted mustache, "we cain't buy that there coffee sack. I'll pay you a nickel apiece for them other two, but I ain't got no use for a coffee sack. You take roasted coffee beans, they weigh light. Why, that there coffee sack would hold three-four hunderd pounds of cornchops. You

86

can leave it here if you want to, son, but I cain't pay you nothing for it. It ain't no use to me."

Waldo carried the coffee sack home and tossed it back in the crib. He had a dime, anyway. A dime was all he needed to write and get himself appointed subscription agent for all the popular magazines. There was established competition in town, to be sure. The Widow Holcomb, for one, was an energetic subscription taker. And there were always those strangers who were working their way through college. But Waldo had his own system. He did not waste time going from door to door as the others did.

Every day he would poke through the postoffice wastepaper barrel, searching for magazine wrappers from which he got names and expiration dates. Thursday mornings, when the early mail was being put up, he would stand in the postoffice lobby until almost school time, watching to see who took the *Saturday Evening Post*. The end of the year was approaching and many subscriptions were expiring. Usually he had only to follow up label clues to get renewal subscriptions.

Two or three times a week he would pass between the polished granite pillars on the corner opposite the courthouse and enter a shadowy, mysterious place filled with the smell of furniture polish and a murmuring quiet apt to be broken briefly by the startling clatter of an adding machine. His metal heel taps clicked on the tile floor. Resisting an impulse to skate, he would march solemnly up and push under the cashier's wicket his subscription money and his small brown leather book inscribed: "Conchartee National Bank in account with R. Waldo E. Ledbetter, Jr." He would glimpse W. S. Winston back in the president's enclosure, sitting as close to his desk as his belly would permit, a big cigar in his mouth, squinting off into space while an anxious cotton farmer sat talking. Mr. Lennox, the cashier, a mild bald little man with rimless eye-glasses, would count the deposit, make a deft entry in the bank book, and pass it back to Waldo.

"You're coming right along, Waldo. How's business?"

"Pretty good, Mr. Lennox. I took six subscriptions to the *Post* and four to the *Ladies' Home Journal* yesterday afternoon."

"Well, that's fine. You stay right in there and pitch!"

His bank balance, two weeks before Christmas, was $17.65. He had more than half enough to pay cash for the Silver Eagle. One night after supper he went in to study the catalogue bicycle pages again. He had about decided on a lower-priced wheel. When he took the lid off his pasteboard box the catalogues were not there. He searched the room. Then he hurried out to ask his mother if she had seen anything of them.

160C3030 SPEED MODEL BICYCLE

"No, darling, I haven't touched your catalogues," she said softly. "But you might ask your father."

His father was sitting in the front room reading the Tulsa *Tribune*. Waldo went in and asked, "Papa, did you see anything of my catalogues?"

His father mumbled without lowering the newspaper, "You don't expect me to try and keep track of your junk, do you?"

Waldo went on searching through the house until his father slammed down the paper, shouting, "Young man, you come in here and get settled down to your home work, or I'm going to give you a dressing down you won't forget soon. Quit tearing up the house looking for some old catalogues that don't amount to the flip of a pin anyhow."

The next morning at breakfast his father said, "Waldo, it's getting cold weather now, and you're needing Winter clothes. You're a big half-grown boy now, and I'm going to let you buy your own clothes this Winter. You've been doing mighty fine here lately."

Waldo was filled with pride at the thought of buying his own clothes, just as if he were a man. He and his father went into the Whipple Mercantile Company, and his father picked out a boy's overcoat, $7.50, and a pair of laced boots, $3.50, and a heavy sweater, $3.00.

Waldo said, feeling his importance, "Gee whiz,

papa, we could buy these things from Montgomery Ward or Sears, Roebuck a lot cheaper than this."

Mr. Whipple, who was waiting on them, laughed and said, "Is that where you been doing all your trading, Waldo?"

His father acted sore. As soon as Waldo had written Mr. Whipple a check for $14 and they had started home with the bundles, his father grabbed him by the arm and said, "Don't ever let me hear you say anything about buying from a mail order company again, young man."

"Why, papa?"

"Because I say so, that's why. You understand?"

After that Waldo tried to forget about the bicycle. He didn't even have enough to make a down payment on one, anyway. He didn't care much. He was having a good time bragging to other boys about his father's letting him buy his own clothes. But sometimes he was sorry that he didn't have the catalogues to play with any more. He had sent off for new catalogues. He watched the post office for weeks, waiting for the catalogues to come. If they ever came, he did not see them.

One day in April Mr. Lennox, the bank cashier, stopped to talk with Waldo on the street. He said, "What's the matter, Waldo, I never do see you in the bank any more? You was making money hand-over-fist there awhile before Christmas. Used to be in ever' day or so."

Waldo said, "Yes, sir, but that was when I was taking magazine subscriptions. That played out after Christmas. That business isn't so good except in November and December when folks are renewing and sending magazines for gifts. There's not much in it for a person now."

"Well, Waldo, you're a pretty bright boy, and I'm going to put you onto a way you can pick up a nice little piece of money. I'm looking for a good reliable boy to drive my cow out to pasture every morning and bring her in every night before milking time. It's Jones's pasture out here a mile and a half north of town."

"When would you want me to start, Mr. Lennox? I have to keep on going to school until the sixteenth of May."

"Oh, this won't interfere with your school, Waldo. You can drive her out about seven a.m. every morning and be back in plenty of time for school. Then you can go get her an hour or so after school's out. I'll pay you a dollar a month, and if you'll get around and see a few others who pasture their cows, you could get a few more to drive and make yourself a nice sum of money this Summer. But April is half gone, and of course I can't pay you but fifty cents for April."

Waldo inquired through the neighborhood and

found four other cows to drive. He went into the Conchartee National Bank on the first of May to collect from Mr. Lennox and to deposit $2.50, his April earnings. Mr. Lennox handed him a statement of his account, and Waldo saw that he still had $3.65 in the bank that he had almost forgotten.

He hurried home that day and went over next door and borrowed Mrs. Draper's new Montgomery Ward catalogue. At first he thought he would only look to see whether the bicycles were still there. The bicycles were still there, all right, and so was the offer: "Easy Payments, Only $5 Down, $5 a Month." Waldo began filling out an easy payment order blank, just for fun:

160C3030   1 *Hawthorne Speed Model   Cherry Red* $24.40

The lower half of the blank, a contract and credit form, had beside the age space: "Minor must have order signed by parent or guardian." Waldo skipped that, making believe that he was a father ordering the bicycle for his little boy. But his five dollars down was real.

The following week he spent most of his time before and after school over at the M. K. & T. depot. He had almost given up hope when one afternoon the 4:30 local came in, and the first crate thrown out of the boxcar held a shining red bicycle. As soon as the freight train had pulled out, Harry Conklin, the station agent, helped Waldo knock off the crate and assemble the bicycle. It had $1.13 freight charges on it, and Waldo gave Mr. Conklin a check.

"This sure is a fine wheel, Waldo," Harry Conklin said. "Did your papa order this wheel for you?"

"Sure he did," Waldo said. "My papa orders me anything I want."

Then Harry Conklin said, "Well, what does the old hypocrite mean then, always carrying on against mail order companies in the *Democrat*, telling other people not to buy from them, and then he goes and buys you a bicycle from Ward's. Why don't he practice what he preaches?"

Waldo, getting set to ride away, said haughtily, "You're full of prunes, Old Man Conklin. My father is not a hypocrite. My father wanted to buy me the best bike going, and Montgomery Ward happened to have the best bike going, so he ordered it from there. That's all."

When he came riding up into the front yard on his new bicycle, his mother said, "Gracious sakes, child, where'd you get that wheel?"

"I ordered it from Montgomery Ward's, mamma. I paid five dollars down, and I'm going to pay it out with what I make driving cows every month. I've only got $19.40 left to pay. Isn't it a swell wheel, mamma?"

"Waldo, your father is going to have a duck fit when he finds this out. You'd better take it out to the barn and hide it until I can have a talk with him and sort of get him talked into the idea."

The first thing his father said the next day at noon was, "Young man, what's this I hear about you getting a bicycle on the 4:30 freight yesterday? Where'd you get the money to buy a bicycle?"

Waldo felt the bottom dropping out of everything, but he said bravely, "Why, I'm making the money driving cows this Summer, papa. So I thought I'd buy me a bicycle on the easy payment plan."

"The easy payment plan? How'd you get credit for any easy payment plan? You're just a minor. You couldn't buy that way without you had a grown-up sign your order. Who signed your order for you?"

"I don't guess they knew I was a minor, papa. I gave Winston's bank for a reference, and I just left the age space blank. So I guess—"

"Who signed your order for you, young man? Your mother?"

"No, sir. I signed it myself, only the place where you sign is so skimpy, and my name is so long, I didn't have room to write my full name. So I had to leave off the 'Junior.'"

"What! You mean you signed *my* name? Lord God, boy, that's forgery! That's a penitentiary offense!"

94

"Papa, I'll send the old bicycle back. I didn't actually want it, anyway. I'll crate it up and send it right back."

"Oh, no, you won't, neither! You're not going to wiggle out of it that easy. You forged my name to get that bicycle, now you'll keep it and take the consequences. They'll send you to the reform school for this little trick, young man! You just wait and see!"

Frightened though he was, Waldo still had hope at first. He mailed early in June the five dollars he earned in May, and a third five dollar payment in July. He was beginning to see his way through to freedom when the drouth sealed his doom.

No rain had fallen since the tenth of June. By the latter part of the month his patrons had begun saying that there was no use in sending a cow to pasture. Every blade of grass was burned crisp. Jones's cattle tanks were broad gray basins of cracked mud dotted with yellow-beaded crawfish mounds. After the first of July people kept their cows in town where at least there was water.

When the fateful dry spell closed in on him, Waldo knew that he could not meet the August payment on his bicycle. He worked every day at his father's newspaper plant, sweeping the floor, distributing type, feeding and cleaning the job press, running errands. His father gave not the slightest promise that these dogged efforts would be rewarded.

95

Montgomery Ward started dunning him about the middle of August. He still owed a balance of $9.40. He dared not send any word of explanation for fear some slip might reveal his forgery.

The collection letters grew less polite, more urgent, and finally one came saying that, unless he sent the full unpaid balance of $9.40 at once, recourse to law would be taken to collect it.

Waldo had been successful in avoiding Sheriff Ferguson for almost four months, ducking round a corner every time he caught sight of the sheriff's portly form striding down the street from the courthouse.

He might have known that God would set a trap for him that Sunday he held back the nickel from the Sunday school collection. The threatening letter from Montgomery Ward had come only the day before.

That Sunday morning Sheriff Ferguson stepped out of Danziger's Pharmacy at the moment Waldo started in to get his ice cream cone.

Some loafers were sitting on the curb watching the dust clouds roll down Broadway. They were talking about the long dry spell.

"Well, Waldo," Sheriff Ferguson said jovially, "are you about ready to start to reform school this Fall? I'm ready to take you any day now."

Waldo stood there stark with fright. The loafers

guffawed. Sheriff Ferguson laughed and ruffled Waldo's hair and walked on. Waldo didn't know whether to run or to stand still. His chin began snubbing.

Herman Gutterman, the booze-ruddy old whiskey-maker, got up from the curb and came over to him. "Don't you never let 'em guy you, Waldo. Your pappy ribbed the shiruff up to say that. I heerd him yestiddy when he done it. You're all right, son. They ain't going to send you to no reeform school. That's jist their idea of a joke." He winked a bleary blue eye at Waldo.

Waldo gave the old moonshiner a suspicious look and walked away. You couldn't believe a word a bootlegger said.

"Herman," Art Smiley said, "why don't you git in your buggy and drive on home now while the goin' is good? You was in town all day yestiddy. That was a Saturday. Today is Sunday."

"Well, sir, I tell you, Mr. Smiley," Herman said, scratching his gray head. "I would go home, but they was something I aimed to do while I was in town this time, and it has clean slipped my mind. I was just waiting around till it come to me what I aimed to do."

"I know one thing you ain't fergot to do," Art Smiley said, "and that's git tanked up. Where did you sleep last night?"

"Oh, I got friends here in town, Mr. Smiley," Herman said in a dignified tone. "I ain't entirely without friends in this town."

"Yeah, I know where you most generally meet your friends and I know where you was visitin' last night—in the back of the Ford Garage, sleepin' off a drunk," Art Smiley said. "So I think you better head for home now. If you stay around town here today you're liable to git drunk again and then I'll have to run you in and your bed in the city jail will cost you $10 and costs tomorrow mornin'."

"All right, Mr. Smiley. If that's the way you feel about it. I don't aim to stay anywhere where my presence is not appreciated. Nobody don't have to hint to Herman Gutterman but once that his company is not wanted. But, like I say, I had something important to attend to while I was in town this time and I ain't been able to recollect yit what it was."

"Well, you go on around in the alley now and unhitch that old mare of yours and git in that buggy and start for home and maybe the ride will jog your memory."

"All right, sir, Mr. Smiley, if that's the way you feel about it."

"That's the way I feel about it, Herman."

Herman Gutterman walked slowly round to the back alley and untied his mare at the hitching rack. He got into the buckboard and turned her head toward home. All along the road he let the lines droop slack. His forehead was furrowed with thought. The mare plodded west.

Just as she was turning in at the lane that led over the low hills to his small farmhouse, he slapped his legs and said, "Dad blame it all! I know now what I aimed to do. I aimed to go see old Matt Keefer and ask him to fiddle for the square dance. After invitin' all them people, I went and clean fergot the music.

"But I reckon if I drive in Monday evenin', that'll be time enough."

PAYMENTS NEVER A HARDSHIP

Do as 75 per cent of the practical home-makers are doing today . . . use your credit to get the things you need and want right away, and pay just a few dollars each month. At Sears, even on good-size orders, payments are never a hardship . . . everything is as simple and easy as A.B.C.

A GOLDEN-SKINNED washerwoman was hanging out clothes in Shannons' side yard. Her big white eyes were peeled round as she stooped and straightened over the clothesbasket. She was keeping sly watch on the clapboard castle across the street. The front door swung open to a silent trumpet blast. W. S. Winston stepped out behind his belly.

"Hee-hee-hee!" she giggled through the clothespins bristling in her wide mouth. "Eight a.m., Mis' Shannon! Double S Winston stahtin' foh he bank. Bettah go set yo' clock, Mis' Shannon. Eight a.m."

"Thank you, Hannah," Mrs. Shannon said from the kitchen window. "Clock's right on the dot this morning. It says eight, straight up."

The sliding doors of Winston's two-car garage stood open on the polished square end of an old Packard. A new Ford coach, jeweled with dew, was parked under a lath carriage porch at the side of the wooden turreted house. But W. S. Winston did not turn toward his cars. His legs carried him to work each morning.

He had nothing to do with his thick legs, toiling like pistons beneath him. Each footstep fell heavy and even on a sidewalk crease. Above the gross flesh he rode serene. An unlighted cigar was tilted against his swollen underlip. His bleak gray eyes were set straight ahead. Shrill sparrows in the catalpas aloft went quiet as he passed. Children at play stood off the walk in awe-stricken silence. The slow parade of W. S. Winston and his vast paunch moved on toward town.

Past the white frame Congregational church on the corner. Left turn. Along Division Street to the mustard brick Baptist church on the corner. Right turn. Past the Long-Bell Lumber Yard and up to the postoffice door. Left turn. He reached round to his belly and got a massive gold watch as he went in. Ten after eight.

His legs, without changing pace, solemnly marched him to Drawer Box 18. He twiddled the combination. The glass-paneled drawer slid open at his pull. He had to reach in twice to get out all the mail that had piled up over Sunday. He shuffled through the hefty clearing-house packets from Tulsa and Muskogee and Kansas City, finding among the long window envelopes one from Montgomery Ward, his copy of *The United States News*, and a red notice card, "Call at Window for Registered Mail."

Two or three stragglers left by the eight o'clock general delivery line fell away from the window mumbling, "Good mornin', Mr. Winston." He did not speak. His bleak eyes gave no sign that he had seen them.

"Oh, good morning, Mr. Winston," Elvira Draper simpered as she hopped down off her high stool.

"Good morning, lassie," he mumbled, groping round front with both hands. He found his big-barreled fountain pen. He pulled forth with a flourish the black cord that held his gold-rimmed eyeglasses.

Elvira Draper took the red card through the wicket and laid out a dog-eared registry receipt book. W. S. Winston clamped his eyeglasses astride the purple blob of his nose and poised his fountain pen over the line where Elvira had her finger. While he was signing, she went to the safe and brought back a thick envelope, heavily splotched with red wax seals. He held it at arm's length and looked at it carefully before he let the eyeglasses go flicking up to the little gold reel on his vest.

Just as he was wheeling his belly away from the window shelf, young Waldo Ledbetter, the printer's devil, ducked in at the postoffice door and almost rammed him. The small boy braked himself by dragging his bare heels on the concrete floor. W. S. Winston gave him a swat on the bottom with the heavy brown envelope.

"There, my lad," he said with a jovial chuckle, "now you can always brag that W. S. Winston once spanked you with $5,000."

The loungers in the postoffice lobby gasped and blinked. The huge sum he had named was not any more astounding than the strange sight of W. S. Winston's giving way to an impulse.

The richest man in town and his great belly went moving off up the side street toward the courthouse square. Cripple Lund sat in his toy wagon on the corner with a stack of Tulsa *Worlds* between his shriveled legs. A smile gashed his broad simple face when he saw W. S. Winston.

"Good mornin', Mr. Winston!" he cried happily as the banker stopped to get his morning paper. "I was waitin' fer you to be along. Yestiddy was a Sunday and I never got to see you. Monkey Ward's sent me a letter yestiddy. They got my order all right."

"What order is that, Lund?" W. S. Winston asked, peering down at the cripple's burly shoulders.

"Oh, don't you know last week, Mr. Winston, I ask you if I could give your name to Monkey Ward's for a credit recommendation? You said it would be all right."

"I probably had something else on my mind. What is it you're ordering?"

"I ordered me that wheel chair."

"Wheel chair? What's wrong with your wagon?"

"Oh, my wagon's all right, Mr. Winston, I guess. Only I have to pole myse'f with this here sawed-off billiard cue. I cain't make the time I could in a wheel chair. It takes me so long to deliver my papers of a evenin', the *Tribune* is threatenin' to give my route to a schoolboy if I cain't find a way to git around better. A wheel chair will be a big he'p to me on my paper route."

W. S. Winston pushed his pouted underlip in and out, chewing his dead cigar. "How much they ask for a wheel chair, Lund?"

"Three dollars down and five dollars a month, Mr. Winston. Jist $29.98 in all. It won't take me but six months to pay it out on their budget plan. Would you want to read the letter I got from them?"

Cripple Lund handed up the envelope he had been holding. W. S. Winston unfolded the mimeographed page and unreeled his eyeglasses.

Kansas City,
August 31

CO

ALVIN B. LUND,
CONCHARTEE, OKLA.
DEAR CUSTOMER:
Thank you for your Time Payment Order.

Ordinarily our credit investigation takes about ten days. We have started this investigation which we hope will enable us to make shipment promptly. It will not be necessary for you to write us about your order. We will handle it as quickly as possible and let you know.

Yours very truly,

IU : DCI   MONTGOMERY WARD & CO.

He let his glasses whip back to his vest and returned the letter to Cripple Lund.

"Hmmm. Well, Lund, ordinarily I'm opposed to instalment buying. But you've always been an enterprising chap, never let your infirmity get the better of you, and I like to encourage enterprise when I see it. Yes, I'll see to it that you get a good credit rating on this."

"I sure do thank you, Mr. Winston. Now if Postmaster Shannon will just promise me, I'll get my wheel chair all right."

"Oh, did you give Shannon's name, too?"

"Yes, sir. They ask for two business references."

"Hummm. Of course I can't give you any assurance what kind of report another reference may turn in. But I'll do all I can for you, Lund." He turned and started on up Broadway.

"I knowed you would, Mr. Winston," the cripple called gratefully after him. "I sure wisht I could do something fer you some day."

105

A wooden pole with faded red-and-white spirals marked the Sanitary Barber Shop in the middle of the block. Albert T. Kimball lay sprawled in the nickel and white-enamel front chair reading baseball news. Tony LaFarge was shaving Old Man Gresham in the warped veneer second chair.

Tony looked toward the blank front door and said mincingly, "Why, good morning, Mr. Winston!"

Al Kimball shot out of the front chair in a flurry of newspaper and smoke. Old Man Gresham reared his lathered face up to see what the joke was, but Tony was laughing too hard to tell him.

"Doggone you, Tony!" Al said, beating at the cigarette sparks on his shirt, "you went and made me burn myse'f. How'd I know he wasn't there? He's five minutes overdue now."

"Sh-h-h! Here he is, sure enough," Tony whispered. "Good morning, Mr. Winston!" he said aloud.

"Good morning, Mr. Winston!" Al Kimball gasped, flinging the rumpled newspaper over on the shoe-shine throne as he sprang forward to open the screen door. He took W. S. Winston's hat and coat and hung them on the rack six hooks away from Old Man Gresham's dust-crusted flour cap. W. S. Winston stuck a finger between his high linen collar and his wattled red neck, beginning the struggle to get off his collar and tie.

Al took down a mug with 𝖂. 𝖘. 𝖂𝖎𝖓𝖘𝖙𝖔𝖓 on it in gold letters. He got hot water at the pedestal lavatory in the center of the shop and mixed lather, busily knocking the brush against the mug. He got clean towels from the cabinet and put a fresh one on the plush neck rest. He glanced at the back mirror and saw that the collar ends were flapping free.

W. S. Winston was at work on the back stud. Al furtively shook a few black grains out of a sensen envelope and put them in his mouth. He squirted a little Lucky Tiger on his hands to take off the cigarette smell. He picked his ivory-handled Wade and Butcher from half a dozen razors that lay on the marble shelf and plucked a hair from his fine black roach to test the blade.

W. S. Winston was draping his collar and tie over a hook on the coat rack. Al grasped the nickeled side-lever and lowered the chair on its greased post.

He stood at attention while W. S. Winston, still panting from his collar tussle, heaved his great bulk up into the barber chair. The banker settled himself with the registered parcel in his lap. Then Al pressed on the lever and gently let W. S. Winston down on the flat of his back.

"Well, Mr. Winston," he asked as he tucked a clean towel under his subject's blue-webbed jowls, "who's going to win out in the World's Serious this year?"

W. S. Winston lay staring up at the embossed sheet iron ceiling. He did not answer. Al Kimball, seeing him in thought, began putting on lather, not with his slovenly wonted stroke, but as daintily as a china-painter. Over at the basin he tested the water with his fingers before he wet the towel. He let an edge of the steaming towel barely touch W. S. Winston's chin and bent down to ask, "How is that, Mr. Winston?" W. S. Winston grunted and Al laid the ends of the towel tenderly over the pouched cheeks. He took up the strop hung from the chair and pulled it taut, running his palm over the leather to moisten it. The narrow shop resounded with his stropping. First he warmed the razor on the horsehide, then he flipped over to the linen web for an edge, and then back to the horsehide for a finish. He lifted off the hot towel and painted on more suds.

"Pullin' any, Mr. Winston?" Al asked softly. The razor, his best Sheffield, was sliding smoothly along the great cheek. W. S. Winston grunted. This caused Al to lay the razor on the strop with redoubled energy.

Old Man Gresham got out of Tony LaFarge's chair and stood fishing in his thin purse for fifteen cents to pay for his shave.

"Speakin' of the World's Serious," he said to Al, "that there Telsy sure had a ball-playin' team this year."

"Yump," Al Kimball said, delicately fingering W. S. Winston's upper lip.

W. S. Winston was sitting up with cheeks talcumed and glowing when Harve Whipple of the Whipple Mercantile Company came in to get a haircut. Al Kimball, shaving W. S. Winston's neck, called out, "Well, Harve, who are you bettin' on to cop the World's Serious?"

Before Harve could answer, W. S. Winston spoke. "Mr. Whipple," he asked, "isn't old man W. F. Slover a customer of yours?"

"Oh, good morning, Mr. Winston. Yes, sir; W. F. Slover does most of his trading with me—what little trading he does these days."

"If he comes in today, tell him I want to see him at the bank."

"All right, sir, Mr. Winston, I sure will. I wouldn't be at all surprised but what he'll be in today. He wasn't in Saturday."

"Okay, Mr. Winston," Al Kimball said, giving the pink-creased neck a final flick of the talcum brush. "I guess that finishes the job for another day."

W. S. Winston eased himself out of the barber chair. He got a crisp five dollar note out of his billfold and handed it to the barber. Al made his daily plea for something smaller. That was the smallest thing W. S. Winston had. Al said that he'd chase into Danziger's Pharmacy next door for change. But

Harve Whipple thought maybe he could break a five dollar bill. Tony LaFarge stepped back with his comb and shears while Harve squirmed in the barber chair and got five limp one dollar bills out of his pants pocket. Al took out fifteen cents for the shave and counted $4.85 into W. S. Winston's hand.

"I sure do thank you, Mr. Winston," Al said, as gratefully as if he had been told to keep the change.

W. S. Winston stood tugging at his collar. Al, not yet having any answer to his baseball question, ventured a more serious topic.

"Well, Harve," he asked lightly, "what're you and the rest of the city dads going to do for the good of the community at council meeting tonight?"

"Oh, we got an important meeting on tonight, Al," Harve Whipple answered. "Voting on a resolution to call a sewer bond election."

"What's that?" W. S. Winston asked with sudden interest. "Sewer bond election?"

"Yes, sir, Mr. Winston," Harve Whipple said modestly. "It's just the resolution we're voting on tonight. Seems like there's been so much sickness this Summer and scavenger fees and all—"

"How much does the city council propose to make this bond issue?"

"Thirty thousand dollars, Mr. Winston. That's about the least a town of this size could—"

"Ye gods! Thirty thousand dollars! How do you men on the city council suppose a town of this size can stand any such outlay as that? This town is up to its neck in debt now—bonded to death."

"You're certainly right about that, Mr. Winston," Al Kimball said earnestly. "It's like I aim to tell the boys at Chamber of Commerce tomorrow—of course a sewer system is a mighty nice thing for a town to have—but you've got to consider how much a proposition like that would raise taxes—and seeing as we've made out this long without no sewer —not that I'm against progress or anything like that—"

"Yes, but, gentlemen, look here," Harve Whipple protested, "the town board don't do anything but vote a resolution to call the bond election. After that it's up to the voters. Personally, I ain't so hot on the proposition myself, but Swede Ledbetter is all steamed up over it. Maybe you read that big editorial he published in the *Democrat*, Mr. Winston? All about how these privies uptown here back of the business district was a stench in the nostrils of a civilized community and so on."

"No, I seldom ever even glance at the *Democrat*."

"Well, anyhow, Swede is chairman of the city council, and seems like he's out to put this proposition over. Personally, I'm in favor of tabling that resolution. But if the people in this town want a sewer system, it does look like they ought to have a chance to vote it or turn it down, just as they see fit."

W. S. Winston snorted as he fastened the collar round his swelling neck. "The people! Irresponsible riff-raff! Yes, they'd vote another $30,000 indebtedness on this town. What do ninety per cent of the voters care? How much taxes do they pay? It's the responsible citizens, the real property owners, that the money will have to come from."

He jerked the knot in his tie so tight that he almost choked. He jabbed his short arms into the coat Al Kimball was holding for him, took up his registered parcel, clapped on his straw hat, and stomped out of the barber shop. The other three men looked at each other with drawn, sober faces.

Before W. S. Winston had stepped over the threshold of Danziger's Pharmacy, Doc Danziger, seeing him coming, had reached into the cigar case and had set out his only box of twenty-cent coronas.

"Good morning, Mr. Winston," Doc Danziger said, dry-washing his plump hands.

W. S. Winston picked out his cigar allowance for the day in silence. He stuck five cigars into his upper vest pockets and carefully pared the sixth with a small gold knife at the end of his watch chain. An everburning gas lighter dangled from the ceiling by a rubber tube. He reached for it and stuck the end of his cigar into the glass-jeweled nickel bowl. As soon as he had got a light, he turned and walked out of the drug store, trailing smoke. Doc Danziger rang up a $1.20 charge ticket on the A drawer of the cash register.

"Double S Winston must be worried in the mind today," he said in a hurt voice to Willis Gresham, the soda jerk. "Did you notice? He didn't even speak to me."

Two Corinthian pillars of polished, barrel-thick granite upheld the narrow brick arch. W. S. Winston passed between them and rapped on the plate glass door with his diamond ring. The green shade was lettered in cracked gold leaf: "Bank Closed. Hours 9 A.M. to 4 P.M." An edge of the drawn shade lifted and Sylvester Merrick's bland black face peeped out. The door swung open at once.

"Good mawnin', Mr. Winston, suh," Sylvester said, bowing him in.

W. S. Winston walked on without speaking.

Mr. Lennox, the cashier, stood by the big aluminum-painted, dynamo-shaped safe in the front enclosure waiting for the time lock to come off. "Good morning, Mr. Winston," he sang out.

W. S. Winston walked along the grille, champing his cigar.

Bud Draper looked up from the whine and clatter of his posting machine and said, "Good morning, Mr. Winston."

The gleaming walnut door of the president's office banged shut on W. S. Winston.

Mr. Lennox blinked behind his rimless glasses. The hands on the wall clock overhead made a right angle. He stooped and deftly began twirling the combination dial. The bolts tocked back as he twisted the handle. He tugged open the thick, pleated-steel door.

Sylvester Merrick went on tiptoe across the clean tile, raising shades. As he eased up the big one at the broad plate glass east window, the sun slipped up over the courthouse and shadows spelled across the white floor: "Conchartee National Bank. Capital Stock $50,000.00. Member Federal Reserve. Deposits Guaranteed."

Mr. Lennox stood in the cashier's cage stocking the drawer with neat rolls of copper and silver and pads of paper money. The president's door opened and W. S. Winston called, "Oh, Mr. Lennox!"

Mr. Lennox passed his right hand nervously over his naked head and hurried back to the president's office. W. S. Winston sat in his big swivel chair with fingertips laced across his belly.

"Lennox," he asked, scowling at his thumbs, "why haven't you kept me posted on this movement to call a sewer bond election?"

Mr. Lennox swallowed and said, "Why, Mr. Winston, I don't know much about it myself. Week or so ago I noticed Ledbetter had an editorial in the *Democrat* about how much this town needs a sewer system. I didn't pay much attention to it, because

Ledbetter always has some hare-brained scheme going and half the time it don't amount to nothing."

"It amounts to this much—it amounts to the city council voting tonight on a resolution to call a $30,000 bond election."

"Oh! Why I didn't have no idea it had gone that far, Mr. Winston!"

"Well, get busy, Lennox. Get Ledbetter in here. How does he stand with us now?"

"We still hold that $2,000 mortgage on the printing plant. It came due last December. But he has kept up his interest payments right along, so we haven't been pressing him for the principal. He had another $50 quarterly interest payment due the first, and I have an idea he'll be in some time this morning about that."

"All right. If he hasn't showed up before noon, better send after him," W. S. Winston said, flipping his right hand.

"Yes, sir, Mr. Winston," Mr. Lennox said, turning toward the door.

"Oh, Lennox! Just a minute. What's the city's present indebtedness?"

"About $135,000, I believe, Mr. Winston."

"Believe? Don't you know?"

"I really ought to check up on it to be absolutely accurate, Mr. Winston."

"Suppose you do. And while you're at it, get all the figures—what the city tax levy is now, how much

115

a $30,000 bond issue would increase it—figure out how much it'd increase taxes on the bank's property here in town and on my residential property—and all that."

There was a faint knock at the door. Lennox opened it. An old man in tattered overalls stood there scratching the brown-streaked gray stubble on his sloped chin. He craned over Lennox's round shoulder.

"Mr. Winston, howdy. Mr. Whipple, he told me you wanted to see me here at the bank. So I come right on up here."

"Yes. Step in, Slover. Bring me those figures right away, Lennox."

Mr. Lennox went out, closing the door silently. Old Man Slover stood turning his tattered felt hat in his hands. W. S. Winston fixed him with cold gray eyes before he said anything.

"Slover, you're not my tenant. You're on that sixty that belongs to Bushager over at the Farmers and Merchants Bank. But that eighty next to you is mine, and that big brush pile down there in the draw is on my land. I want you to get that straight."

"Yes, sir, Mr. Winston, I knowed that was your land all right."

"Then what did you mean by driving Sylvester away from there Saturday afternoon? I sent that nigger out there to set fire to that brush pile. I want it cleared out of there. Sylvester comes back and reports to me that you and some of your neighbors threatened him with a shotgun and wouldn't let him do his work. What do you mean acting like that, Slover?"

"Well, sir, Mr. Winston, it's like this. That bresh pile jist about kept me and my neighbors in meat last Winter. Rabbits swarm there. When they wasn't nothing in the house to eat, we could always go rustle that bresh pile and scare out a few rabbits. We couldn' 'a' got through last Winter without that bresh pile, and we was countin' on it he'pin' the same this Winter. So when me and some of the neighbors seen the nigger down there startin' to set fahr to that bresh pile, we jist naturally told him to git on away from there."

"Slover, you don't want to go to jail, do you?"

"No, sir, Mr. Winston, I don't," the sharecropper said stubbornly, "but it ain't as if that bresh pile was on good land. It's down there in the draw whur they ain't nothin' but rocks under it, and if you was to burn it, you couldn't use the land it's on no way."

"Look here, Slover: you're not deciding for me what I'll do with my own land. I'm going to send the bank's nigger out there again in a day or so to burn that brush pile. If he meets with any more threats from you or any of your neighbors, I'll send the sheriff out next."

The old man began to whine. "Mr. Winston, that

117

little old rocky patch won't do you no good—and it's food for three families next Winter."

"That's all, Slover." W. S. Winston turned his back and began slitting open envelopes in his morning mail.

The old man plodded out. The door had scarcely closed behind him when brisk footsteps clicked on the tile outside. There was a short knock and the door opened on the gangling frame of R. W. E. Ledbetter, editor of the Conchartee County *Democrat*.

"Good morning, Mr. Winston," he called breezily. "All right to come in? Mr. Lennox said you wanted to see me."

"Yes. Close the door, Ledbetter, and have a seat."

Ledbetter sat nervously on the edge of a director's chair. "About that mortgage, Mr. Winston—I guess that's what you wanted to speak to me about. I come in this morning to make my interest payment. I know I ought to be paying something on the principal but—cotton will be coming in soon now and I'll be able to collect some advertising accounts. There'll be the farm auctions this Fall—job printing business always picks up in the Fall. I think by October I can start paying off the principal. I've kept caught up on the interest right along."

"Hmmm," W. S. Winston said coldly. "Ledbetter, I'm afraid we're going to have to call on you to do something about that mortgage before October.

Personally, I don't doubt that the investment is safe enough, but it's poor banking policy to let a mortgage run on like this. This mortgage became due and payable last December. If you can't make some arrangement to liquidate it at once, I'm afraid—very much afraid—"

There was a soft rap at the door. W. S. Winston looked up and said come in. Mr. Lennox opened the door and came tiptoeing over to the big flat-topped desk. He laid a slip of paper before W. S. Winston and silently withdrew. Ledbetter crossed his legs and with his eyes down began plucking at a run in his silk sock. W. S. Winston, sitting as close to the desk as his flesh would allow, stealthily studied the penciled figures Lennox had brought.

"Ledbetter," he asked suddenly, "what's all this hullabaloo you're kicking up about a $30,000 bond issue for this town?"

The editor jerked his head up, looking startled. "Why, Mr. Winston, I— Of course, it's not just me alone. Although I do think that a newspaper is not serving its highest purpose without it strives for community betterment—and it strikes me that this town cannot go forward much until it puts in a first-class modern sewer system."

"All very fine, Ledbetter. If this town had the money. But, as chairman of the city council, you must be aware that this town already has a bonded indebtedness of $135,000. That this town is having to set aside $7,000 every year of the world for its sinking fund. Have you ever stopped to think that a $30,000 bond issue would make a per annum appropriation of $8,250 necessary? That the present city tax levy of 24 mills would have to be raised to about 29 mills on the dollar? This town has a population of about 1,500 people, not counting the niggers. Well, say we count the niggers, and make it an even 2,000. Simple arithmetic will show you that this means a per capita indebtedness of $67.50 right now, and if we load on another $30,000, this will be increased to $82.50 owed by every man, woman, and child in this town. Now perhaps you can tell me who is going to bear the brunt of this added expenditure?"

"Well, sir, Mr. Winston, I'm not up on it well enough to call the figures offhand like you do. But I do think there's a lot to be taken into consideration. You know there's been a lot of typhoid around this Summer with all these open privies and—"

"Hrrumf! Who's had typhoid this Summer? None of your family, have they? None of mine, I know. Only typhoid cases I've heard of have been among that riff-raff down there along the creek. They live like hogs anyway; sewer system wouldn't be any use to them. Nobody in this town who amounts to anything has had typhoid this Summer."

"No, sir, Mr. Winston, I guess not. But you can't never tell where typhoid is going to break out next.

Especially with the unsanitary conditions that exists in a town of this size. Take out there back of the Sanitary Barber Shop where their waste water puddles up in the open alley. Or go the whole length of these back alleys uptown here. What a smell! Whee-oo!"

"Yes, Ledbetter, but this town could stand a lot worse smells before it would be justified in frittering away $30,000. But I'm not disposed to argue the point with you. I take it you're determined to carry on with this crusade of yours to call a bond election?"

"Well, sir, Mr. Winston, I don't hardly see how I can back down on it now—not after the editorial I run in the *Democrat* two weeks ago. The resolution is scheduled for council meeting tonight, and person'ly I feel like I ought to vote the way my convictions lies."

"Hmmm. All right, Ledbetter. Let's get back to what we were talking about before we got off on this sewer question. As I was saying, I don't see how this bank can carry that mortgage on your printing plant any longer. Not with the unsettled conditions that prevail just now. Nobody regrets a foreclosure more than I do, but the government requires us to follow strict banking regulations nowadays."

"Mr. Winston, to tell the truth, Postmaster Shannon was the one who suggested that sewer bond idea to me here awhile back. He asked me if I wouldn't

121

get behind it and I promised him I would. He's kept after me to get the city council to act on it. Of course I thought it was a sound proposition at the time, but I don't know—if it's your opinion that it'd raise taxes too much—that it might not be to the best interests of the community right now—why, I—"

"Do you suppose you can put the kibosh on that resolution?"

"I think maybe I can, Mr. Winston, if I work it right. I'll go around and see the other council members this morning. Harve Whipple never was so hot on the proposition. And Old Man Gresham usually votes like I tell him to. I don't know how much influence I can have on Dave Pollock, but all I'll need is my vote and two others."

"All right, Ledbetter," W. S. Winston said, getting up to usher him to the door. "You get busy and take care of that. And if I can give the directors some assurance that we're not going to be taxed out of existence in this town, I believe I can persuade them to let that mortgage ride indefinitely. So long as you keep up the interest payments."

Mr. Lennox was hovering outside the door. "Mr. Winston," he asked mildly, "did you—ah—get those clearing house items with the mail this morning?"

SUPERTONE PURE SILVER WOUND

Violin G Strings. Highest grade sheep gut wound with pure silver wire and brought to a high polish. Gut carefully stretched and trued before being wound. We guarantee this string absolutely against rattling or buzzing. Very durable and correctly gauged. The tone is rich, melodious and of great carrying power. Shpg. wt., 1 ounce.

12F1299 *Each Was* 69¢ *Now*..............59¢

FOUR well-dressed people sought their way across the dust-filled ruts. They paused at a rickety, bucket-weighted gate, their ears intent on the violin. Beyond a dark huddle of cedars stood a ramshackle house. Music—thin, spirited, insidious music—came swirling through a broken window.

The slender woman sang under her breath, "Get out of the way for old Dan Tucker, he's too late to get his supper."

The two large women gave her startled glances. The man in black frowned.

"Don't that beat all!" he groaned. "We traipse all the way out here through the heat and dust while he sets at home—*fiddling!* The fable of the grasshopper and the ants all over again. Matt Keefer has fiddled all through the fat years, and now when the

123

lean years come, honest folks has to get out and feed him."

"Country people say," murmured the woman who had sung, "that old Matt Keefer would rather fiddle than eat."

One of the large women bridled. "Humph! I guess old Matt has got to the place now where he'd just as soon do a little eating. Am I not right, Reverend Grotts?"

"No, Mrs. Winston," the Reverend Harley Grotts said pontifically, "that's just the trouble. Matt might be hungry, but I say he's not hungry enough. If ever he gets hungry enough, I claim he'll mighty soon quit that fiddling. No starving man would set around sawing on a fiddle. I say this: make him get out and strike a few licks of honest work!"

"Maybe old Matt hasn't ever worked," the slender woman said, "but at least he has kept the countryside in music all these years."

The other large woman snorted. "Music! My dear Mrs. Ledbetter, I hope you don't call fiddling for square dances *music!*"

"I don't know why not, Mrs. Whipple. Personally, I'd just as soon hear Matt Keefer play as I had Fritz Kreisler. I don't know—I might enjoy Matt's violin even more."

"Hunh-huh!" the two large women said.

"Of course, it may not be the kind of music you

ladies of the Delphian Club enjoy," the slender woman went on sweetly.

"Well, all I've got to say for you, Mrs. Ledbetter," Mrs. Winston said, "is that you've got mighty strange taste in music."

"Ladies! Ladies!" the Reverend Harley Grotts said, holding up two pacific hands, palms outward. "Remember that we are on a Christian mission."

He knocked on the warped gray front door. The music stopped abruptly. Footsteps sounded within. A grizzled, red-faced little man in tattered overalls opened the door. He blinked a moment. Then, tucking his fiddle and bow under one arm, he greeted them.

"Well, well; this here certainly is a surprise," he cackled cheerfully. "Come right on in, folks, and make yourse'ves to home!"

The four well-dressed people crowded into the bare, uncarpeted room. It was furnished with an iron bedstead, gaunt under its ragged quilts, and a splint-bottomed hickory chair, polished by years of energetic sitting.

The two large women sidled past into the kitchen.

"Why, I ain't had so much company since my old womern passed on, five year ago come Janerary," the little old man said, bustling about. "Here, won't you take this cheer, Mis' Ledbetter. Reverend, I reckon you'll have to set on the bed."

"We didn't come here to visit, Matt," the man in

125

black said brusquely. "We're the relief committee from town. You understand: we pass on those wanting aid and, if counted worthy, we enroll them to receive aid in the form of flour, lard, doctor's prescriptions and so on. Few days ago a report come in that you was out here all alone, starving to death. Any truth in that?"

The old man straightened his drooping shoulders. "I'm by myself here; that's true, Reverend," he replied with cool dignity, "but I ain't starved to death yit—and I ain't put in fer no free aid, neither."

The slender woman interposed, smiling, "We heard your music all the way out past your front gate, Mr. Keefer."

The bristling little man unbent at once and beamed on her.

"Did you, shore enough now, Mis' Ledbetter?" he asked eagerly. "I bet it sounded awful, now didn't it? Doggondest thing happened last week—I broke my 'G' string a-tunin' of it. I ain't been able to git a new one yit, bein' as the 'G' string is the most costliest fiddle string they is, wound with pure silver wire and all. I tried to mend it, but it ain't no use tryin' to mend a 'G' string—she'll rat and buzz on you ever' time. I don't know what I'll do next time folks wants me to play a dance. What you heard was me playin' on jist three strings. I guess you noticed what was wrong, didn't you? Didn't sound much like music, did it, Mis' Ledbetter?"

126

"Of course it did, Matt. It sounded beautiful to me. But what we came out for, really, was to see whether we—"

"Not much point to it in this case," the Reverend Harley Grotts interrupted, "but it's part of the form we go through. Have you got any money?"

"Yes, Reverend, I got a little money," the fiddler answered mildly.

"Oh, so you *have* got money! How much?"

The old man went over to the bed and dug a red tobacco tin out from under the mattress.

"It ain't much," he said. "Just some Indian-head pennies and a buffalo nickel my old womern had tucked back when she was alive. Twelve cents in all. I been sort of holdin' them coins, seeing as how they was my old womern's keepsakes."

He emptied the green-tarnished coins out into his thin hand.

"That's all right, Matt," Mrs. Ledbetter said tenderly. "You keep the coins that belonged to your wife. What we're most interested in is whether you have been getting enough to eat?"

Before he could reply, the two large women came marching out of the kitchen, one carrying an empty lard pail and the other, between thumb and fore-finger, a shriveled potato.

"No food in the kitchen," Mrs. Winston said. "Only this potato."

"Lard pail is empty," Mrs. Whipple said. "So is his flour bin."

"Tell us the truth, Matt," Mrs. Ledbetter asked softly. "How long has it been since you have had anything to eat?"

The old man hung his head and toed the floor.

"Yestiddy morning, I had a little snack, Mis' Ledbetter. I was just savin' that pertater back. I could of ate it any time I took the notion."

"Now, looky here, Matt," the Reverend Harley Grotts said in a generous tone. "We want to put you on the relief rolls. This little investigation of ours has showed us that you *need* aid all right. Now it's up to you to show that you *deserve* it. Now you put that fiddle away and git to work—around here on your own place if nowhere else. There is still plenty of time before frost to put in a late garden, especially if we git a little rain. All right then—chop wood, mend your fence out there, git some glass in these broken windows—do anything, jist so it's work.

"We give out food at the courthouse one day a week—on Wednesdays. It is Monday morning now. Wednesday is day after tomorrow. Now if you start doing some work around here, you can come in day after tomorrow and we'll fix you up with twenty-five pounds of flour and fill your lard bucket and maybe give you a piece of salt meat and some beans. But I'm telling you right now, Matt, if you don't quit the fiddling and start to work, I'm going to see to it that you don't git an ounce of relief. We'll be going now."

The man in black held the front door open while the two large women filed out. The slender woman hesitated, fumbling with her purse. The old fiddler stared wistfully out the doorway.

"Here, Matt," she said. "You take this. It's little enough, but maybe it will see you through until Wednesday."

She hurried out. The forlorn old man stood gazing after the four well-dressed people who trooped along between the blasted hollyhocks that fringed his dusty path. He watched them get into a big sedan. Mrs. Winston sat at the wheel. The car was fogging down the lane before he came to and looked down at the fifty-cent piece in his palm.

"Oh, Mrs. Ledbetter!" he whimpered.

He turned quickly and ran over to the bed. On his hands and knees, he grabbled under it and pulled out a large book. He thumbed the pages frantically and marked a place with a grimy envelope. Then he scrambled up and hurried, hatless and coatless, off toward town.

Postmaster Shannon was tending the stamp window when old Matt Keefer came hurrying into the lobby with the big book under his arm.

"Mr. Shannon," he panted, clinging weakly to the window shelf, "would you mind making out a little order for me? I've got the money right here."

129

The old fiddler pushed under the wicket an envelope and a little mound of coins.

"Sure, I'll be glad to fill out your order for you, Matt," the postmaster said, counting the coins. "But what's all this money for? You figuring on buying out Sears and Sawbuck with sixty-two cents?"

"No, sir, Mr. Shannon," Matt Keefer said earnestly. "All I want is their Supertone silver-wound 'G' string."

A BOON TO SUFFERERS

Comfortable arm rests and folding footboard. Back adjusts to many different positions from upright to full reclining. Seat, back and leg rests are durable veneered panels. Hand rims on wheels— easy to propel. Golden Oak finish. ¾ in. rubber tires. Height of back 31½ in.; seat from footboard 18 in.; depth of seat 19½ in.; width of seat 18 in.; diameter of large wheels 26 in.; small wheel 10 in.; width over all 26 in. Weight 65 lbs. Ship. wt. 105 lbs.

153D9372—Cash Price....$26.98 Easy Terms $3 Down, $5 a Mo. $29.98

W. S. WINSTON sat alone in his office reading his morning mail. He crumpled circulars and dropped them into a square metal wastebasket painted to look like mahogany.

Now and then he would look up from a letter to stare broodingly out across the quiet side-street at the Farmers and Merchants Bank building. The Farmers and Merchants Bank was of red brick, too, but it had only one granite pillar at its corner doorway.

He came to the Montgomery Ward inquiry about Cripple Lund's credit standing. After glancing at it,

131

he put it under the top flap of a brown morocco "work organizer" on his desk. The top section had a celluloid tab labeled: *For Immediate Attention.*

Postmaster Shannon put his leathery face in at the door without knocking. "Did you ask to see me, Mr. Winston?"

"Oh! Why, yes, Mr. Shannon, I believe I did mention to Lennox that I'd like to have you drop by when you came in today. Lennox said you usually didn't come in until afternoon."

"That's right. Usually I come in to get a draft for the central accounting post office in Oklahoma City, just so I get it off on the evening mail. But we got so busy Saturday afternoon—new mail order catalogues came in, the *Democrat* was two days late, and one thing and another—I didn't get to remit my postal funds. So I had to come in for a draft this morning so I could catch the noon train."

"Pull up a chair there, Mr. Shannon. We haven't had a chat in a long time. Mr. Shannon, how long is it now that we've been neighbors?"

"Why, I guess I could count it up, Mr. Winston —I reckon it's more than twenty years we've been living across from you all on the corner there. Let's see—I came to Oklahoma in nineteen-aught-three and I built that house across from you there in—"

"We've always got along mighty well as neighbors, haven't we, Mr. Shannon?" W. S. Winston put in mellowly.

132

"Why, yes, Mr. Winston, we have. Only complaint I ever had against you is your cesspool. I've spoken to you about it several times, if you recall. I had to call it to your attention again last Spring." W. S. Winston slapped his plump knees and chuckled. "That's right! You did sort of jack me up about that cesspool. I'm glad you reminded me of that. Sylvester is supposed to keep that cesspool cleaned out, but you know how you have to keep right after a shiftless nigger. I'll rake Sylvester over the coals about that cesspool this very day. But that reminds me of something I wanted to talk over with you. They tell me you're back of this movement to call a $30,000 sewer bond election."

"Well, Mr. Winston, I hope I'm not the only one in favor of it," Postmaster Shannon said stiffly, frowning over his halfmoon spectacles. "But, yes, I've been urging the city council to pass a resolution calling this sewer question to a vote. I understand they're going to pass on it tonight. I don't have any doubt about the bonds carrying if it's ever put to a vote by the citizens of this town."

W. S. Winston ran his thumbs slowly back and forth on the green edge of his plate glass desk top. "Mr. Shannon," he said in an injured tone, "I certainly wish you had discussed this matter with me before you went to the city council with it. I think maybe together the two of us might have threshed out some sort of solution. I believe I could have presented some figures that would have proved to you that a $30,000 bond issue is out of the question just now."

"The figures are available to any citizen who cares to consult the records, Mr. Winston. I know what the figures are. And furthermore, I don't see how you and I could decide a matter that's the public's interest."

"Mr. Shannon, frankly now, in light of this town's present bonded indebtedness, do you feel it can stand an additional burden of $30,000? How much taxes do you pay per annum now, Mr. Shannon?"

The postmaster had begun to get white around the corners of his jaws, but he kept his voice steady. "Altogether I pay $58 a year on my property here in town and I don't begrudge a penny of it. As for a $30,000 bond issue increasing taxes, why, the amount ordinary people, people who can't afford cesspools, have to pay out in scavenger fees now would more than cover the extra tax. Besides, the health of this community ought to be valued above a four mill tax increase."

"Mr. Shannon, the city tax levy is already 24 mills. Taxes on my property there next to you are $107 a year, almost twice as much as yours. The bank pays a total of almost $600 a year taxes on its office building here and its rent property in town. So you see who has to bear the brunt of all this excessive taxation."

Postmaster Shannon stood up and jammed on his hat. "I hardly expected you to be in favor of anything that might take a few nickels out of your pocket instead of putting a few in, Mr. Winston," he said dryly. "Why should you care about anyone else? You're all fixed up. You've got a cesspool— a cesspool that drains down the alley and keeps half my garden plot so sour nothing'll grow on it. Cesspool with an old rotten board cover that's a menace to the safety of anyone walking down the alley. No! If the rest of the community wants to get the same sanitary conveniences you enjoy, you're opposed to it."

W. S. Winston's face went white, then turned red. "Mr. Shannon, you'd do well to alter your tone toward me," he growled. "I'm not entirely without power in this community, you know."

"Humf," Postmaster Shannon said waspishly. "If you're thinking of your power to get me thrown out of the post office, I'm not going to let that worry me. Hop to it. Meanwhile, it's a simple matter for me to transfer the postoffice account over to the Farmers and Merchants Bank. There's one man in this town that you can't dictate to and that's me. And if you don't do something about that cesspool draining down on my place, I intend to take legal steps against you for maintaining a public nuisance."

"Good day, Mr. Shannon!"

"Good day, Mr. Winston!"

Postmaster Shannon stumped out, leaving the door open behind him. W. S. Winston, breathing hard, glared at the open door, and moved as if to get up and close it. He creaked back into his swivel chair. He reached up and pulled a soggy cigar butt out of his mouth and glared at it a moment before he flung it toward a tall brass spittoon. He sat pushing his lips in and out furiously, blood darkening in his face.

As soon as he began to get his breath better, he got up and went to the door. Sylvester was washing the big front window. W. S. Winston put up his right forefinger and wriggled it. Sylvester propped the squeegee against the glass and came trotting.

"Sylvester, how long has it been since you cleaned out the cesspool at my house?" he asked angrily.

"Hit's been about fo' months now, Mr. Winston —las' May, I think. But don't you recollect, Mr. Winston, I repo'ted to you about that cesspool needin' repair. That boa'd top is all rotted out. And the bricks has all fell o'ten the sides. It ought to have some masonic work done on it right away. I esspeck hit'll take right at $25 to put that cesspool back in shape again, Mr. Winston."

"Hmmm. Well! That's all, Sylvester. Go on back to your work."

136

As Sylvester turned away, R. W. E. Ledbetter came striding in through the front door.

"Well, Mr. Winston," he began breathlessly, "I went around and talked to Harve Whipple and Dave Pollock and they—"

"Just step inside my office, Ledbetter, and close the door."

R. W. E. Ledbetter followed W. S. Winston in and closed the door. The banker lowered himself into his swivel chair. Ledbetter stood with his hat in his hand.

"Now, what was it, Ledbetter?"

"I've got it all fixed, Mr. Winston. It didn't take hardly any argument at all. First I talked to Harve Whipple and he said he'd seen you this morning at the barber shop and that he was in favor of tabling the proposition. I told him I'd just about decided that way, too. So we both went to see Dave Pollock and Dave said he was for whatever the rest was. And Old Man Gresham will do what we tell him to. So I believe I can manage to keep that resolution tabled indefinitely if we can sort of keep the thing quiet."

"Good, Ledbetter," W. S. Winston said with his chin tucked down. Suddenly he raised his head and fixed his bleak gray eyes on the editor. "Ledbetter, how would you like to be postmaster?"

R. W. E. Ledbetter blushed and stammered. "Why, I don't know, Mr. Winston. I mean—of

CATALOGUE

course, if they was to throw Old Man Shannon out
and there was a vacancy, why, I guess I'd go take the
examination, being as I'm an ex-service man and
would get the preferred rating. I have often thought
that the post office and my printing business would
go very nicely together. Only trouble is, I backed the
wrong man for Congress in the primaries last year,
so I doubt—"

W. S. Winston flipped up a meaty hand. "Con-
gressman Roscoe Stubbs is a personal friend of mine
—under plenty of financial obligations to me. He's
going to be in Tulsa Friday. How'd you like to go
up and have a talk with him? I'll give you a letter
to him. If you want the post office here, I think it
can be arranged."

"Why, Mr. Winston, this is such a surprise to me,
I don't hardly know what to—"

"That's all right, Ledbetter. You make arrange-
ments to be in Tulsa Friday to see Stubbs and I'll
take care of the rest. That's all now."

After Ledbetter had gone out overcome with grat-
itude, W. S. Winston pulled open the lower drawer
of his desk. He reached down and lifted a thick mail
order catalogue to his lap. He got his eyeglasses on,
found "S" in the yellow index section, and murmured "six-four-nine" as he flipped over a hundred
pages in the back of the catalogue.

138

281D8210 SEPTIC TANK

A white-on-black caption was spread across page 649:

A MODERN SEWAGE SYSTEM
NO MATTER WHERE YOU LIVE

"Ummmm," he bumbled, reading slowly with pursed lips:

Indoor plumbing—city-like in its sanitary, carefree operation—is easy to have! Once in the ground it practically never requires care—just occasional cleaning at 1- to 5-year intervals, depending on soil conditions. No odors, no chemicals, no moving parts. Natural bacterial action destroys all matter—liquids pass off through drainage bed. Complete instructions included. We recommend you order one size larger than actual requirements. . . .

He unscrewed the cap on his fountain pen and tore a perforated order blank from the back of the catalogue. He filled in the order blank:

281D8210 *One Sanitary Septic Tank* 300 *gal. cap.* $17.95

Opposite "indicate How You Want Order Shipped" he put an X in the square beside "Freight." He made out a check for $17.95, folded it with the order blank and tucked it into one of the mail order company's brown print-addressed envelopes. He was licking the flap when Bud Draper came to the door with a shorthand notebook.

"Mr. Winston," he asked, "did you want me to take any letters before noon?"

W. S. Winston looked at his watch. "It's a quarter after eleven now," he said. "Yes, we might work in a few letters before I go to dinner."

Bud Draper sat down on the other side of the desk with his shorthand notebook open and his pencil ready. W. S. Winston puffed out his cheeks and folded his hands across his belly and leaned back in his chair with his eyes closed.

"Take one to Honorable Roscoe J. Stubbs, Mayo Hotel, Tulsa. 'My dear Roscoe.' Ah— Harrumf! No, make that 'My dear Stubbs.' Uh—"

W. S. Winston leaned forward in his chair and scratched his head and grimaced. He stared out the window. Across the way Postmaster Shannon came out of the Farmers and Merchants Bank and started down the street. There was a sound of metal wheels trundling on the cement sidewalk and someone crying hoarsely, "Mr. Shannon! Mr. Shannon!" Cripple Lund, poling his toy wagon for all he was worth, came into view. Postmaster Shannon turned and came back to meet him. W. S. Winston could see Cripple Lund talking earnestly and Postmaster Shannon nodding and smiling. He and the cripple shook hands and parted. Bud Draper looked up from his shorthand notebook and saw W. S. Winston sitting there with his mouth open.

"Just let that letter to Stubbs go for a while," W. S. Winston said, reaching to get a letter from the top flap of his leather desk file, "and take one to Montgomery Ward, Kansas City.

"GENTLEMEN: Your inquiry of the thirty-first ultimo received and contents duly noted. As regards credit standing of Alvin B. Lund, this man is a hopeless cripple without steady income, and it is our well-advised opinion that he is a very poor credit risk. . . ."

IT COSTS US

more than a dollar to place this catalogue in your
hands. We send it to you gladly without charge, con-
fident that you will recognize its worth. Look it
over carefully . . . read the story of value it brings.
In a spirit of fairness to us as well as to yourself,
we ask you to give it your careful consideration.

TUESDAY noon, after everyone had finished his small dipper of banana-nut ice cream and slice of pound cake, Veronica Smiley, popular manageress of the Broadway Café, came in with the extra help she hired on Tuesdays and Saturdays to clear away the dirty dishes.

Up at the head table Albert T. Kimball, Chamber of Commerce president and proprietor of the Sanitary Barber Shop, hummed to give the other boys the pitch and started them off to the tune of "Pack Up Your Troubles":

Kick all the grouchers off the old green earth
　And roar, roar, roar;
For they've annoyed us ever since their birth,
　Roar, boys, make them sore;
What's the use of worrying and fretting to the core?
So kick all the grouchers off the old green earth
　And roar, roar, roar!

142

The roars were not so loud as they might have been, so Al Kimball shouted, "Come on, fellas—if you cain't sing, jist he'p make a noise!"

He swung them into a rousing parody of "There Are Smiles":

There are clubs built just for hoboes,
    There are clubs built just for Japs;
There are clubs made up of Poles and Dagoes,
    And a dozen other foreign maps.

There are clubs where niggers mix with white folks,
    There are clubs that travel in reverse,
But the club that always boosts Conchartee
    Is our Cham-ber of Com-merce.

Then they sang a comic after-luncheon favorite about Greedy Nellie, who ate some oysters, clams, marmalade, and johnnycake, and then drank some beer, each thing she ate or drank making a verse. Nellie never knew what made her feel so queer, and the Chamber of Commerce members all tried hard to keep from laughing about it when they joined in on the final stanza—*up* came the oysters and *up* came the clams, and *up* came everything, a verse at a time, that they had sung about Nellie's having eaten in the first stanza.

After that song everyone was laughing and in good humor. Harve Whipple tried to start a necktie pulling. But before many ties had been yanked, Al Kimball stood up and made his empty water glass ring by tapping it with his knife.

"Boys," he said, as soon as everyone had quit scuffling, "today we are going to hear a message from R. W. E., better known by his alias of 'Swede,' Ledbetter, our popular newspaperman. Now if 'ye ed' will kindly stand up, I'll let him speak for hisself, which will be better than me talking for him. How about giving Swede a hand, boys?"

Al Kimball started clapping his hands and the others joined in riotously. The Chamber of Commerce was chuckling and grinning, but when R. W. E. Ledbetter stood up he was not smiling. His long pink cheeks were set and his eyes were serious back of his hornrimmed glasses.

"Boys," he began, brushing back his hempen forelock, "I guess you have all heard that poem about where a certain community in the olden times was so infested with rats that nobody couldn't hardly live in it. So the town dads calls in a fellow to rid out the rats and it seems like this fellow claimed to be able to get them out, I mean the rats out, by playing music on his pipes and had made quite a rep for himself, being reputed far and wide as the Pied Piper of Hamburg. Well, I don't know as this has got much to do with what I'm going to say. But I was reminded of it, because if you boys don't dub me the Pied Piper of Conchartee [Laughter] when I get done outlining this proposition I have worked out

144

in the interests of this town, I'm going to be mighty disappointed, and uh—

"The point I am making is, I guess you all know that the plague of Monkey Ward and Sears Sawbuck [Laughter] catalogues has descended upon us once more again this year. Now anyone who read my editorial in last week's *Democrat* will appreciate my attitude on this subject.

"Men, year after year we are confronted with this situation of our farmers' and fellow citizens' money being milked out of our trade territory. It seems to me like, as I look back on it now, we have been taking this tough situation laying down and thus far have not done anything about it. Oh, yes: we have tried to knock the mail order companies by making fun of them and so on. But what effect does that have? Men, I think it was about time something actually was *done* to correct this situation of Kansas City and Chicago mail order firms taking this business right out from under our noses and—and uh—taking thousands of dollars out of our trade territory, and—and so forth.

"Boys, there is nothing like a little gray matter applied to these situations. Someone has said, if I remember right it was Arthur Brisbane, who makes $50,000 a year, the highest paid editorial writer in the world, has said, 'It takes a combination of four G's to put anything across: Gumption plus Grit plus Git-Up-and-GO!' [Laughter and Applause.]

145

Well, there is this to be said: I think this scheme of mine has the Gumption. Now all we need is the Grit and Git-Up-and-Go to counteract a tough situation.

"Just to be brief, my idea is to get hold of every one of these mail order catalogues that came in here last week and get them out of circulation. Absolutely destroy them. That is the one and only way we can manage to keep home town money at home.

"Now I see some of you looking doubtful already, and you're probably going to ask me: 'O.K., Swede; but how're you figuring to put this proposition through to final completion? Boys, right there is where the Home Town Industry Jubilee and Bonfire enters in! Which I thought would be a good name for this scheme.

"Last Friday afternoon when I saw that truckload of mail order catalogues coming in, I says to myself, 'R. W. E., that is just like a truckload of pests being brought in to be turned unloose on the community.' And then I said to myself, 'If the State was able to almost rid this country of coyotes by paying a bounty for coyote pelts, why could not the merchants of this town work the same scheme and get rid of mail order catalogues?' Now the mail order firms claim that it costs them better than a dollar apiece to get those big catalogues out. I don't doubt it a bit, because I know printing prices.

"What I want ever' merchant in town to do is

146

agree to pay one dollar in trade for each one of these catalogues that is brought in to them. Don't worry about whether the country people'll bring 'em in. Just depend on me for that. By working fast, there is no question in my mind but what we can clean up ever' single one of the six hunderd catalogues, which I understand was the number shipped in here, in a week's time. We can't take a day longer, because every day means just that much more money being drained out of our trade territory. And to keep from causing any ill-will among the country folks, we end up on the deadline set for bringing in the new catalogues by having a big Home Town Industry celebration with a big bonfire made out of the catalogues.

"Now all I want to know is, are you boys with me with the Grit and Get-Up-and-Go to put this proposition over?"

R. W. E. Ledbetter sat down and there was loud applause. Then there was a moment's silence until Harve Whipple spoke up.

"What about financing the proposition, Swede?" he asked doubtfully. "A proposition like that would need some financing."

Two or three other men who had been looking dubious, nodded their heads and said, "Yeah, what about the finances, Swede?"

"I'm glad you brought that question up, Harve!"

147

the editor said, springing to his feet before the discussion became general.

He pulled a folded sheet of paper from his hip pocket.

"Now about buying in the catalogues. Some merchants, of course, will have more brought to them, some less, depending on the number of customers he has. But with every business in town that stands to lose by mail order competition lined up on this—no reason why a single merchant should hold out—we'll have twenty businesses taking catalogues in trade. This would make each take in around thirty catalogues apiece, more or less, and thirty dollars is not going to break anybody up. More especially thirty dollars in trade, which you can figure as representing about ten or fifteen dollars actual outlay at wholesale. Why, it would be a keen trade-stimulator even if you wasn't getting shed of the catalogues. But what I'm pointing out is that you can count on this money coming back ten-fold with your increase in business when we cut off the mail order competition, by getting the catalogues out of the people's hands.

"Now I have here a two-page advertising layout. Down the center runs a full explanation of the Home Town Industry Jubilee, explaining in big type the catalogue trade-in idea. All around this is space for twenty small ads. I want ever' merchant that comes in on this deal to have an ad in one of

148

these spaces. We'll run this, a double-page spread, in the *Democrat* this week. Also we'll want to run off some 30 by 22 circulars, about a thousand, which I'll print at cost, and we'll circularize the town and this entire trade territory.

"I contribute the idea free of charge. Of course the *Democrat* will join right in and take catalogues in payment for subscriptions or on job printing work. So don't suspicion that I'm trying to make any big profit on this deal.

"Today is Tuesday, August the twenty-eighth. Now to put this over right, we ought to have those circulars printed and in the mail by tomorrow morning. The *Democrat* will follow on Thursday with its big double-page ad. I'll leave it up to the rest of you to set a date for the Home Town Industry Jubilee, but if you take my advice you'll make it just as quick as possible—I'd say a week from tomorrow, which is September fifth.

"Now by all of us pulling together on this, we can put it across in fine shape, and the financing hadn't ort to worry anybody."

ALLURINGLY LOVELY—

does HE say that about your complexion? Is your hair the shining crown of glory you'd like it to be? Hands . . . nails . . . eyes . . . do they proudly meet the test of his critical glances? . . . Every woman has some "best" feature! Are you dramatizing Nature's gift or hiding it with the wrong kind of make-up? . . . These are the problems millions of women are facing every day. To help you solve them, Sears have secured the services of Mlle. Lorraine de Barker, well known beauty specialist. Whatever your particular problem—oily skin, large pores, drab lifeless hair—she is ready to give it individual attention and advice. . . .

THE Widow Holcomb came flouncing into the post office Tuesday afternoon. She had her hair tucked under a wide, floppy-brimmed hat and the hat was fixed on with three long hatpins. She walked right on past Gladys Ferguson and Elvira Draper sitting at the stamp and money order windows, without speaking. She stopped at the parcel post window. Postmaster Shannon was standing there.

"Mr. Shannon," she asked, "did I get a package on the noon train?"

"Why, no, Mrs. Holcomb—we get very little mail

on that train and seldom ever any parcel post. Our big mail comes in on the 5:45 and at night."

"Mr. Shannon," she said sharply, "that package ought to be here right now. I asked Mr. Slemmons about it this morning out on the route and he said that he hadn't seen anything of it. So I thought maybe it might have been left here in the office."

"Why, no, I don't think so, Mrs. Holcomb," Postmaster Shannon said with unruffled calm, "but I'll go look in the package rack for you. I usually handle all the parcel post myself and I believe that if it had come in I would have seen it."

He turned to the long wooden rack that was divided into alphabetical compartments. "No, Mrs. Holcomb; only one package in the H box and that's for Charlie Hargris here in town. Where were you expecting the package from?"

"Kansas City," she snapped. "It's an order from Sears."

"Well, maybe you're expecting it a little too soon. I've noticed that lots of times when people come in here all heated up over not receiving a package they think is overdue, the package usually comes in on the next mail in record time."

"No, sir! This package of mine should of come in Monday afternoon, or Tuesday morning at the very latest. I've had lots of dealings with Sears Roebuck and they're very prompt."

"Do you remember what day you mailed your

151

order, Mrs. Holcomb?" Postmaster Shannon asked mildly.

"I certainly do. I distinctly remember. I got that order off on the noon train Saturday. That would have put it in Kansas City the first thing Monday morning and it should have got here this morning at the very latest."

"Well, yes—you're not allowin' any too much time, but the customary thing is for a mail order company to fill orders the same day received. It would have just about had time to get here last night on the midnight train. What was in the package, Mrs. Holcomb?"

"Why, it was—oh, it was just some little things I was needing. Anyway, I don't see that it's anybody else's business but mine what was in the package."

"It's the post office's business any time it wants to know what's going through the mail," Postmaster Shannon said, losing his temper a little. "Not that the post office department is particularly interested in what you are ordering. I just thought maybe it might help to know what size package you were expecting, whether it would be shipped outside the sack, and so on. Sometimes a very small package gets caught in the sack when we're shaking out the mail, gets sent back to the mail sack depository, and isn't found for months or even years. Do you have any idea what size package yours will be?"

"Why, I suppose you would call it a small pack-

152

age. It's not likely to be in a very large package, but it won't be tiny, either. Just a medium small package."

"Then I'll go back to the sack pile and shake out the sacks again," Postmaster Shannon said. "It might be there."

The widow stood tapping her toes, nibbling her underlip.

Postmaster Shannon came back to the window in a few minutes.

"Nope! Isn't there, Mrs. Holcomb. And I'm reasonably sure that no package for you has come into the office within the last few days."

"Oh, Mr. Shannon," she wailed, on the verge of tears. "I got to have that package! I've *got* to! I can't go any place until I do get it! Tell me what to do, Mr. Shannon. I've got to have it right away. I can't wait any longer. What can I do?"

"Well, I don't know what it is you've ordered, Mrs. Holcomb, but you're in such urgent need of it, why don't you try to buy it here in town and then return the duplicate to Sears when it finally comes."

"No, it's nothing I can buy here in town— Oh, I suppose I *could*—but, no, I *can't* buy it here in town."

"If it's as important as you say it is, I suggest that you write, or even telegraph, to Sears and ask them to check up on your order. I think possibly it'll come in tonight or in the morning, but just to guard against any possibility of oversight write to them and—"

"I have written to them," the Widow Holcomb said grimly. "I've got the letter right here in my hand to mail. And maybe you think I don't burn them up! I bet you they never hold up another order of mine. What I mean is, I'm getting them told. I never needed anything so bad in my life and then they go and take their own sweet time about getting it here, when they've never took over two days before. Somebody's to blame for this and it's either them or the post office—I don't know yet which."

She turned and stuffed a letter through the drop and her high heels went clicking out of the lobby.

Postmaster Shannon winked at Elvira Draper and Gladys Ferguson. "I'll bet her package comes in on the next mail, what do you bet?" he said.

"Heck, I know what it is she's got ordered," Elvira said, arching her eyebrows. "She don't need to make such a secret of it. Ever'body knows she dyes her hair, only she don't know they know it."

"I guess you wouldn't have been sure of it, either," Postmaster Shannon said acidly, "if you hadn't pried into that package of hers last Winter."

"Gee whiz, if it was me and I was needin' it that bad," Gladys said, "I'd get on the 'bus and go to Tulsa and buy me a bottle."

"You don't know, kid," Elvira said. "When you

154

think you've got ever'body fooled as bad as she thinks she has, you don't even want to face a strange drug clerk any more than you do a drug clerk who knows you."

R. W. E. Ledbetter came hustling into the post office. He slapped a greenback down at the stamp window.

"Elvira," he said, "can you give me ten dollars' worth of pre-canceled ones right quick."

"Yes, I can, Mr. Ledbetter," Elvira said, opening the stamp drawer and counting out ten sheets of one-cent stamps. "But you'll have to wait until I can go run the canceler over them."

"Oh, hello, there, Ledbetter," Postmaster Shannon said coolly. "I hadn't seen you yet today."

"No, sir, Mr. Shannon—I don't know whether you've heard about it yet or not—I've got this Home Town Jubilee business on my hands and I'm jist about run to death."

"I was talking to Dave Pollock this morning, and he tells me that the city council tabled that resolution to call a sewer bond election. I certainly was surprised to hear that, Mr. Ledbetter."

"Yes, sir, Mr. Shannon. It come as a surprise to me, too. But that seemed to be the will of the majority, so they wasn't nothing I could do about it."

"Then I suppose that means that this town must

go through another Summer without a sewage system?"

"Well, I guess it does, Mr. Shannon. But you know how I feel about it person'ly—I sure hope it don't. Only thing was, I just couldn't buck the other three boys on the council and do any good."

"Are you right sure that Double S Winston wasn't the one you were afraid to buck?" Postmaster Shannon said cruelly.

"Why, no, Mr. Shannon, I don't see how you could suggest such a thing. Of course Mr. Winston has got a right to register his opinion, just like any other responsible citizen— But, no, I think I can speak for the other members of the council in saying that we was all sincere in acting for the best interests of the community when we tabled that sewer bond issue—for the present, anyhow."

"I suppose you know that the city council can be forced to act by petition?"

"Well, sir, to tell you the truth, Mr. Shannon, I hadn't thought much about it. You see, I've got so much on my mind with this Home Town Industry Jubilee proposition—we're working overtime tonight to get the circulars printed. Going to mail out a thousand circulars first thing in the morning. I jist haven't got time to think about nothing else."

"If you Chamber of Commerce boosters would spend more time on trying to make this town a decent place to live in instead of a stink hole on the face of the earth, and less time fooling with these addled-brained schemes to stimulate trade, you might halfway justify your existence," Postmaster Shannon said testily.

"Why, Mr. Shannon!" R. W. E. Ledbetter said, shocked stiff. "Sometimes I think you're a downright Red, even if you are a Republican postmaster. Just to be frank with you, Mr. Shannon, you could be a leading citizen in this town if you wasn't so radical. What you lack is civic pride. I'm just telling you man to man, now, Mr. Shannon."

Postmaster Shannon got a grip on himself and went back to the ice water keg and drew himself a long cold drink.

OFFICIAL BOY SCOUT HANDBOOK

For boys who love the out of doors. Indispensable to boy scouts. Durably bound in limp blue keratol. Illustrated. 650 pages.

3F1657 .... 50¢

LATE Tuesday afternoon Art Smiley came stalking into the postoffice lobby with the nape of Bill Huggins in one hand and a smoldering United States flag in the other.

"We shore guessed right, Mr. Shannon," the town marshal said through the stench of burnt cloth. "He stolen the flag, jist like we suspicioned he did. I caught him out back of Hugginses' barn and I bet you cain't guess what he was doin', Mr. Shannon. He was a-burnin' the flag, Mr. Shannon. Yes, sir; he was *burnin' up the flag.* I didn't have a minute to spare. I nabbed him jist before he destroyed the evidence. He already had the flag on fahr, and it ain't quite put out yit. You ort to seen him fight when I tried to stomp it out!"

The postmaster left his wicket and came to unlock the partition door. "Bring him right in here to my desk, Art," he said, "where we can have this out quietly."

Art Smiley shoved the youth through the door and

flung him into an office chair. Bill Huggins slumped down sullenly. Little spasms kept jerking his flat chin back against his neck.

"He won't talk, Mr. Shannon," Art said. "I tried to make him tell me how come he done it, but he won't talk. I cain't get a word out of him. But he fit like a bobcat when I tried to stomp the fahr out of that flag."

"You just let me attend to him, Art. He'll talk to me all right." The postmaster turned to the sniveling youth and said with heavy sarcasm, "Now ain't you a pretty specimen! You'd better speak up while you've got the chance."

Bill Huggins gave him a surly glance and kept still.

"So you stole the postoffice flag, did you?" the postmaster went on. "Boy Scout! And then went and set fire to it. Without using any matches, I reckon. Boy Scout! A great big overgrown lout like you! I guess you learned to burn up flags in the Boy Scouts, eh? Well, I don't know what you learn in the Boy Scouts, but *I'm* going to see if I can instill a little genuine respect for the U. S. flag in you."

At this Bill Huggins jerked himself up in his chair, bridling. "The United States flag!" he cried. "You're a fine person to be talking about respect for the United States flag, Mr. Shannon. You've got a fat nerve to be talking like that, I must say.

159

Who're you to be talking about respect for the United States flag?"

The postmaster was thrown off his guard by this savage onslaught. "Who am I to be talking about respect for the U. S. flag? Why I'm the U. S. postmaster here, that's who I am, you young smart aleck, you! Don't you get fresh with me, young fellow! I'm the duly constituted representative of the United States Government in this town, that's who I am. If you only knew which side your bread is buttered on, you'd address me with respect as such, sir!"

Postmaster Shannon was rigid with anger. Bill Huggins sneered openly.

"Well, all I've got to say is, Mr. Shannon, you've got plenty to learn about your job."

The postmaster, on the defensive now, snapped back, "Oh, I have, have I? Why, young man, I'll venture to say that there's not a postmaster in this State that knows his job better than I do—that has made a more thorough study of the Postal Laws and Regulations. Anyway, I know enough about my job to know this: you're facing a federal charge right now for stealing and mutilating government property."

Art Smiley, who had been standing there gaping, dumbfounded by this sudden strange turn of things, came to. "You don't have to take no more sass offen him, Mr. Shannon," he said anxiously. "I'll haul him right on up to jail now."

160

"You better not put me in jail," the Boy Scout said with a menacing leer. "I know too much."

"Leave him right there until he has said his little say, Art," the postmaster said. "Now, young man, just you explain that last statement, please. Then we'll decide how to deal with you."

"All right, Mr. Shannon," the brazen youth said, taking on a pompous tone. "You claim you know so much about respect for the United States flag and the Government for which it stands—well, Mr. Shannon, I guess I ought to try and refresh your memory a little. Let me just read you a few lines from the Boy Scout Handbook."

It was plain now that he had the upper hand. He pulled a blue, limpbacked book from his pocket and flipped it open. "This here is the chapter on *Respects Due the Flag of the United States of America*," he said, giving his elders a brash look.

Postmaster Shannon turned red. "Just a minute," he said hotly. "If you mean we left the flag out all night last night, if that's what you mean, that was an oversight, and I regret it as much as anyone. But if you think you can sneak out of stealing and burning the postoffice flag on a slim excuse of that kind, young man, you've got another think coming."

"Naw, that's not what I mean at all. You just let me read this. 'Number one: *Cautions, Do not permit any disrespect to be shown to the flag of the United States of America.*' All right. Them's our orders in

161

the Boy Scouts. The Boy Scouts of America is the strongest patriotic organization in the country. Maybe you didn't know that.

"Now here on page 72 it says:

WHAT TO DO WITH WORN-OUT FLAGS

Old or worn-out Flags should not be used . . . *hmm.* When a Flag is in such condition that it is no longer a fitting emblem for display, it should not be cast aside nor used in any way, but should be destroyed as a whole, privately, preferably by burning . . . (from Flag circular issued by War Department April 14, 1923).

"Preferably by burning, it says. Now, Mr. Shannon, if you had been up on your job as much as you let on like you are, you would of seen that flag was no longer a fitting emblem of display. That flag— anybody except a blind man could see it—is all faded and frayed and whipped out at the edges. Mr. Shannon, you ought to of taken that flag out and burned it yourself two weeks ago. When you didn't do it, I just done my duty as a Boy Scout and burned it for you. So how do you get that way—claiming I stole the flag?"

The Boy Scout sat back in his chair and perked his head in triumph. Art Smiley's jaw was hanging low. Postmaster Shannon was looking blank. After a moment the postmaster reached over and took the Boy Scout Handbook.

162

"Let me see it," he said. He read in silence a little while. Then he said, looking puzzled, "That's what it says, all right. I just can't figure it out. All that about worn-out flags is here, but right over on the next page it says, 'The two flags flying over the Capitol are replaced every six months.' Well, that's all the oftener the Department issues me a new flag. I'm only allowed to put in requisition for a new one every six months. And that flag Mr. Smarty here burnt up still had a good three months left to go. I guess these sand and wind storms out here puts more wear on a flag than it would get up in Washington, D. C. Anyway, it sure says here that a worn-out flag is supposed to be burnt."

The town marshal suddenly began whooping with laughter. "Well, Mr. Shannon, I reckon the boy has got you there, all right. Bill sure knows his stuff about respects to the flag, don't he, Mr. Shannon? We never get too old to learn, eh, Mr. Shannon?"

A self-satisfied smirk covered Bill Huggins' face. "And furthermore," he said easily, "I don't mind telling you, Mr. Smiley, that when you stomped on that United States flag, you desecrated it, and according to Regulation 12 of the proclamation made by the president, April 6, 1917, you are subject to arrest and punishment."

Art Smiley stopped laughing and pondered this accusation.

Bill Huggins got up and swaggered toward the

partition door. "Well, if that's all you had to ask me," he said brightly, "I guess I'll be going."

Postmaster Shannon jumped across and grabbed him by the seat of the pants. "Hold on! Don't be going yet, son! I sat and listened while you read to me out of your little book. Now you just sit down and listen while I read to you out of a book I've got."

He pushed the youth back into his chair. He turned to his desk, picked up a thick, paperbound book, and ran his forefinger down a pink index column.

"Page 400," he murmured, turning to the middle of the mail order catalogue. "Now listen close to this, Bill:

"United States Flags

"Forty-eight stars sewed on each side. Double-sewed seams. Heavy canvas headings with grommets. Size recommended for public buildings, 5 x 8 feet. All wool flags. 6F2603 *Price*, $6.45

"Now, Bill, it'll be three months before the Department issues me a new flag. Meanwhile I don't propose to have this post office going without a flag. So you see that push-broom over there in the corner? And you see that drum of floorsweep right beside it? Well, you take that broom and a scoopful of floorsweep and you get out there in that lobby and start sweeping. And you keep that lobby clean every day until I tell you you've worked out what it's going to cost me to get a new flag for this post office."

Bill Huggins sprang out of his chair, protesting, "Mr. Shannon, you haven't got no right to try and make—"

Art Smiley interrupted him. "And if you don't keep that floor clean," he said, stepping up and shaking his fist under Bill Huggins' nose, "until Mr. Shannon tells you you can quit, I'm gonna take it out of your hide. You blamed little old stuck-up rascal, you, trying to accuse me of shamin' the United States flag! I don't keer if you did read it in a book somewheres—I never done no sich thing. All I was doing was trying to put that fahr out, and you know it. Dern your hide, anyway, trying to make out like *I* insulted the United States flag!"

Bill Huggins cowered before the town marshal's threatening hands. Then he walked meekly over and took up the broom and a scoopful of red floorsweep. He went out into the lobby. They heard the broom start swishing over the littered concrete floor.

Art Smiley stood there with his jaw set hard, clenching and unclenching his big hands. Postmaster Shannon grinned and winked at him.

"Well, Art," he said, chuckling, "I guess there ain't much I can teach that boy about respects to the flag, but I bet you I can give him a good course in respect for public property."

THE FIRST CATALOGUE,

published in 1872, was a single sheet affair, resembling a handbill more than anything in the catalogue line; and in comparison with our present catalogue, listing approximately 75,000 articles and containing 25,000 illustrations, is almost ridiculous . . . 1874. This year the price sheet was superseded by an eight-page catalogue three by five inches in size . . . 1875. This year the catalogue contained seventy-two pages and, for the first time, illustrations—a few wood cuts showing a "Grange" hat, a bed spring, farm wagon and a line of trunks and valises . . . 1876. The catalogue was a book of 152 pages . . . 1878. The catalogue page size was increased to 6 by 8½ inches and the wood cut illustrations included one woman's dress—the first mail order fashion picture . . . 1883. The page size was increased to 8½ by 11 inches . . . 1889. The catalogue listed 25,000 articles . . . 1896. Halftone illustrations, engravings made from photographs of merchandise, appeared in the catalogue for the first time. Children's hats and a line of corsets on living models were shown in halftone on a heavy, highly coated paper insert . . . The fall catalogue of this year had a three-color process page showing a line of children's caps in actual colors . . . 1897. A few fashions were shown by halftone on the regular catalogue paper stock, evidence that the halftone was

166

now becoming recognized as a practical thing for the mail order catalogue. . . . The circulation and size of the catalogue increased so fast that a time soon came when no printing establishment in the United States carried enough type of one kind to prepare the catalogue. To meet this condition, special type faces were designed and cast for catalogue work . . . 1904. Up to this time customers had been required to make a small payment—fifteen cents—in order to insure that the books would go to people who were genuinely interested. But this year it was decided to change the method of supplying catalogues. Three million catalogues of 1,130 pages, weighing approximately four pounds each, were distributed free of charge. . . .

A MORNING breeze moved down the long cool tunnel of the Whipple Mercantile Company. It swayed gently the dangling clusters of bandannas, work socks, tinware, and bologna. It mingled the odors of calico, leather, coffee, kerosene, tobacco and cookies.

Two or three loafers were already sitting round the cold iron stove in the center of the store. The long swish of a broom sounded in the grocery department, where Harve Whipple was sweeping out for the day.

CATALOGUE

A lean man came in through the side door with a catalogue under his arm. He stood blinking his flat eyes a moment, getting them used to the shady store after the bright sunlight outside. Harve Whipple propped the broom against the grocery counter.

"What can I do for you, Emory?" he asked.

"Harve, I seen them circulars pasted up in your front winders where you say you'll give a dollar apiece for new mail order catalogues. Is that right?"

"That's right, Emory. Dollar apiece in trade for all you bring in."

"Well, here's a Sears Roebuck catalogue for you then." He turned and winked at the loafers who sat round the potbellied stove chewing solemnly. "We don't hardly do no tradin' with Sears anyhow."

"Fine, Emory, fine!" Harve said. "I wisht there was more people like you in this town."

"Naw, we don't do much business with Sears. We git most of our stuff from Ward's."

The loafers, who had been put on the alert by Emory's wink, guffawed in chorus. Emory plopped the thick catalogue down on the grocery counter.

"That's O.K. by us, Emory," Harve said, getting a slight edge on his voice. "Just so long as you bring in the new Fall-and-Winter catalogues, we'll give you a dollar in trade for ever'one you bring in, whether it's Sears' or Ward's. Now what did you want to get this mornin'?"

"Why, le' see— Gi'me a cut of Horseshoe, Harve.

I cain't think of anything else right now. Jist gi' me a due bill for the balance." Emory winked at the loafers again. "My old womern is goin' to raise hell whenever she finds out I've made off with her Sears catalogue. Maybe a ninety-cent due bill would sort of pacify her."

Harve got down a plug of Horseshoe from the lozenge-shaped display frame that held the chewing tobacco. He took it over to the nickeled tobacco-cutter and sliced off a ten-cent cut.

"You want it in a sack, Emory?"

"Naw, jist gi'me here—I want to start eatin' it right now."

He bit off a chew and took his place in a tilted chair beside the other loafers. The circle chewed in silence for a while, spitting toward the brown-stained sawdust frame at the foot of the cold iron stove. Harve Whipple went on sweeping out.

"How many of them catalogues you got a'ready, Harve?" one of the loafers asked presently.

"Emory's jist now was the first one this morning," Harve said. "We jist put them circulars up last night. Swede Ledbetter delivered me a bundle at seven o'clock and the ink wasn't dry on 'em yit."

"What are you folks goin' to do with all them catalogues after you git 'em?" another loafer asked.

"It tells about it right there on the circular," Harve said shortly. "Cain't you read? We're going to have a big bonfahr at the end of the celebration a week from tonight, and we're goin' to burn 'em all up."

"Hell, you all cain't burn them catalogues. Did you ever try to burn a catalogue? Hardest thing to burn you ever saw."

"We'll git 'em to burn, all right, don't you never worry about that," Harve said. "Soak 'em in coal oil and they'll burn."

"What I ain't never found out," a third loafer said, "is why you want to git shet of the catalogues anyhow?"

"Why, ain't you heerd, Tobe?" Emory said, chewing away. "It's a scheme for these here merchants to git a corner on all the strikin' paper in this part of the country, and after they git all the catalogues burnt up they're goin' to sell all of us this here toilet paper and make us use it like they do at Double S Winston's house."

A murmur of chuckles moved round the circle. One of the loafers let his tilted chair down and leaned forward with a confidential air.

"Say, I heerd that there at Winston's folks dungs right in the house," he said, rubbing his stubbled chin. "Do you reckon they's anything to that?"

"Why, of course they is, Ote," Emory said easily. "Ain't you never heerd of that before? Old Double S Winston has got him one of them turd machines in his house and it's all connected up so's the water washes it right out back into a hole in the ground. All rich folks has contraptions like that."

"Yeah?" Ote said, propping his chair back again. "What're you tryin' to do—guy *me?*"

"Hell, no! If you don't believe me, go right up to the hardware store and ask Carl Bussett—he put in the plumbin' work there at Double S Winston's and I guess he ort to know."

"Yeah, sure, go ask Carl Bussett," Ote scoffed. "Then he sends me to ask somebody else and then—you're jist tryin' to git me started on one of them wild goose chases like lookin' fer a left-handed monkey wrench."

"Why, you blamed fool you! I'm not neither. Ask Harve, there, if you don't believe me. Ain't that right, Harve?"

"Ain't what right?"

"Ain't Double S Winston got him one of them there turd machines right in his house?"

"Well, I guess if you want to call it that, he's got one. He's got a toilet in his bathroom, just like I've got at my house."

"Now, you see there, Ote! Harve's got one in *his* house. Don't be so backward. You've been livin' down there on that crik bank all your life and you think ever'body else lives jist like you do. I bet you don't know half of what's goin' on in the world."

"Well, I don't keer what you guys say," Ote said

171

positively, "I don't believe no sich thing. Turd machine! Dung right in the house!"

"Listen at the fool! Harve, hand me that catalogue. They've got 'em in there. Ain't you never looked at a Sears Sawbuck catalogue, Ote?"

"Hell, no!" Ote said.

"That's right, Ote!" Harve Whipple said. "You tell 'em. Ote's got better sense than most of you fellers. He trades right here in town where he can git the most for his money."

"What do I want to look at one of them mail order catalogues fer?" Ote said proudly. "I cain't read."

"Well, fer Christ's sakes," Emory said, "I cain't read very good neither, but I can show you the pitchur." He leafed hurriedly through the catalogue. "Now looky here," he said, stopping at a page of bathroom fixtures. "Here's a pitchur of one, right here."

Ote glanced at it. "Yeah?" he said. "That's what *you* say."

"S-sh!" Harve Whipple whispered. "Stop that rough talkin' now, boys. Here comes Reverend Grotts."

The Reverend Harley Grotts came walking sedately into the store. The men sat up respectfully and spoke all around, "Hidy, Reverend . . . Hidy, Reverend . . . Hidy, Reverend . . . Hidy, Reverend . . . Howdy do, Reverend."

"Good morning, gentlemen," the Reverend Har-ley Grotts said. "Mr. Whipple, I want to get a little bill of groceries this morning."

Emory, seeing a Tulsa *World* under the preacher's arm, asked brashly, "What's the news in the paper this mornin', Reverend Grotts?"

"Oh, lots of news in the paper these days, Mr. Hubbard. War and rumors of war."

"That's what this here country needs all right—another good war to put business back on its feet," one of the loafers piped.

"You said it!"

"It shore would he'p things!"

"Yes, I guess if the truth was knowed, we're moving at a faster pace today than at ary other time in the world's hist'ry."

"Mr. Whipple, I want a quarter's worth of navy beans and a tube of rolled oats and the medium-size tin of Hershey's cocoa—and a bottle of Garrett's snuff—that's for the nigra woman who comes in to help Mrs. Grotts, she dips snuff, a dirty habit, but Mrs. Grotts has it on the list, so I suppose I'd better get it—and a nickel's worth of those triple-X mints, I find they help my throat, gets husky preaching a long sermon, and a quart bottle of Welsh's grape juice, that's for communion, and a can of pink salmon—do you make those two for a quarter? . . ."

"Didn't see you out to Chamber of Commerce luncheon yesterday noon," Harve Whipple said,

173

hustling about behind the grocery counter to fill the order.

"No. I had a funeral out in Shady Grove district yesterday afternoon and I didn't get out. But I was just talking to Mr. Ledbetter and he tells me that all the merchants have agreed to take in mail order catalogues for a dollar each in trade. I notice that you already have the circulars posted in your front window."

"That's right, Reverend Grotts. It was Swede's idea and I guess it's going to work all right. Anyway, we'll get a few catalogues out of circulation."

"How have they been coming in? Have you got many yet?"

"Well, slow. But I think maybe they'll start coming in faster as soon as the word gits norated about. Of course the circulars were jist printed last night."

"It's a splendid idea—a splendid idea! I can't see any reason why it shouldn't be very successful. It shows real enterprise on the part of the merchants— and enterprise is what puts a town on the map. Enterprise and co-operation. Co-operation, a wonderful force in the world. I told Mr. Ledbetter that I am going to take 'Co-operation' as a subject for my sermon next Sunday morning—and I'm going to suggest to my flock that they contribute their catalogues toward getting a new carpet for the front room of the parsonage. I hope all you gentlemen will be out to hear me."

174

There was an embarrassed murmur of assent from the circle round the cold iron stove.

"Now would that be all, Reverend Grotts?" Harve Whipple asked.

"Yes, I believe that's the bill," the preacher said, taking up the cardboard box filled with groceries. "We have two mail order catalogues at home, but I didn't go back to get them after talking with Mr. Ledbetter. Mrs. Grotts will probably drop by with them this afternoon. I believe that bill came to two dollars even, Mr. Whipple, but if there's anything due, you can just hand Mrs. Grotts a note of it. Good day!"

He went out with the box of groceries under his arm. He passed at the door a stoop-shouldered old man with cotton lint on his shapeless felt hat and faded overalls. An overgrown boy in new overalls followed him into the store.

The old man held out a shoe box to Harve Whipple. "Mr. Whipple," he said, "these here shoes is too tight on my boy's feet. And besides they're little old thin patent-leather slippers not no good anyhow. I want to trade 'em on a good stout pair of work shoes."

"Aw, pa, I don't want none of them old heavy work shoes," the boy whined. "I got a good pair of work shoes I'm wearin' now."

"You shet up, Homer! You'll git what I tell you. Them shoes you got on is almost wore out."

175

Harve Whipple stood turning the shoe box in his hands.

"Why, Mr. Slover," he said, "you didn't buy these shoes here, did you? This here looks to me like the line of shoes Sears Roebuck carries."

"That's right, Mr. Whipple. He went and ordered them shoes from Sears Roebuck. I told him when I seen the picture in the catalogue they wouldn't do, but he was hog-wild after 'em and went on ahead— wouldn't listen to his pappy. Then when they come they was so tight on his feet they nearly killed him and his feet sweat and galled and he's got the aw- fullest foot on him now you ever seen. So I brung 'em to town today to trade 'em for a pair of shoes he could wear."

"Why, Mr. Slover, you'll have to wrap these shoes up and send them back to Sears Roebuck if they don't fit."

"Wrop 'em up and send them back? You mean you wouldn't take 'em in on a trade fer a good pair of work shoes?"

"Why, no, Mr. Slover, I couldn't do that. I wouldn't have a shoddy pair of shoes like these on my shelves. And besides they're all scuffed up on the bottoms."

"Yes, Homer went and wore 'em to church Sun- day. I told him not to wear 'em to church, but he did and we like to never got 'em off his feet when he

176

come home. They nearly killed him, being patent leather and all, his feet sweat and—"

"Well, if I was you, Mr. Slover, I'd just wrap those shoes up and shoot 'em back to Sears Roebuck and tell them they're no good—that you want your money back. Here, I'll wrap them up for you myself."

Harve reached for the wrapping paper roll at the end of the counter and tore off a strip.

"All right, then, Mr. Whipple, if you don't figger you can take 'em in on a trade. But I would like to look at some good stout work shoes for this here boy."

"Yes, sir, Mr. Slover!" Harve said, wrapping up the shoe box. "You've sure come to the right place for work shoes. We're headquarters for work shoes. What size does Homer wear, Mr. Slover?"

"Aw, pa," Homer said fretfully.

"Why, I reckon he'll take a 11½ anyway, Mr. Whipple. Maybe a 12. Them patent leather slippers he got was 11's and they was way too small fer him."

"Aw, pa," Homer said again.

"What is it, Homer?" the old man barked.

"Pa, I don't want no work shoes. I want a pair of shoes I kin romp in."

TESTED WITH 210 LB. WT.

Sash cord clothesline. Extra quality, non-stretch, thread line of high quality cotton fibers. Hard smooth finish, won't stiffen. $\frac{7}{32}$-in. diam. 50 or 100 ft. only in one piece. Ship wts. 1 lb. 4 oz.; 2 lbs. 4 oz.

86D897—100*ft.* ....56¢

AN UNSHAVEN man with yellow eyeteeth came pulling a rusty tin wagon down the side street. The wagon was loaded with a bundle tied in a dirty sheet. Its squeaking wheels stopped in front of the post office. The stubble-faced man tongued a quid out of his cheek and tossed it on the sidewalk. He propped the wagon-tongue back and went into the post office.

He stopped at the general delivery window.

"Any-mail-fer-C. R. Butts?" he asked, running his words together.

Elvira Draper reached up and got the letters from the B slot of the general delivery case and ran through them without paying much attention.

"Nothing!" she said airily, stuffing the letters back into the slot and taking up her magazine again.

"I was expectin' a order. It ort to been here yestiddy," he said stubbornly.

Elvira Draper slapped her magazine face down

178

and reached up to the B slot again. She went through the letters more slowly.

"Oh, yes; I guess there is a package here for you. Just take this notice back to the parcel post window and give it to Mr. Shannon. He'll hand you your package."

C. R. Butts shuffled back to the parcel post window with the package notice.

"Mr. Shannon, you got ary a parcels post package here for me?"

"Oh, yes, Butts," Postmaster Shannon said, taking the package notice. "Came in last night, I believe." He stepped back to the wooden compartments that held the packages. He looked at a label and lifted out a rubber-rollered clothes wringer with a tag wired on it.

"This what you were looking for, Butts?" he said, lifting the iron-rod wicket and shoving through the clothes wringer.

"Yes, sir, Mr. Shannon. My old womern claimed she had to have a new clothes wringer. It looked to me like she could of made the old ern do awhile longer. But you know how it is—you cain't argy with a womern."

"Well, there it is, Butts. Take it away."

"You all ain't never changed your mind about lettin' us do your warshin' fer you, have you, Mr. Shannon?"

"Why, no, Butts. I spoke to Mrs. Shannon about

CATALOGUE

it, but she says she's got Hannah Merrick doing the washing now and that she's perfectly satisfactory. Comes to the house and does it."

"Uh-hunh, I know, Mr. Shannon, I know. They's lots of white people in this town jist like you all are, I don' aim to complain nor nothing, Mr. Shannon, but did you ever stop to think that they's a heap of white folks in this town that will give niggers work and let the hard-workin' white folks starve?"

"I never did hear of you hurtin' yourself workin', Butts," Postmaster Shannon said in a peppery tone. "Hardest work I ever saw you do was trail that little old wagon around full of dirty clothes. I don't doubt that your wife works hard enough—washin' six days a week for other people. And there's your oldest daughter—her name's Hattie, ain't it?—got a pretty good job, night central in the 'phone office. So you ought to consider yourself pretty well off. Got your women folks all workin' to support you and I guess you don't have no trouble h'istin' a bottle, do you?"

"Mr. Shannon, when I was deppity shirruf here, I served this county and I served it well. If old Shirruf Ferguson hadn't throwed me out when he come in, I would a still been servin' it. Fu'thermore, I might a had the niggers doin' my work, too. But I don't believe in givin' the niggers work when they's honest white folks needin' work."

"Well, Butts, a nigger has a right to work and

180

live just like anybody else, I always say. And if they're as industrious and self-respecting as the Merricks are, I believe in giving them all the encouragement I can."

C. R. Butts drew away from the parcel post window, appalled.

"Mr. Shannon," he said, "you ort to be ashamed! I knowed you was a Republican—but all Republicans ain't necessarily nigger-lovers, I don't keer what they say. I'm broad-minded enough to know that. But you—why, I bet you think a nigger is jist as good as a white person."

"That's according to which white person you mean, Butts—and which nigger. Now Sylvester Merrick—well, I don't know a better man than Merrick, even if there are smarter men. But my opinions will scarcely interest you, Butts."

A newly-painted Model-T Ford stopped with a rattle and a bang at the postoffice door. Sylvester Merrick climbed out of the open front seat. He came into the post office with a jaunty step.

"Talk of the devil," C. R. Butts muttered. "Drivin' right up in an automobeel."

"Mistah Shannon, Mistah Winston tole me they was a pahcels post package hyah foh me. Is that right, suh?"

"Why, yes, Sylvester. You've got a large package here from Montgomery Ward. It came in last night on the 5:45."

"What're you buyin' from Monkey Ward's, black boy?" C. R. Butts asked in a surly voice.

"Oh, Mistah Butts, jist a few little things we was needin'."

"Come on! Come on! Don't stall me! I ast you what you was buyin' from Monkey Ward's."

"Well, Mistah Butts, if it really intrusts you to know, I'm gettin' some dress goods for my wife and a toy foh my little guhl and some laun'ry soap and a len'th of clothesline and so on. Things lak that."

"Yeah? Well, you better be careful you don't wind up with your neck in one end of that clothesline rope, black boy."

Sylvester tilted up his moist black face, showing two rows of perfect white teeth, and guffawed too loudly.

"I sho' will, Mistah Butts. I sho' will be keerful about lettin' anything lak that happen! I *sho'* will!"

"What do you mean, buying soap and stuff from a mail order house when you can git it here in town, anyhow?" C. R. Butts growled. "Ain't the merchants in this town good enough fer you?"

Sylvester pointed at the clothes wringer the white man was holding. "Mistah Butts, ain't you been doin' some out-o'-town orderin' yo'sef? Ain't that a Sears Roebuck tag I sees on that clothes wringah you got theah in yo' hand?" he asked amiably.

"Watch out how you talk to a white man, nigger! You git fresh with me and start askin' me questions,

182

and I'll mash that black face of yourn in. I'll learn you your place if you mess with me much."

Sylvester's beaming face fell. "All right, suh, Mistah Butts," he said meekly. "I didn' mean to sound sassy, and if I did, I hopes you won't hold it agin me. I'm a black man, Mistah Butts, and I knows my place. You're a white man, Mistah Butts. You keep yo' place and I'll sho' keep mine."

Sylvester Merrick picked up his package and walked out to his car. He cranked it and went banging away in a fog of smoke and dust. C. R. Butts stared out the door after him.

"The idea of that nigger ridin' around here in a automobeel when they's white folks cain't make a honest livin'," he said.

"He sure told you off, Butts," Postmaster Shannon said. "And he was exactly right, too. It wasn't none of your business what Sylvester Merrick had in that package. You forced him to tell you. It's too bad he had to be so meek about it. It would have suited me just as well if he hadn't called you a white man."

"Yeah, the impident black— If I 'a' done what I ort to, I'd 'a'—"

"You better be gettin' on home with that bundle of washin' you got out there in your little wagon, Butts. Your wife's waiting for you."

"Let 'er wait. I guess she's waited before."

"Well, get on out of the lobby, anyhow. You've

183

got your package, haven't you? There's nothin' else here for you. What're you waitin' on. Get on out of here."

"Listen, Mr. Shannon, you cain't order me outn this here post office. This post office is a public place."

"That's just all you know about it, Butts. There's strict gov'ment rules against allowin' any loafin' in a post office lobby. Sometimes I don't enforce 'em as strict as I should, but I don't like to have a man like you around—and I'm putting that rule in effect right now."

"You cain't talk to me like that, Mr. Shannon. I'm a respectable citizen. You ain't nothin' but a public servant—and a nigger-lover at that."

"Listen here, Butts—I'm coming round on the other side of this partition to clean out the lobby— and if you ain't gone by the time I get out there, I'm going to sweep it out with your carcass!"

C. R. Butts began moving very slowly toward the front door, carrying his clothes wringer.

"You better not tetch me, Mr. Shannon, or you'll be sorry. I could whup you with one hand tied behind my back."

The Yale lock on the partition door snapped back and Postmaster Shannon came charging out. C. R. Butts skipped nimbly out of the post office. He ran out into the center of the street and stopped. Postmaster Shannon came to the door and gave the rusty tin wagon a kick that sent it rolling down the sidewalk toward the Long-Bell Lumber Yard. C. R. Butts ran cursing after it.

Elvira and Gladys were pale and wide-eyed when Postmaster Shannon stepped back into the building. "What's the matter, Mr. Shannon?" they asked. "How did it start? What did that old Butts say to you?"

"He said too much," Postmaster Shannon said, closing the partition door.

"That C. R. Butts is a mean man, Mr. Shannon," Elvira Draper said. "Him and Hattie, that oldest girl of his that works in the 'phone office—why, I jist cain't tell you the awful things ever'body knows for a fact about them. And Mrs. Butts, she works so hard, takin' in washing. But I wouldn't git in no fuss with that old C. R. Butts, Mr. Shannon. He's mean. He's li'ble to sneak around and do you harm."

"Yeah, I know," Postmaster Shannon said. "The ornery skunk. I've lived too long among people just like him to get worried now about what he might do. The only thing that gets me is, how can anybody that low-down get the idea that they're better than a self-respecting, fairly intelligent man like Sylvester Merrick."

"Why, Mr. Shannon!" Elvira gasped. "Sometimes you jist scare me with the things you say."

"Yes, I guess so," Postmaster Shannon said wearily. "The older a man gets the less he knows about how to keep his mouth shut."

"Mr. Shannon, you've got a daughter off to college," Gladys Ferguson said keenly. "Would you want Helen to marry a nigger?"

"That would depend on who the nigger was," Postmaster Shannon said, going back to the water cooler.

C. R. Butts ran down the street after his small wagon. He caught it in front of the Long-Bell Lumber Yard and turned round with it, making a wide arc before the front of the post office. He moseyed off down the back alley, cursing under his breath.

Back of the Conchartee County *Democrat* building he halted. Through the open double doors he could see Red Currie sitting at the linotype keyboard. The faint click of the matrices falling and the long clank of the elevator arm lifting a clip back to the magazine floated thinly out. C. R. Butts turned and went toward the building.

"Hidy there, Red," he said, standing in the doorway.

Red looked up with his ink-blackened fingers still moving lightly over the keys. He eased over on one side of his low chair and farted above the sound of the linotype machine.

C. R. Butts stood watching him awhile without speaking again. When Red got up and went round back of the linotype to take out a matrix that had stuck in the jittering distributor, C. R. Butts asked, "You workin' hard, Red?"

"Yeah—can't you see I'm workin' hard?" Red said, stooping to toss a bright pig of type metal into the melting pot. "What did you want?"

"Red, I was jist wonderin' if maybe you didn't have some launder work to be done. My womern is washin' today and I'd go pick up your dirty clothes fer you if you wanted me to."

"Naw," Red said shortly. "I got a nigger woman to do my washin'."

"Which nigger womern, Red?"

"Hannah Merrick."

"Has she already got your launder this week?" C. R. Butts asked.

"Yeah. She gits it on a Tuesday and delivers it back Friday afternoon."

"Red, what do you want to let a dirty old nigger do your warshin' fer? You doan want to give a nigger work when they's honest white folks cain't make a decent livin' in this town, do you?"

"Hell, a nigger gits my clothes jist as clean as anybody would—and maybe a little cleaner for all I know. All I keer about is gitting my clothes done up nice—it don't make me no diffrunce what color skin the woman that does it has got."

"Red, you wouldn't want to feed a nigger and let a white man starve, would you?"

187

"You ain't starvin', are you, Butts? My understandin' was that you're still able to keep in drinkin' liquor. Got two women supportin' you. Wife takin' in washin' and Hattie night central in the 'phone office. What're you gripin' about?"

"What does the nigger charge you fer shirts, Red?"

"Nickel apiece, I think."

"My womern'll do 'em for four cents apiece if you'll give us a trial."

"Well, I'll think about it, Butts. Not this week, though. Hannah has done been and got my launder this week."

"Where you roomin' at now, Red?" C. R. Butts asked.

"Right where I always was—over at Widow Tinsley's roomin' house."

"Wha' ya say I come by and pick up your clothes next week, Red. I'll gar'ntee you satisfaction or your money back. That's fair, ain't it?"

"I told you I'd think about it, didn't I, Butts? I'll let you know. Go on now and stop botherin' me about it," Red said harshly.

C. R. Butts sauntered on down the alley with the small tin wagon screaking behind him.

SEARS SPEEDY SERVICE

Your order is handled in the quickest possible time when you send to Sears. . . . The minute your order is received, things start happening. . . . Skilled experts fill it, pack it and ship it. . . . Most orders are on their way in considerably less than 24 hours. . . .

THURSDAY morning Slemmons' car stopped at the Widow Holcomb's R.F.D. box. The widow came dashing out of the house, trying to hold her pink kimono about her bare legs as she ran down the walk to meet the mail carrier.

"Did you bring my package?" she called eagerly.

"No, ma'm," Slemmons said. "They wasn't a sign of a package for you, Mrs. Holcomb. Postmaster Shannon has been watching exter careful ever since you jumped him about that package day before yestiddy, and he says he's shore they ain't been no package come fer you. But here is a post card from Sears that maybe'll tell you something."

"Oh!" the widow said faintly, taking the card.

Slemmons sped away. She stood reading, squinting at the card in the strong white sunlight:

Kansas City, Mo.

August 29

Our records indicate that we have not received your order of August 25. We believe this is the order you wrote about.

Orders are handled promptly and your merchandise, or some word from us, should have reached you before now.

If you have not received your order or word from us about it since writing, kindly return the bills with this card. If you have no bills, be sure to send back this card, and give us a complete copy of the order.

Yours very truly,

26030   SEARS ROEBUCK & CO.

157/79/825/KC

"Oh, the fools!" she raged, tearing up the card. "If they haven't got my order yet like they say, how could I return any bills to them? Boy, if I don't write them a letter that'll set 'em on fahr!"

Blanche, the black girl, came to the front door and called through the wire screen, "Talaphome, Mis' Della!"

The Widow Holcomb hurried back into the house, whispering as she passed Blanche in the front room, "Who is it, Blanche, who is it?"

Blanche rolled her eyes and shook her head. "I doan know, Mis' Della, unless hit's that Injian man that's been callin' up ever' day now."

The widow went on into the kitchen and took up the dangling receiver at the wooden telephone on the wall. She put an elbow on the small varnished shelf. She got her mouth set before the black mouthpiece.

"Hell-yoe," she said sweetly. . . . "Oh, Eagle! How are you, hon? . . . Oh, I'm still feelin' pretty blue, but it sure does cheer me up to hear your voice again. . . . No, Eagle, I jist cain't go any place this week. . . . Oh, I know it would be fun, I jist think those country square dances are more fun than anything. . . . I sure wish I could go with you, but I cain't go tomorra night, Eagle, honest I cain't. Not unless I'm feeling better than I am now. . . . Of course I'm not stalling you, why would I be stallin' you? . . . Well, I don't care who saw me, I don't feel like going anywhere. . . . Why don't you call me tomorra and I can tell you for sure then. . . . Oh, if you feel that way about it, go on and take Irene Pirtle. But I'll bet you Ira won't let her go with you. . . . Oh, a little bird told me. . . . Well, that's jist perfectly all right with me, big boy. I don't know what I can do to he'p it. . . . Good-by!"

The 'phone bell jingled, ringing off, but she stood a moment holding the receiver. Then she jammed it on the hook and turned away. The bell rang again before she was out of the room. She went back to it.

"Hello!" she said shortly. "Oh, Ira! Where have

you been keeping yourse'f, Ira? You haven't called me up in a coon's age. . . . No, Ira, I'm jist as sorry as I can be, but I cain't. . . . I jist cain't. Honest, I cain't, Ira. . . ."

Ira Pirtle tore the wrapper off the small brown package and took out three shiny collars. He walked over to the mirror above the white-enameled wash basin in the corner of the filling station office. He turned up his tucked-in collar-band and fastened on one of the rubber collars. Before the mirror he stood, turning this way and that, stretching his sinewy neck, smirking at his reflection in the mirror.

After a few minutes of this he took off the collar and put it back in the box. He tucked his soiled neck-band under. Then he went over and cranked the telephone.

"Give me 1-3-9," he said. . . . "Hello! Is that you, Della? . . . Why, I been keeping myse'f right where I always been. I didn' know where you wanted me to call you up, seems like you won't go nowheres with me no more lately. . . . Say, Della, how about you and me steppin' out tomorra night? Old Herman Gutterman out here west of town is th'owing a big square dance and we'd have the time of our lives. . . . Oh, come on, Della, why cain't you? You could, too, if you jist wanted to. . . . I know what's the matter with you—you're so struck on that big old fat Eagle Catoosa that you won't go

anywheres with me no more. . . . Aw, I know
better than that. Don't give me that stuff. . . . He
did! Why, he's a liar and the truth's not in
him. . . . Irene's not going nowheres with him, I'll
gar'ntee you that. . . . Yes, ma'm, I've strictly put
my foot down with that young womern. She's stayin'
strictly to home tomorra night. . . . No, she's not
goin' to go nowheres with Eagle Catoosa. . . . I
don't keer what he told you, I reckon I've still got
more say-so about Irene than he has. . . ."

XTRA RANGE

Increases killing range by 10 *yards. High brass cup adds to strength and safety. Progressive burning powder. Instantaneous ignition—Non-corrosive primer. Powder in* 12-*gauge Xtra Range Sportloads produces velocity equal to* 3¾ *drams of smokeless powder. Two genuine hair felt wads. Powder is carefully tested for velocity and strength. Scientific machines load shells with exact quantity of powder, correct amount of wadding, and correct weight of spherical and sized shot. Shells waterproofed inside and out. Non-mailable; can be shipped by freight or express only.* 4 *boxes or More Shipped Prepaid.* 12-*Gauge—*2¾ *in. long after fired.*

6F475...Box of 25......................99¢

THE SUN was blistering the sanded green paint of the M. K. & T. railway station. A gray farm wagon drawn by two mousy mules turned off the dust-cushioned road and came gritting along the graveled platform. It stopped on the shady east side of the depot. The driver eased his blue hulk to the ground and went into the waiting room for whites.

He gaped a moment at the empty slat benches. Flies droned against the paint-sealed windows. There was a muffled chatter of telegraph in the room beyond. The ticket window was shut; so he lumbered on through to the sunny side of the station. He went round and stuck his head in at the Negro waiting room, off which the office door opened.

"Hello, Mr. Conklin! Hello!" he bawled.

The station agent, sweltering in a balbriggan undershirt, came to the office door.

"Mr. Conklin, is ary a passel here yit for W. F. Slover?"

"Sure is, Homer; come in on the 4:30 local this evenin'."

"Hot diggety! I shore am proud to hear that. We been lookin' for our ship-mint over a week, and it riles pap to have me lay out and drive to town so much."

"O.K., Homer. You sign right here on this waybill—if you cain't sign, make your mark—and I'll go get your freight."

Homer clamped his tongue in a corner of his mouth and painfully began tracing his name on the wrong line. The station agent rolled back the freighthouse door and brought out a small red-labeled box.

"Careful how you handle this, Homer," he said. "It's marked explosives. What's that bulshevik pappy of your'n fixin' to do—start him a bumb factory?"

"No, sir, Mr. Conklin; them is shotgun shells. I been waitin' on them so as I could go huntin'."

"Well, if you was so anxious for a few shotgun

shells, looks to me like you'd 'a' bought some here in town. The hardware ain't quit handlin' shotgun shells, has it?"

"Shucks, Mr. Conklin, my pappy won't buy nothin' here in town if he can order it. Why, I recollect onct the old womern had the neuralgy in her jaw and she had to suffer it six days while pa was makin' up a order to Sears Sawbuck for some aspireen tablets. Anyway they charge too much for shells at the hardware. And you got to figger, too, nothing like that cain't be sent in the mail; so if anybody orders four boxes, why Sears pays the freight. But that's jist on shotgun shells, because they cain't come by mail."

"All right, Homer; there's your shotgun shells. Now you can get on back to your cotton pickin' instid of pesterin' the life out of me about whe'r your freight has come."

"I ain't goin' to pick no more cotton this day, Mr. Conklin. I'm goin' huntin' tonight—and maybe take in the dance."

"Where's the dance at? Odd Fellows Hall?"

"No, I didn't mean no round dance. I meant the big square dance out to Gutterman's place. I allowed you'd heard about Gutterman's dance, Mr. Conklin. You know Bessie, that's Gutterman's old womern, she got ketched a-sellin' bootleg here last Spring and Judge Throgmorton give her six months in the county calaboose. So Bessie's gettin' out today, and Herman is th'owin' a big square dance to celebrate."

"Well, Homer, if you aim to get home in time to put on your best bib and tucker, you're going to have to h'ist your tail some, ain't you?"

"Aw, I don't know wh'er I'll even go to the dance or not, Mr. Conklin. I jist said that. I wanted to go, but you know how set in his notions pap is. I was jist schemin', though, on the way to town—maybe if I went huntin' tonight I could slip off and look in up at Gutterman's and maybe dance me a few sets. But don't you never name it to pap, or he'd take the hide off'n me!"

"O.K., Homer. Give them gals an exter swing for me."

"I shore will, Mr. Conklin. You come see us some time."

IF YOU WISH

write in your own language. Wysylajcie wasze listy po polsku jerzeli wam się podoba. Schrijf uwe brieven in het Hollandsch als het u past. Ecrivez en français si vous préferez. Se Lei preferisce scrive in italiano. Napište vaši psani v Českém jasyku jestli si tak přejete. Schreiben Sie uns Ihre Aufträge in Deutsch, wenn Sie wünschen. Skrifva dere brefva på Svenskt om detta är lättere for dere. Escriba en español si lo desea. Skriv paa Norsk eller Dansk hvis det er lettere. . . .

ONLY one passenger got off the 5:45 that afternoon—a blond lank man who wore a new straw hat and a wrinkled Palm Beach suit. Spike Callahan, the jitney driver, did not even seek a fare. He raced his motor and swung his Dodge sedan away from the station. The lone passenger yelled and struck up a loose-jointed sprint down the platform. Spike put on his brakes.

R. W. E. Ledbetter panted alongside the car.

"You drivin' over to town, Spike?"

The hawk-faced jitney driver grunted, "Yah."

"Care if I ride over with you?"

"Naw. Get in," Spike said, but he did not move to flip open a door as he would have for a paying passenger.

198

Ledbetter trotted round and climbed into the front seat. He mopped his face as the car sped away. "I could've walked it in ten minutes, but it's so all-fired hot today and I'm anxious to get back to the *Democrat* office and see if Red Currie has got the paper out yet. I was called to Tulsa on business today. I hate to leave Red Currie with so much responsibility, but this was just a case of have-to. Red's a good boy, all right, but he is like ever' sorrel-top ever I saw: little too quick on the trigger."

"He's too damn' smart-alecky to suit me!" Spike snarled. His blotched lean face was set and his bitter lips had gone white. "Soon as you learnt him to run that linotype he got too big for his britches. I went in there today with a piece for the paper and he got awful smart with me. Said I'd have to pay to get it in."

The editor was indignant. "He did! Red Currie said that? What was the piece about, Spike?"

The taxi driver cleared his throat and kept looking straight ahead. "It was just something the wife wrote about our baby."

Ledbetter's face took on a funereal expression and he reached over and laid his hand on the jitney driver's shoulder.

"Spike," he said, "I sure was sorry to hear about your baby last week. That sure was tough. I didn't get out to the funeral myself—we was a day late with the *Democrat* last week—but Mrs. Ledbetter went, and she said it was beautiful. This makes the second you've lost, don't it? Well, I always say it's just as tough to lose a child right at the start as it is one ten or fifteen years old."

The hard look flickered out of the jitney driver's dark eyes for a moment. "Yeah," he murmured, "it's tough."

"Have you got it with you, that what the wife wrote? Red Currie ain't editor of the *Democrat* yet by a long shot."

"I didn't aim to mention it again," Spike said bashfully, "but the wife wrote it herself and she thought maybe you'd appreciate it enough to print it in the paper." He fumbled in his shirt pocket and drew out a blue-lined leaf of pencil paper.

The editor unfolded it and began reading in a rapid mutter:

We wish to thank our many friends, neighbors, singers, and Bro. Batenfield for their kind deeds and sympathy shown during our bereavement of our beloved baby daughter. Also for the beautiful floral offerings.

> She was a little angel,
>   Sent to us for only a day,
> God wanted another angel,
>   So He taken our Baby away.
> Last Wensday Arlene was born,
> Ere Friday she was gone.

WRITE IN ANY LANGUAGE

She never knew no worldly harms
Ere Jesus taken her to his arms.
(Signed)
MR. AND MRS. C. H. CALLAHAN
CHESTER JUNIOR CALLAHAN

The jitney driver said uneasily, "I told the wife she'd ought to sign it 'Spike Callahan and wife,' so folks'd be sure to reco'nize the name, but she held out that just the initials was more proper. What about that?"

"Either way would be nice," R. W. E. Ledbetter said. "Now, Spike, we can run the missus' poem free of charge, but fact of the matter is, Red was right— we do make a small nominal charge for cards of thanks. Only twenty-five cents."

Spike Callahan's face went hard again. He gave a little sneering sniff. "I guess you was going to pay me two bits when you got in my taxi to be hauled over to town?"

Editor Ledbetter gulped. "Why, no, Spike; I just thought so long as you was coming over to town anyway and didn't have no load you wouldn't mind me riding with you. But—well, sure, if that's the way you look at it, why, I'll waive our customary charge. That reminds me, though—before I forget I want to jot down another item."

He reached in his coat for a pencil and scrawled hastily on the scrap of paper: "Ye ed. businessed in Tulsa Friday."

HERE'S A SIZZLING STYLE

*They're a WOW! No fooling! these pants have
"IT!" They're really trousers and semi-vest combined and are they stylish? Say! they were born in
Hollywood and in two weeks they had spread like
a conflagration all the way to Fifth Avenue! The
double-breasted vest effect is what they're all raving
about. Vest is a part of the waistband! Fancy but-
toned sidepockets, adjustable strap in back, and 22-
inch cuff bottoms carry out the stylish scheme. All
wool and silk in a rich brown stripe. Sizes 28 to 36
in. waist and 28 to 34 in. inseam. State measure-
ments.*

45F8575............................$3.65

Red CURRIE came down the back alley carrying two pleated gray blocks of Conchartee County
Democrats. The ink was still moist on the newsprint.
Fivefinger Earp's mail truck was parked at the back
door of the post office and Fivefinger was going back
and forth, unloading the 5:45 mail.

The mail order merchandise was piling in.

As Red walked round the truck to get in the back
door with the papers, he noticed Irene Pirtle standing at the front corner of the post office. His large
ears turned crimson and the color seeped over his

peaked face. She was the prettiest girl in his high school class.

"Oh, Red," Irene called, "are you going in the back way to mail those papers? Would you do me a favor?"

The blush deepened on Red's face, but he answered smartly, "Sure! Any flavor you want—lemon or vanilla?"

Shrill laughter parted her bright doll mouth. She gave her hempen bob a backward toss to show the warm curve of her throat with its little creases of moist powder.

"Cr-r-a-a-zy!" she shrieked.

Red Currie, saffron-faced, walked over to where she was.

"Say, Red," she said in a low, sober voice, "I'm expecting a package on this mail. I want to be sure and get it before papa comes for the mail. So would you please ask Mr. Shannon if anything come for me and if it did, get it for me while you're in there?"

"Sure I will, Irene. I'm expecting a package myself and I have to ask about that anyhow. So I can get yours easy if it comes."

"I cer'nly would appreciate it, Red."

She idled against the alley side of the building while he went into the post office through the back way. A few minutes later he was back with a large brown envelope and a wide cardboard box.

"Yours sure is light," he said, handing her the envelope. "What's it got in it?"

She giggled. "That's for me to know and you to find out! What you got in yours?"

"Tell me what's in yours and I'll tell you what's in mine."

"I'd show you what's in mine if you'd show me what's in yours!"

"Aw, naw. You'll see mine on me soon enough. I guess I'll put mine on tonight and take in a square dance out here in the country. Just to give the hicks a treat."

"I'd wear mine to a square dance," she said, wistfully arching her plucked brows, "if I had anybody to take me."

"Heck, what's the matter with me? I'll take you!"

"It's funny you never did ask me before."

"I would of ask you before, but I thought you was stuck on Eagle Catoosa."

"Gosh, no, kid! Papa won't let me go with Eagle no more. Besides Eagle is sparkin' the Widow Holcomb now. That big old fat Indian slob ain't nothing in my young life."

"Well, would you go with me to this square dance if I was to come by for you tonight?"

"Maybe. But you got to let me see what's in your package."

"All right—if you'll show me what's in yours."

She tore open the envelope flap and pulled out a

garment of flesh-tinted rayon. She brushed it lightly with her finger tips to restore three small silk rose-buds. He bent forward and peered closely at the shimmering cloth.

"I don't see yet what it is," he complained.

She laughed boldly. "Step-ins, you foolish!"

"Aw, do things like that have rosebuds sewed on 'em?"

"You wouldn't kid me, would you? Now let's see yours."

Still a little shocked, he broke the paper tape that sealed his cardboard box. He took off the lid and tore the tissue wrapping away from a fold of brown cassimere with gaudy silk stripes interwoven.

"What's that?" she breathed.

"Sizzle pants," he said proudly. "The latest thing out."

"Sizzle pants?" she gasped. "I bet they look funny on you."

"Funny! Wha' ya mean, funny?" he asked huff-ily. "They're a Hollywood sensation. Trouble with this town is, it don't keep up with the styles. I don't expect these mossbacks around here to appreciate snappy clothes."

"Well, I cer'nly am anxious to see them on you."

"Ain't you got nothing better to do, little missy, than to stand here in the alley talking to a boy?"

They both jumped and looked round at the scrawny man who had slipped up behind them. He had watery pink eyes, and tobacco darkened the sour creases at his mouth.

"Oh, hello, papa," Irene Pirtle said faintly.

"You march right on up to the filling station, little lady," Ira Pirtle said in a crabbed voice. "I'll attend to you there!"

"Oh, foot!" Irene said, and in a quick whisper to Red added, "Seven-thirty."

IF YOU WISH

to return this merchandise—Write us just a brief note telling us what is wrong and what you want us to do about it. Remember we want the order to be perfectly satisfactory to you. If you want to return the item and have your money refunded, we are ready to do it, but it helps us to know why the order has not pleased you. . . .

THE SAD banshee whistle of the 5:45 came trailing across the flatlands south of town as Spike Callahan's Dodge rustled over the white chat drive beside his rented bungalow. He got out stiffly and walked round by the sunny back porch. A baby boy in clean gingham rompers was knocking toys about in a play-pen.

"Daddy's home, Junior," Spike called in an oddly gentle voice. "You got a big old fat kiss for daddy?"

The little boy turned his head toward the voice and gurgled. As he looked up, the western sun struck him in the face. The child met the strong light without blinking his milk-blue eyes. He was blind. He stretched out his arms, groping for his father. One of his tiny hands was a stub with five red buttons in place of fingers.

Spike fondled his son and played with him awhile before he went into the house. His wife, a large blonde woman, stood at the gas range frying steaks. She was dressed in a crisp, green wash-frock, and she looked pale and cool even in the sultry kitchen. A breakfast nook between the kitchen and the parlor was laid for a meal.

"How you feel by now, Kate?" Spike asked as he hung up his hat.

"Pretty good, I guess," she said without looking up. "The heat makes me feel a little faint at times."

"Well, don't go and overdo yourself." He drew water at the sink and began washing his hands. "Say, did you get that stuff fixed up to send back to Monkey Ward's?"

She was lifting hot biscuits out of the oven. She did not answer at once. He was opening his mouth to speak again when she said quietly, "This is only the second day I've been out of bed."

"Yeah, I know, but if we put off sending that stuff back much longer we're li'ble to have trouble getting our money back. And we sure could use that $4.59 we got tied up there. Business is punk."

"I'll get the box ready tonight," she said.

"Did you save them papers that come with the order?"

"Yes, the papers are stuck in the catalogue."

They sat down at the breakfast nook and ate in silence. After the meal Spike lighted a cigarette. He

208

sat moodily picking his teeth. The gray stalks of smoke trailed from his nostrils. She began taking up the soiled dishes.

"Aren't you going to eat your salad?" she asked.

"Naw," he said, chirping through his teeth, "you know I never do touch that rabbit fodder."

She put the dishes in the sink. Then she reached up and took from the shelf above a nickeled alarm clock. She began winding it.

"What time does your watch say?" she asked. "I've got to set the alarm so I'll be sure to give Junior his medicine tonight."

He took out his watch and glanced at it. "Five after seven. How is Junior, you think?"

"Those sores don't seem to be healing up at all. Don't you reckon we ought to have Dr. Jenkins look at him again?"

Spike twisted his lips and gave a sardonic snort. "Hell of a lot of good Doc Jenkins done me! You wait and see wh'er this dope we got now don't help. —Say, I give Ledbetter that piece you wrote. He bummed a ride over from the 5:45 this afternoon. Then he had the nerve to want to charge for printing what you wrote in his lousy paper. First that Red Currie in there wanted two bits to put it in the paper. He got awful sassy—if he'd 'a' said much more I'd 'a' slapped me the snot out of that red-headed brat. I got Ledbetter told all right. He said it would be in next week's paper. Person'ly, I don't much care."

209

Her back was turned, but he could tell from the way her large shoulders were quivering that she had started crying again. She stood at the sink weeping softly. There were tears in his eyes, too, as he got up and started toward her. Then he scowled and crossed over to where his hat was hung. He crammed it on and went out the back way, banging the screen door.

She blew her nose and went to the door. "Spike," she quavered, "why don't you stay home tonight and help me put Junior away."

"Aw, naw," he said, getting into the car. "I better get on up town awhile and see if I cain't pick up a few nickels. Look for me back when you see me comin'."

SHINE AS THE STARS DO . . .

in Hollywood Autographed Fashions. Authentic up-to-the-minute styles worn by famous film stars. These copies of your favorite stars' very own dresses, coats, neckwear, shoes, hosiery, foundations, and bathing suits are offered only by Sears Roebuck. You'll know them on the pages of this catalogue by the actual photographs of beautiful film stars. . . . You'll know them by their special labels bearing the signature of the popular star who wears it. . . .

IRA PIRTLE sat propped back in a hickory chair outside the door of his three-cornered filling station office. He held in his lap a new mail order catalogue. He licked his lips as he leafed slowly through it, drooling over the buxom women pictured on the underwear pages.

A car drove into the pool of light. Ira hurriedly stuck the catalogue behind his chair. He lowered himself to the concrete floor and went over to the gas pumps.

"Give me three gallons of the white, Ira," Spike Callahan said, getting out of the car.

Ira, his moist eyes on the graduated glass, unhooked the hose and began lowering gasoline into Spike's tank.

211

Spike had his pant-legs pulled up slightly, looking at his shoes under the light. "Ira," he said, "my car is leaking oil on me some way. You got an old rag I could wipe off my shoe with?"

Ira hung the gas nozzle back on its hook. "I don't know wh'er I got ary rag here, Spike. Seems like I get so many calls for rags, I just cain't keep any on hand."

He went into his office. A moment later he came to the door and said, "This be all right?" He tossed out a begrimed wisp of cloth.

Spike caught it. "Yeah, this is all right. But what the hell! Say, Ira, you're getting pretty ritzy, ain't you, handin' out women's silk undies for customers to wipe their shoes on. How come that, Ira?"

Ira Pirtle did not smile. "I'll tell you how come that," he said grimly. "That daughter of mine's gettin' to where I cain't do nothin' with her. She come walkin' in here tonight and she had a parcel in her hand. I ast her what she had in that parcel and she claims she's got dress goods. I ast her to let me see and she says she ain't a-goin' to do it. So I snatched that parcel away from the little missy and looked for myself. And that's what was in it—that there what you got in your hands. Looky what it's got sewed on it! Rosebuds. Yes, sir, rosebuds! Dogged if I'm goin' to have ary a child of mine shamin' me by wearin' a garment like that. So I jist

212

naturally ripped it up and throwed it right down on the floor and scrubbed it in the grease. I swan if I can figger out what the young uns of today is comin' to. Course that'n of mine ain't got no mother now to look after her, but I can tell you, she's not a-goin' to disgrace herse'f while I'm here to he'p it."

"That's right, Ira. You got to watch 'em close these days."

"Put that rag in your car, Spike, if you got any use for it. I'd just as soon not have it layin' around the station here."

"O.K., Ira. Now lend me your pliers and I'll see if I cain't tighten this cable up some way to stop that oil from workin' out."

"Here's some pliers. But pull over there by the greasing-rack so as other customers can drive up to the pumps."

Spike ran his car round to the other side of the station. While he was down on the floorboards, working, a long red roadster stopped at the curb. A broad swarthy face called low, "Hey, Spike!"

Spike walked over to the other car, peering into the darkness.

"How's-a-boy, Eagle?"

"Sh-h-h!" Eagle Catoosa whispered. "Not so loud. I don't want Old Man Pirtle to know I'm out here. Listen, Spike, this is on the Q.T., see. I got a little job for you."

"How much is they in it?" Spike asked guardedly.

"What you say to five bucks, hunh?"

"Five bucks will be all right. What is it—murder?"

The big Indian chuckled and shoved a five-dollar bill into the jitney driver's hand. "Naw! Listen, guy, Old Man Pirtle won't let Irene go with me no more because I cut the old man out with Mrs. Holcomb, see. Well, I want to take Irene out tonight anyhow. But she's went out to Gutterman's square dance with the red-headed guy that works in the printing office, see. So all I want you to do is drive out there and get Irene away from the square dance for me. I got reasons for not wanting to show there at Gutterman's tonight. All you have to do is just get Irene off to one side and tell her I'll be waitin' down there at that culvert below Gutterman's place with my parkin' lights on. She'll come right on down there. That kid is nuts over me."

"You say she's with Red Currie? I'm goin' to like this."

"Yeah, that bird thinks he's a hot rock. Well, you'll take care of that all right for me, won't you, Spike?"

"Sure, I'll take care of that for you, Eagle."

"Better take a few drinks on old Herman while you're out there. He's started up again and he's got some pretty fair stuff."

"Naw, I'm off of it, Eagle; doctor's orders."

"A few snorts of Herman's whiskey never hurt nobody."

"You might be right at that. Drive on ahead and I'll pass you on the way."

IF IT'S TWINS

Wards will send you an Exact Duplicate Layette Free. Twins are apt to happen . . . even in the best of well-regulated families! Not that they aren't welcome, no indeed! Because if there's anything better news than a brand-new baby—it's TWO brand-new babies!

TWILIGHT deepened in the bungalow. After she had put the baby to sleep she wandered through the hot dark rooms. When she came to the bedroom she went over to the clothes closet and took down from the top shelf a cardboard box. She brought it into the living room and snapped on the silk-shaded table lamp.

She sat down and reached under the mission table for the mail order catalogue that lay on the footboard. The large book opened at a place where a thin fold of wire-stapled invoice papers had been put away.

Tears wetted her cheeks as she began reading again—

Provides His Necessities

2 *Bishop dresses, Cotton batiste, Lace trimmed.*
3 *flannel bands about ¼ wool, balance cotton.*
12 *birdseye diapers Hemmed 27 by 27 inch size.*

216

31D4512 LAYETTE

1 *Dress Hand Smocked Fine Quality Cotton Batiste.*

2 *Gertrudes, Amoskeag 1101 cotton flannel. Shell stitched edges in pink or blue.*

2 *pairs hose mercerized cotton. Cream white.*

1 *baby book "Health and Care."* . . .

31D4512......39-*piece Layette*.......$4.59

She turned with sudden resolution to the pink index pages in the back of the book. Then she opened the catalogue on another page. It was headed in large letters:

ORDER WITHOUT EMBARRASSMENT . . . BY MAIL!

She read the page again. Again she puzzled over the curious inklings she found there. Unlike those on any other page of the catalogue, the description of each item here was a little nest of hidden meanings.

She mumbled the bewildering words slowly as she read and her eyes were blank with despair.

"When used as directed, affords a source of satisfaction to discriminating and enlightened women. . . ." "A powerful, quick-acting germ-killing agent. Will not injure delicate tissues. . . ." "Supplies the germ-destroying action of chlorine in convenient form, assuring its effects without harmful

217

action. . . .*" "Kills germ-life in organic matter,
but contains no irritating or dangerous chemicals and
will not cause injury to delicate membranes."
LANTEEN. LYGEL. LACTIKOL. LYSOL.
VERALIN. ORTHO-GYNOL. LORIS. LIBER-
TIES. SAFETEES. Order your feminine hygiene
needs from this page. SAVE MONEY! SAVE
EMBARRASSMENT!*

After a long time she lowered her head and laid
her face on the open catalogue. She began to pray.

"Oh, dear God," she prayed, "I'm not sure, and
I've got to be sure. . . . You see everything that
happens in the world, God, so won't you please help
me . . . help me . . . help me, God, help me. . . ."

PUT YOUR MODEL "T"

back on its feet! Replacement parts for Model T-TT Fords. Exact duplicates of original equipment. They fit perfectly. When ordering repair parts find the Ford part number in the picture shown here. Then find that number in the numerically arranged table listing below and order by our article number.

FRIDAY evening at dusk C. R. Butts, having made his deliveries and collections, came up the back alley trailing his empty tin wagon. He stopped back of Danziger's Pharmacy and pulled the wagon in through the back door. Doc Danziger stood under the shaded light back of the partition mixing a prescription on the little marble slab.

"All right fer me to park my wagon here a little while, Doc?"

"Yeah, that's all right."

"Give me a bottle of them Hostetter's Bitters, will you, Doc?"

"I'll sell you a bottle for a dollar."

"That's what I meant, Doc—sell me a bottle."

C. R. Butts counted out the coins on the prescription counter. Doc Danziger left the prescription he was mixing and got a bottle of Hostetter's Bitters from a shelf near the back of the store.

"Take it on out in the alley," Doc said, handing C. R. Butts the pasteboard carton that held the bottle. "I ain't allowin' no more drinkin' here in the back of the store."

C. R. Butts took the privy key from the nail where it hung by a wooden paddle and went out the open back door into the darkness. A few minutes later there was a sound of a padlock grating on its hasp and then the tinkle of glass breaking in the alley.

C. R. Butts came back in wiping his shrunken lips on his shirt sleeve.

"Wowie!" he said. "That makes me feel like a new man. That hits me right where I live. I ain't had no supper."

"That Hostetter's Bitters will make you want to laugh and play," Doc Danziger said.

"Shore does. If I had me a way to go, I believe I'd go out here to Old Herman Gutterman's to the big square dance tonight."

"They ort to be plenty goin'," Doc said. "Why don't you git on out there on the street and inquire around and I bet you'd have a way to go in five minutes."

"That's a good idea, Doc. I'll go out and look around and see if I cain't find somebody that's got a car goin'."

"They'll be plenty to drink out at Herman's."

"Yeah, they sure will. That's what I want to go fer."

220

C. R. Butts went out through the front of the drug store with Doc Danziger keeping an eye on him through the peephole in the prescription partition. The screen doors slammed.

Butts wandered on up Broadway toward the colored lights of Pirtle's filling station. There was a car standing in the shadows. Peering into the darkness he saw Spike Callahan stooped over fixing his car.

"Hi, there, Spike!" C. R. Butts said boozily. "What you doin'?"

Spike stood up and scowled. "Who wants to know?" he asked.

"I do—C. R. Butts."

"How you like the way you found out?" Spike said, bending over his work again.

"Spike, I thought maybe I could talk you into going out to Gutterman's square dance with me tonight."

"With you?" Spike asked without looking up. "How was you goin'?"

"Well, that's jist it. I ain't got no way to go, but I thought maybe I might ketch a ride with you out there tonight."

"Naw. I got a drive to make for another fella pretty soon now. I cain't take you to no square dance."

"Which direction you headed? If you're headed

221

west, I'll give you two bits to drop me off at Gutterman's."

"Where's the two bits?" Spike asked, straightening up again.

"Right here it is," C. R. Butts said, handing Spike
a quarter.

Spike held the coin over to the light and looked
at it before he put it into his pocket. "O.K., Butts.
Crawl in the back seat there. I'm goin' to start jist as
soon as I can put these floor-boards back in."

C. R. Butts got into the car. Spike Callahan fitted
the floor-boards in and spread the rubber mat over
them.

"Here's your pliers, Ira," he called, scooting them
along the concrete floor of the filling station. Ira
came out and picked them up.

Spike got into the car and slammed the door. The
starter whined, the motor roared, and he swung the
car backwards out into the dark street at a high
speed. A Model-T Ford came jolting along at the
same moment. There was a loud crash. Spike jammed
on his brakes.

"What was that?" he asked.

"I think you must of hit somebody," C. R. Butts
said, picking himself up from the bottom of the
back seat.

"God damn it all!" Spike said, climbing out.

Sylvester Merrick stood in front of his broken,
spouting radiator, ruefully scratching his head. Spike

took one look at the crumpled rear fender on his own car.

"God damn you, nigger, where in hell did you think you was goin' with that wreck anyhow?"

"Mistah Spike," Sylvester said politely, "didn't I have the right of way?"

"Hell, no, you didn't have nothing."

"Yas, suh, Mistah Spike. You can jist call anyone around hyah and have 'em look at my tracks and then look at yourn. They'll tell you I had the right of way."

"Don't dispute my word, nigger, or I'll cold cock you with a tire tool."

The sound of the crash had brought men and boys running up the street. They crowded round, watching the fun by carlight.

"All right, nigger. Fork up," Spike said. "You're goin' to pay me for gettin' this fender straightened. It'll take about a dollar."

"All right, suh, Mistah Spike. I'll pay foh yo' fenduh if you'll git me a new radiator foh my cah in place of the one you busted up."

C. R. Butts slipped up behind Sylvester and pinned his arms. The Negro did not struggle to get free. He stood rigid.

"I got him, Spike!" C. R. Butts cried. "Go ahead and mash his face in."

"Naw, let him go," Spike said. "I'll mash his face in without you holdin' him."

223

C. R. Butts let go and Sylvester threw up his arms, but not in time. Spike's fist struck him full in the face and blood jutted from his nose. C. R. Butts clipped him one behind the ear. The Negro staggered but did not fall. A great jeer went up from the men crowded round.

Art Smiley came elbowing through the crowd. "Here, you fellas, what's goin' on?" he said loudly.

"Nigger gittin' smart," someone said.

"Nigger run into Spike's car."

"This nigger smashed my rear fender all up," Spike said.

"Well, this ain't no way to do," Art Smiley said. "If he run into you, you can make him pay for the damage, and if he won't pay for the damage you can take it to law. But this here fightin' on the street, that ain't no way to act."

"Hell, I ain't goin' to fool around tryin' to git him to pay for the damage he done me," Spike said. "I already got my satisfaction."

"You said it, Spike!"

"Did you see old Spike jist double up his fist and rare back and smack that impident nigger one?"

"You tell 'em, Spike, you shore got your money's worth."

"Git on, then! Git on!" Art Smiley said. "You all boys bust up this crowd and git on back to where you was loafin'."

"Come on, Butts!" Spike said. "Git in the car if you're goin' with me."

"We learned that nigger a lesson, didn't we, Spike?" C. R. Butts said, getting into the front seat.

"What do you mean, *we?* You sneaked up behind him," Spike said, stepping on the starter. The car roared away.

Sylvester stood with the blood running out of his nose, dazedly running his hands over the dished-in radiator.

"What's the matter, Sylvester?" Art Smiley asked, not unkindly. "Your nose is all bloodied. Did Spike Callahan whup you?"

"Yas, suh," Sylvester said stolidly. "I reckon he did."

"Well, are you bad hurt? Are you able to drive?"

"Yas, sah, I's able to drive, if my cah'll go. I doan know if my cah'll go with the front all smashed in lak that."

"Git in, then, and try it. You'll have to git it off the street. I wouldn't let it worry me if I was you. Accidents will happen, and it don't do a man no good to lose his temper about it."

"Yas, suh," Sylvester said, stooping to crank his car.

COLOR MAGIC

Color has strange powers! The sight of it suggests life, warmth, beauty . . . the very mention of it fires our imagination! We're "fussy" about dyes—insist that so far as possible all dyes shall be, not just good dyes, but the best dyes known. . . .

I**RA** PIRTLE sat drowsing in his slat-bottomed chair. It was almost nine o'clock and there was no business. The lights along Broadway shone on a silent street. Ira was thinking of closing up for the night when the telephone rang. He got up and went to it.

"Pirtle Service Station! . . . Oh, hello, Della. What's on your mind? You ain't changed it yit, I reckon. . . . Why, I reckon she's at home. I sent her home from here about six o'clock. She was still there when I went down and et supper. . . . Now, I think you're wrong about that. I think you jist got your suspicions aroused. . . . Sure I'll take you anywheres you say. Be tickled to death to. . . . In jist a few minutes, Della. I'll close up right now. . . . Sure I'll come by your place and pick you up. But le' me go past home first and see if she ain't there. . . . Oh, now, Della, I'm pretty sure you're wrong about that. I forbid her to go with Eagle any

226

more, and she knows when I say a thing I mean it.
. . . Well, if she's disobeyed me, I'll take me a
strap and wear her out, you mark my words. . . .
All right, Della. It won't be but a few minutes. . . .
Good-by."

Ira hung up the receiver and began scuttering
about, moving inside wire display racks of canned
motor oil, locking the gas pumps, scooping silver
change out of the cash drawer. He stuffed the canvas
money bag into his hip pocket and took a wild
glance about before he pulled down the electric
switch to cut off the lights.

His Ford coupé was parked at the side of the
filling station. He jumped in and sped off down the
darkened street.

The car stopped in front of a small bungalow.
Ira got out and ran into the house. It was in darkness.

"Irene! Irene!" he called, stumbling through the
rooms, bumping into furniture.

He snapped on a bedroom light. The bed was
empty. He turned and ran through to his own bedroom. Squinch-eyed before the mirror glare, he seized
a collar from the open parcel on the chiffonier,
clamped it round his crinkled neck, and fastened it
with the steel clips of a ready-made bow tie. He
smeared talcum powder on his day-old whiskers.
Then, without stopping to turn off lights, he ran
out of the house to his car.

The Widow Holcomb was standing at her front gate with her head swathed in a white veil. The car had scarcely stopped when she came running out to it. Ira flipped open the door for her. She sprang in.

"I guess you was right, Della," Ira said. "She sure ain't at home. But I sure don't know where she could of went."

"Drive out to Gutterman's," she cried. "That's where he wanted to go tonight. They've went out to that square dance of Gutterman's, that's where they've went!"

Eagle Catoosa sat at the wheel of his big car, smoking a cigarette. Footsteps sounded on the culvert. A girl came slipping out of the darkness.

"What did you want?" she asked coldly.

"Did Spike call you out?"

"Yeah, he told me you was down here. What did you want? I got to be gittin' right on back. I've got a date."

"Come on and git in the car. I want to talk to you."

"No, I ain't goin' to git in no car with you."

He reached over and opened the door. "You git in this car like I told you to."

She walked round the darkened car and slipped into the low front seat. He grabbed her and squeezed her to him and kissed her violently. She made gurgling noises and pushed him away.

228

"Eagle," she said sharply, "I'm off a you like a dirty shirt. Goin' smellin' around after that old Widow Holcomb. I ain't goin' to have no more to do with you."

"Hell, I jist had one date with her to git back at your old man."

"That's all right. You can jist go on and go with her. I wisht you would. Maybe if you did Papa would git wise to hisself."

"Act like you had half-sense, Irene. I jist dated the widow cause your old man won't let you go with me. Come on, let's take a little ride."

He started the motor. She leaned forward suddenly and turned off the ignition and snatched the keys out of the lock.

"Hey! What's the matter with you?" he said.

"I cain't go on no ride," she said. "I told you I had a date up there to the dance. He'll be out lookin' for me in a minute."

"Let him look. If he comes down here, I'll poke his face."

He put his arm round her and pulled her to him. "Come on, gi'me them keys."

"Now, Eagle, you quit," she whimpered. "I ain't goin' to have no more to do with you. You don't respeck me enough."

"Hell, I do too respeck you, Irene. I told you I'd marry you any time you said."

"Gosh, no, Eagle! Papa would kill me."

229

"He wouldn't do nothing to you after you was my wife. I'd take keer of that."

"I know. But, gee—I— Oh, I jist couldn't, Eagle. Not right now."

He reached for her again, but she drew back saying, "Watch out! Watch out! Here comes a car!"

She shrank down into the seat. The Ford coupé went on by, but the brakes on it squealed and it stopped about a hundred feet up the road.

"Le' me out! Le' me out! That's papa!" she said frantically.

"Here," Eagle said, reaching behind and lifting the cover on the rumble seat. "Climb in back there so he won't see you."

She scrambled over the back of the seat and crouched down.

The car ahead went into reverse and came grinding back down the road.

"Whaja do with the keys? Whaja do with the keys?" Eagle whispered hoarsely. "Gi'me the keys and I'll drive on away from 'em."

"They're there in the seat or on the floor somewheres," she whispered back. "I dropped 'em somewheres."

The Ford came alongside. A woman jumped out.

"Is that you, Eagle?" the Widow Holcomb called.

"Sure, it's me. Wha' ya want?" Eagle said, striking a match and peering down to find the keys.

"Who you got with you?" Ira Pirtle's voice asked.

230

"That's some more of your business," Eagle said, cursing when the match burnt his fingers.

There was a murmur of talk over at the other car. Ira Pirtle got out and came walking over to the big car.

"Irene ain't with you, is she?" Ira asked.

"Cain't you see they ain't nobody in the car but me?" Eagle said, striking another match. The keys, pushed down in the crack of the seat, glinted in the match light. Eagle picked them up. Ira Pirtle leaned over the rumble seat.

"I cain't see nobody with you in the front seat," Ira said, "but who's this here in the back seat?"

Eagle turned round and laid the lighted match against the back of Ira Pirtle's collar. The rubber sizzled and burst into flame.

"My God! I'm on fahr!" Ira Pirtle shouted, staggering back into the road, clawing at his throat.

"Roll in the dust! Roll in the dust!" the widow screamed.

Ira Pirtle dropped to the ground and wallowed in the road. Eagle's motor roared, the lights went on, and the car leaped away. It went thundering down the rough country road.

"Oh, honey! Oh, sweetheart!" the widow cried, sitting down in the road and pillowing Ira Pirtle's singed neck in her lap. "Did that mean old Indian hurt you?"

231

Ira Pirtle opened his eyes and looked up at her. "Is the fahr out?" he asked.

"Yes, you put it out," she said. "Only a savage Indian would think of a trick like that. I wouldn't have nothing more to do with a savage Indian that would pull a trick like that. Oh, honey, he ain't kilt you, has he?"

"Ah," said Ira Pirtle, snuggling his head down into the widow's warm lap.

IMPORTED CUCKOO CLOCK

Sears Cuckoo Clocks are Imported from the Black Forest of Germany. Stag's head and maple leaf top and front ornaments are hand-carved by families who have been doing carving for generations. Beautiful walnut finish. Ht., 19½ in., width 13 in., 5 in. dial. Cuckoo appears to call hours and half-hours. One-day weight movement.

5F9314¼ $14.45

THE FINEST room in Gutterman's three-roomed house was the built-on kitchen. The big brass oil lamp that hung from the ceiling had a mountain scene hand-painted on its white glass shade. The linoleum-covered floor seemed to be tessellated with blocks of red marble and green onyx. Splendid with nickel, huge with hot-water reservoir and overhead warming closets, a six hole range took up one side of the room. The other side held a varnished oak kitchen cabinet with a vast, oval-windowed flour sifter and a polished zinc top.

Over on the wall near the kitchen cabinet a cuckoo clicked out of its ornate little hut and called once for the half-hour.

Spike Callahan put the big jar of whiskey back down on the kitchen table and looked at his watch.

233

He went over to the cuckoo clock and moved the hands forward ten minutes.

He was alone in the kitchen. The door leading to the front room was open and through it came sounds of feet thudding on bare boards, shrill giggles and hoarse guffaws, the squeak and twang of fiddle and guitar being tuned, and glimpses of men and women milling past in their Sunday clothes.

Old Herman Gutterman's hearty voice could be heard calling: "Git yore podners fer a quadrille!"

The hubbub got louder, backs thumped against the wall, and then the noise went down. Old Herman was shouting them into their places: "Four couple right this way. Three more couple right over here. Two more couple this way. One more couple. . . . All set now!"

Spike Callahan took another long pull at the whiskey jar, shuddered, and wiped his mouth on the back of his hand. He sat and stared moodily at the open back door.

Homer Slover came sneaking in out of the darkness carrying a double-barrel shotgun. When he saw Spike, a foolish grin spread over his big moon-face and he bobbled his head. "Reckon it'd be all right for me to go in there and dance jist wearin' these here overhalls?"

Spike gave him a drunken nod. "Sure, that's O.K., Homer! You're all right. Go right on in there and pitch!"

234

Homer propped his shotgun carefully beside the back door and tiptoed through to the other room just as the fiddle and guitar swept into the dance tune.

The furious swirls of "Hell Among the Yearlings" came flooding out into the kitchen. The house quivered as the dance began. Someone began clapping loudly in four-four time. The thunder of footfalls filled the house. Herman Gutterman was bellowing:

> First couple out to the couple on the right,
> Lady around the lady with the gent behind,
> Lady around the gent and the gent cut a shine.
> Couple up four in the center of the floor—
> Two little ladies do-se-do
> One more heel and one more toe,
> One more swing and on you go. . . .

Red Currie, dressed in his sizzle pants, came out into the kitchen and glanced anxiously about.

"Where'd Irene go?" he asked.

Spike turned his bitter, pocked face up at Red. "Where'd you get them pimp's pants, bright boy?" he asked.

"I seen Irene come out here to the kitchen with you awhile ago," Red said. "Where is she now?"

"Oh, you mean you want to know where your girl went! Why, bright boy, I thought you knew all the answers already! So your girl has stood you up, has she, bright boy? Well, what're you whinnyin' around me for? A bright boy like you ought to be able to see that I haven't got your girl."

Red gnawed his lips. He had his fists doubled up. He hesitated a moment. Then he turned and strode out of the house. Spike picked up the whiskey jar and took another drink. A slight spasm twitched his shoulders. He sat there dozing a little.

> All the way to Arkansaw
> To eat cornpone and 'possum jaw—
> At 'em on the left with the old left hand,
> Right and left with the right and left grand.

Spike jerked his head up and saw Red Currie standing in the back door. Red was holding out a grimy wisp of cloth with three artificial rosebuds on it.

"I found these in the front seat of your car," he said quietly. "I know who they belong to, all right." Then he skinned his lips back over his teeth and screamed, "Now, God damn you, Spike Callahan, you better tell me where my girl is!"

In the room beyond Herman Gutterman was shouting above the wild music and scuffling feet:

> Neck yoke down and double trees draggin',
> Once and a half and keep on raggin';
> Gals swing hard, but gents swing harder,
> Swing that gal by her old rag garter.

236

Spike peered at the clue with bleary-eyed wonder. All of a sudden he began laughing. He banged the table with his hands and whooped. Red stood stark in his accusing pose and glared at Spike a moment longer. Then he put his arm down and shifted his eyes nervously.

> Once and a half and the other half too,
> Once and a half go all the way through;
> Come to your podner and meet her in the shade,
> Come to your podner and all promenade.

Spike held his sides and gasped, "Bright boy, if you keep on, dern if you ain't goin' to be a reg'lar Hawkshaw."

Red Currie reached over beside the door and picked up the shotgun. He pointed it at Spike and said calmly, "I guess this'll make you tell me where you taken Irene!"

Spike's face suddenly grew sober. "You put that gun down, you damn smart aleck, you," he snarled, lurching to his feet.

"Not till you tell me where Irene is!"

"I'll slap some of that smartness out of you, you little red-headed simp!"

He came staggering across the room with his open hand outstretched. Red's face puckered up and he began to weep.

"Don't you lay hand on me, Spike!" he sobbed,

cringing against the wall. "If you lay hand on me, Spike, I'll shoot you, you see if I don't!"

Then with tears streaming over his peeled face, he cried, "You take one more step towards me, Callahan, and I'll blow your guts out!"

He had the shotgun to his shoulder now. Spike halted a few feet from the end of the barrels.

"Put that gun down before I grab it and whap it over your head," he said, talking with his teeth clinched.

"You tell me first where Irene is."

"O.K., then. I guess I'll have to take it away from you."

"Stop, Spike, stop!" the boy cried as he pulled the trigger.

After the gun went off there was a deep silence. The music stopped in a long whimper and then no sound at all came from the other room. Spike Callahan stood at the cook stove, against which he had been blown, with a bewildered look on his face. He grunted once and his body folded neatly to the kitchen floor. Red Currie carefully set the gun back where he had got it. He slipped out the back door.

The carved wooden clock over by the kitchen cabinet whirred and the cuckoo popped out at its little door. Its jerky calls fell on the silence ten times.

A woman screamed in the other room. The dancers came swarming out into the blood-spattered kitchen.

LET OUR PERSONAL SERVICE

solve your buying problems. A bit of friendly advice is always helpful on an important purchase. Our Personal Service is free and does not obligate you in any way. It is strictly personal. . . .

THE BULKY catalogue was sodden with her tears and sweat. She kept her face pressed against its musty pages and went on praying.

"Oh, God," she prayed, "it just can't be right. Blind and crippled and still-born, God. Why must I keep on bringing children like that into the world, God? Oh, God, won't you please let me not ever have another child by him? Please, God, help me . . . help me . . ."

The alarm clock in the kitchen began ringing. She got up quickly and hurried into the kitchen to shut it off. As she turned on the light and walked across to the kitchen shelf she saw that it was just ten o'clock.

CONCEALED SPRINGS

Long-Wearing Non-Elastic Rayon-Cotton Web Suspenders. All Brass Trim. Concealed rust-proof bronze springs give extra stretch and relieve strain on trouser suspender buttons. Cord ends 1½ in. wide. 40 in. long. Assorted patterns and colors. Crossback style.

35D1413—*Ship wt. 4 oz*..................37¢

THERE was perfume in the wood-shed.

It was a warm night and the fires were out. Even while the dance was on, shadowy forms lurked about the yard, scuffling, laughing, quarreling, and drinking. But no one would be coming for firewood on a night like this.

They were in the wood-shed when the gun went off. The wood-shed was a lean-to built on one side of the kitchen. Lead shot peppered through the thin kitchen wall and rustled among the split sticks of stove wood. The charge went too high to strike them.

She put both hands against his hulking shoulders and pushed hard.

"Git up! Git up!" she whispered frantically. "That's Orin!"

He staggered to his feet and hobbled toward the

240

wood-shed door, trying to tug his trousers up over the pimpling knobs of his knees.

"I told you! I told you!" he whimpered in the dark. "Doggone you, Birdie! I didn't want to come out here with you. You went and got us into this yourse'f. Now he's got us trapped in here and he'll kill us both."

He stood fumbling his trouser buttons with one hand and trying to lift the oak bar on the wood-shed door with his other hand. Birdie slipped lithely under his arm and wrenched the bar away. The door banged against his face as she pulled it open and fled into the night.

He heard a woman scream, then the rumble of feet trampling through the house. He yanked the door open again and went plunging and crashing through the blackjack scrub that covered the hillside.

There was a metallic screak. Fiery pain deadened his adam's apple as he fell backward. He rolled over on his large belly, groaning for breath, waiting for the death blow. Then he knew that he had run into a wire clothesline. He began to crawl on his knees toward the barbwire fence.

Someone came to the kitchen door and called, "Who's out there?"

The hubbub in the kitchen quieted.

He was climbing through the barbed wire strands. He did not answer, but the sound of his pants ripping on the barbed wire crackled out in the silence like a lightning stroke.

The man on the back porch step called, "Stand right where you are or I'll shoot."

He plunged madly on, stumbling through the brush. He heard the footsteps running out into the yard. Then the gun was fired. The explosion rang in his ears. Overhead the fine shot sang and whispered among the dry leaves. He did not stop.

His dangling suspenders caught on a scrub oak bush. He ran on and the suspenders stretched as far as they would go. As they tore loose from the oak twig they flipped toward him and struck him in the small of the back with a stinging pop.

He gave a great groan. "Oh-h-h-h! I'm shot!"

He reeled onward and he did not fall.

He came to the small canyon of Cedar Creek and he went sliding and scrambling down its rocky side. Small stones and dirt rattled after him. He did not wait to listen for sounds of pursuit as he surged up the opposite bank.

His breath was coming in dry painful heaves. The sound was like that of a horse with the blind staggers. His long warty face was turned up, pale in the starlight.

The trailing suspenders caught on another oak twig. They stretched as far as they would go and sprang back to strike him on the butt with a loud smack. His flagging feet quickened and he spurted forward again.

The lights of town appeared, a faint white mist above the low sand hills.

He came to another barbwire fence. He was upon it before he could stop. He fell on his stomach and went slithering under it, down into a dry gravelly ditch. The suspenders caught on the fence.

A long roadster came roaring along the road. He lay quiet until it was past.

As he climbed out of the ditch, with the gravel stinging under his finger nails, the suspenders snapped back again.

"Oh-h-h!" he groaned. "He's got me! I'm shot again. I cain't run no more."

But the dirt road into town lay white in the starlight and he did run on. He ran faster than he had been able to run through the brush and over rough land, his fists clenched, his pale long face thrown back, and a cloud of dust funneled after him.

"Squish-sqush-squish," his warm shoes went.

"Bl-l-l-uh-d!" he wheezed.

He came into niggertown and he sped past the darkened shacks without slowing down. When he reached the M. K. & T. railway cut, instead of going on up the street that led to the courthouse square, he swerved down the steel tracks, glimmering under a green switch light. He ran on, shielded by the high

243

clay walls of the railway cut, his large feet clanging the white ballast against the rails.

He came to another street crossing and turned into it. But the street, a quiet residential one, was dotted with corner electric lights, and he turned down the first alley he came to, loping blindly toward his home.

He saw beyond the tree shadows the black hulk of Banker Winston's house. Only three more blocks to go. A tin can went skittering away from his toes. He staggered on. There was a sound of wood breaking. The ground gave way under him and darkness closed round him.

"This is the end!" he gasped as he sank into the earth. "Orin Hollinsworth killed me back there and now I'm goin' to hell!"

W. S. Winston was aroused from his sleep by someone yelling outside. He sprang out of bed and went to the window where a breeze was soughing the draperies back and forth. He stood there in his nightshirt listening.

"Fire! Fire! Fire!" the cry came again. It came from right out back of Winston's garage.

Without even stopping to get into his dressing gown and slippers, W. S. Winston went rushing out of the bedroom. He bulged up to the wall telephone in the kitchen and cranked it frantically.

"Wilbur, what on earth is the matter?" his wife called sleepily when she heard the telephone bell.

"Fire!" he bellowed. "The garage is on fire!"

And to Hattie Butts, the sleepy telephone central, at last aroused, he hollered, "Ring the fire bell, woman, ring the fire bell! My garage is on fire."

He had scarcely put the receiver back on the hook when the iron clangor of the fire bell jelled the silent night.

Hattie Butts got into her soiled pink crêpe de chine nightgown and let her hair down. Only the night light was burning. She sighed and stretched out on the army cot beside the switchboard. She had no more than got her eyes closed when a drop fell and the bell rang. She grunted and rose up slowly.

She went over to the switchboard and jammed on the wire clamp of the headphone and flipped back the drop that was W. S. Winston's home number. She pulled out a plug from the back row and stuck it into the answering jack.

"Hallo," she said wearily. "Number, please. . . . Oh! *Fire?* All right, Mr. Winston!"

Hattie jerked off the headphone and sprang down from her high chair. She ran over to the open window and began tugging the fire bell rope. The fire bell, on its wooden platform just outside the second-story window, creaked over on its wheel and its doublequick clapper beat out the loud alarm.

Some nightowls loafing in the Passtime Pool Parlor and in Danziger's Drug Store came piling out into the back alley.

"Where's the fire at, Hattie?" they called under the telephone office window.

"Banker Winston's garage!" Hattie screamed down at them.

They went stampeding down the alley to the barn where the fire engine and hose carts were kept.

Hattie, with her hair streaming down over her nightgown, hurried back to the tall varnished switchboard. The whole front of the switchboard was in movement. The drops came clicking down. Hattie, working hand over fist, began jabbing plugs into the answering jacks as fast as she could. A thick tangle soon covered the switchboard, even though the cords kept writhing down.

"Banker Winston's garage. Banker Winston's. Winston's," she kept saying over and over into the hanging mouthpiece.

The volunteer fire squad—first come, first take a hand—dragged out the hose carts, grasped the pulling ropes and went careering off toward Winston's house.

All over town sounded the rumble and roar of motors being started, going to the fire.

The first hose cart came clattering down the alley back of Winston's house. Automobile headlights made the scene as bright as day. W. S. Winston, his nightgown tucked down in his trousers, stood shivering in the backyard.

"I don't see any flame," he was saying in bewilderment after the hose had been connected to a corner fireplug amid shouted advice from onlookers. "I don't see any flame, but I certainly heard someone call 'Fire!' right out here in the back. I *know* I wasn't dreaming. I had just got to bed and then I heard someone shout 'Fire' several times. It seemed to come from right out here in my garage."

"Maybe it was jist somebody's idea of a joke, Mr. Winston," one of the men suggested.

"Oh, no!" W. S. Winston said. "Whoever it was yelling 'Fire' certainly was yelling in earnest. No question about that."

The flat canvas firehose stiffened and rounded and writhed like a live thing as the men at the fire plug, a hundred yards away, turned on the water.

"Wait a minute, boys! Hold the deal! Shet 'er off! False alarm!" the shouts went up.

Then the anguished cry, like an echo, came again, "Fire! Fire! Fire!"

"Why, it sounds like it's coming from right out here in the alley!"

"Sounds like it's comin' from down underground."

The men, wan and ghastly in the strong white light, gave one another frightened looks. Everyone was silent for a moment.

"Fire! Fire! Fire!" the cry was raised again.

"Here he is, boys! Here he is!"

"Well, be dogged if he ain't fell in the cesspool."

"Watch yer step there you don't fall in your-ownse'f!"

"Who is it down in there?"

"Cain't see. Somebody run fetch a hook."

"Whew! What a stink."

"Hand him down a rope there."

They crowded round the broken boards of the cesspool, cautiously keeping a safe distance away. Someone appeared with a length of rope.

"We're th'owing you down a rope. Ketch it now! You got it?"

The hollow voice came from the hole in the ground. "Yeah!"

"All right, boys. Grab holt the rope! Ever'body pull now. Out he comes."

The line of men on the rope heaved away. The rope tightened and then went slack. There was a loud splash in the depths of the cesspool. The men on the rope went staggering over into a heap.

"Uh-oh! He must a lost his grip. Try 'er agin, boys. All right, Mister. Ketch on the rope. Take a bend on 'er. We'll git you out of there if it takes us all night."

This time the line surged away and a sodden, bedraggled form came popping out of the hole and slid for a few feet along the ground.

248

"Turn the light on him!"

"Turn the hose on him!"

"Look and see who it is!"

"Well, be dogged if it ain't Slemmons the mail carrier!"

"Whee-oo. Slemmons, ain't you a mess now!"

"What was doin' down there this time of night, Slemmons?"

Slemmons got slowly to his feet and glared at the crowd around him.

"What I want to know is," W. S. Winston said, in an angry cold-laden voice, "Slemmons, what's the idea of yelling 'Fire!' when there wasn't no fire?"

"Mr. Winston," Slemmons said mournfully, "do you reckon anybody would of come if I'd a yelled 'Shit!'?"

SMART FANCIES

Hits! Spicy Checks—Swanky Fifth Avenue Stripes—Peppy novelty effects. A splendid assortment of the latest fancy patterns. Designs that bring twice the price in metropolitan shops. You'll look a long time to find newer style—let alone such a saving. Extra fine weave cotton broadcloth. Preshrunk and fade-proof. Expert tailoring, distinctive styling, perfect fit. Attached collar model. Fancy Patterns are all similar to illustration. State size. Shpg wt. 11 oz.

33D340—*Shirt was* $1.19. *Now......*$1.09 *Each*

A LIGHT went on in one of the bedrooms at the Widow Tinsley's boarding house. Red Currie stood in the center of the room. A fit of trembling seized him and his teeth chattered like castanets. He began pulling off his clothes, clawing at his shirt. Then he stopped and stood rigid. Slowly he pulled up, inch by inch, the front of his blue-striped shirt.

He saw with horror that his shirt front was spattered with blood.

He pulled the shirt off and carefully rolled it into a neat ball. He began moving quietly about the room, looking for a place to hide it.

A bundle of freshly-laundered shirts, opened, but

250

still in their newspaper wrapping, lay on the bureau. Red stared at the clean shirts a moment.

Dazedly, he held the rolled-up blood-spattered shirt between his knees while he took one of the clean shirts and put it on. He pulled the newspaper out from under the bundle and got the piece of twine it had been tied with.

The newspaper was the front page of a month-old *Black Dispatch*. He used it to wrap round the blood-spattered shirt. He tied the wrapping with twine. He snapped off the light and slipped quietly out of the house with his small bundle under his arm.

A light was burning in the southwest corner of the courthouse. The sheriff's office was crowded with men. They stood smoking and spitting, talking in low voices.

"I tell you, shiruff," C. R. Butts was saying, "they ain't no question about who done it. Wasn't I right there this evenin' when Spike whupped that Merrick nigger for strackin' his car?"

"Yeah, I know all about that, Butts," Sheriff Ferguson said indifferently. "But we'll jist wait till the dogs gits here."

"Where's the bloodhounds comin' from this time, shiruff?" another man asked.

"Eufala, I reckon," the sheriff said. "I telegraphed that man down there that keeps the dogs and he sent me a telegraph right back that he'd be here on the midnight train."

"It ain't long now till the midnight train runs."

C. R. Butts began complaining again, "Shiruff, that nigger will be clean out of the country before ever you git them dogs here. Ask Bert, there—he seen the nigger runnin' through the blackjack and taken a shot at him."

"I shore did, shiruff. I heerd somebody climbin' through the fence out there and I called to him to stop and when he didn't stop I grabbed up that very shotgun he done it with and let him have the other barrel. I ain't sure whe'r I hit him or not, but—"

"I know, I know," Sheriff Ferguson said. "You told me that before. But you say you ain't prepared to swear it was the Merrick nigger."

"No-o-o, I didn't see him good enough to tell which nigger it was, shiruff," Bert said slowly. "But I will say this—it was *a* nigger all right. I'll take my oath on that. He run like a nigger—you know how a nigger runs—sort of splay-footed?"

Sheriff Ferguson sighed. "Well, wait till the dogs gits here. That Merrick nigger has always been a right respectable nigger—workin' there at the bank. Without I got more evidence than you fellows give me that he's the guilty party, I ain't goin' to run over there in niggertown and arrest Sylvester Merrick and then have Double S Winston on my neck for arrestin' his nigger without sufficient evidence.

And besides that have folks laughin' at me if I git the wrong nigger."

"Hell, shiruff," C. R. Butts began again, "you ain't goin' to git the wrong nigger when you git that Merrick—but if you keep on waitin' I doubt whe'r you'll be able to ketch him. You don't have to take my word for it. They's men right here that seen Spike hit him. Art Smiley told you the same thing. Spike knocked him down and drove off. Then the nigger got in that Ford of hisn and follered us on out there. He parked it right down there below Gutterman's and sneaked up there to the kitchen where Spike was settin', grabbed up that shotgun and killed him in cold blood before old Spike could lift a hand. Anyhow, that's the way I got it figured out. Revenge pure in simple."

"Yeah, I know," Sheriff Ferguson said. "That's the way you got it figured out, Butts. That's not sayin' that's the way it happened. All I say is, jist wait till the dogs git here. We'll pick up that trail quick enough when the dogs git here."

"Where's Jim Humplehauser? He's county attorney, ain't he, shiriff?" another man asked. "Looks like he'd ort to be here."

"Yeah, I been tryin' to git a-holt of Jim all evenin'. But he's out on a big drunk somewheres tonight."

C. R. Butts waggled his head. "Now if I was shiruff, I'd—"

"Yeah, if you was shiruff, you'd do wonders," Sheriff Ferguson said sarcastically. "You was sich a brave deppity."

"I don't keer," C. R. Butts said. "If us men here done what we'd ort to do, we'd all go out and ketch that nigger ourse'fs without waitin' on you, shiruff. And when we ketched him, we'd jist string him up to a telephone pole and save the county all that expense of tryin' him."

"Listen here, Butts," the sheriff shouted angrily. "If I hear any more of that kind of talk out of you, I'll sling your ass in jail. I ain't goin' to have no lynchin' around here while I'm shiruff. Now you jist set down there and shet up. I've told you and told you, and I ain't a-goin' to tell you no more—jist wait till them dogs come."

"If that nigger had his car parked down there on the road, how's a bloodhound goin' to foller his trail? A bloodhound cain't foller no rubber tire trail. They ain't no bloodhound can do that."

"Butts," the sheriff said coldly, "air you goin' to shet up or am I goin' to have to shet you up?"

One of the men looked at his watch. "It's ten till twelve, shiruff," he said.

The sheriff stood up and pushed his tilted broad-brimmed hat down on his head. He started out of the room and the other men came crowding after him. "Them dogs will be here pretty quick now," he said as he went out.

254

HOME CULTURE

books. Supreme Letter Writer. Over 200 *guides for business correspondence of all kinds and social letters, both formal and informal. Helpful for everyone. Cloth bound.* 226 *pages. Size* 5¼ *by* 8¼ *in. Ship. wt.* 1 *lb.* 4 *oz.*

57D4567 .... 85¢

R ED CURRIE sat at the linotype keyboard. One of his jaw muscles kept twitching, but his pink face was stiff and expressionless. He took a piece of new copy from the spike and folded it before he slipped it under the copyholder. He began setting:

CONCHARTEE, OKLAHOMA,
AUGUST 2

WHEREAS, it has come to our attention that a brutal crime is supposed to have been committed by one of our race; and

WHEREAS, that friendly and mutual relationships that have so long existed among the white and colored citizens of our fair county has been interrupted by such a brutal act;

BE IT RESOLVED, that we, the colored citizens of Conchartee, Conchartee County, Oklahoma, do here and now place our stamp of disapproval on such an atro-

255

cious act, and assure the widow that she has our deepest sympathy and the law our unstinted support in bringing the guilty to speedy justice.

We do not condone crime in any form. We believe in, teach our race to be, law-abiding citizens. We trust that the brutal act will not break the friendly and mutual relationships that exists among the white and colored people of this, our good county. We have the utmost confidence in the white citizens of this county, and trust that you have the same in us. We shall ever strive and teach our race never to betray that trust. We pray that the guilty will be punished and that the innocent will be protected.

Your humble citizens,

L. J. COREY
F. HAMMICK
T. R. JONES
B. P. PEARSON
V. C. EDWARDS
G. W. SHIRES
A. P. HARTSHORNE
I. B. SHERMAN

Red stuck the copy on the hook. He picked up the stick of warm type and carried it over to the stone composing block. R. W. E. Ledbetter came hustling back.

"Red," he asked hurriedly, "have you pulled the proof on that piece I wrote about the murder?"

"Naw, I ain't pulled no proof," Red said in a surly voice. "There it is, right there on the block." He picked up his ink-sodden cigarette and moved back to his machine.

"Wha' ya mean, there in that story," he asked without looking toward Ledbetter, "where you say that shirt they found was gaudy like niggers always wear?"

R. W. E. Ledbetter pulled a galley proof and held up the strip of thin paper.

"I don't know which part you mean, Red. Where is that?" he said. He began reading the proof under his breath:

Feeling ran high in Conchartee all day Saturday against Sylvester Merrick, Negro, who allegedly shot and killed C. H. Callahan, taxi driver, at a square dance west of town Friday night. Mr. Callahan was reported to have become engaged in an altercation with the Negro as the result of an automobile accident early Friday evening and the motive is thought to be revenge, but there was some doubt as to the Negro's guilt by the sheriff's office at first and Merrick was not taken into custody until Saturday noon by which time feeling was running so high that the Negro was taken into custody at his own request.

What was regarded as conclusive evidence of guilt however was discovered Saturday afternoon when small boys playing in a culvert near the M. K. & T railway

CATALOGUE

tracks near the Negro section of town found a bundle containing a blood-stained shirt wrapped in a newspaper bearing Merrick's address label. The shirt bore the trademark of a mail order house which the Negro is reputed on good authority to have been a customer of and also was a gaudy striped affair which Negroes so often wear. . . .

"Oh, yes!—I see what you mean. Here it is right here." The editor read the line over again aloud. "Why, what's wrong with that, Red?" he asked innocently. "Niggers do wear gaudy shirts."

"Nothing wrong with it, I guess, if that's what you wanted to say," Red mumbled.

"Red, what in the world's the matter with you here lately? You're gettin' so grouchy nobody can't hardly get along with you."

"Aw, I'm all right," Red said in a low voice.

His fingers moved over the keyboard and a thin hail of matrices came tinkling down:

COLORED MAN WRITES ANENT RECENT
CRIME

Conchartee, Okla.

August 2

To the White Citizens of Conchartee County:

Just a few lines to let you all know that we good colored citizens of Conchartee County don't feel no sympathy for the nigger that murdered the white gentleman. No! we haven't felt that he did right because he should stay in his place, and since he did such as he did, we are not feeling that we have a right to plead to you all for mercy.

It make us chagrined and feel that he has ruined the good colored people that try to behave themselves.

I feel very bad over it myself to see that we have such a fellow in the Race and I am among the good colored people that feel just like I do toward him. I talked with them and they can't see how they can have any sympathy for him.

But I am writing to let you know that we leave it to you all to do what you all see fit to do to him. But still asking you all not to be too hard on your good servants that have been honest and faithful for the time that we have been working with you for the other fellow. Because we good colored people want to thank you all for favors and the chance that you will have given us to let us have schools for our children and teachers to teach them and jobs for us to work and to get bread for them that they can have a chance. Also we thank you all for making it easy.

Because if it wasn't for the good white citizens, we realize that many of our girls and boys could have been mobbed for nothing they done, but for the brutal act that was done. I also thank the sheriff for working so faithfully to get the right man.

Your faithful servant
JASON CALLOWAY

still pleading for a chance for the better class of colored people and not to punish us for him, because if he do wrong he is wrong, and we have no sympathy for him!

Red turned and called up toward the front where R. W. E. Ledbetter sat at his desk.

"Are we goin' to have room to run this long-winded letter from that old nigger, Calloway?"

His voice trembled.

"Why, yes, I think we ought to try and get it in, Red. It seemed to me to be pretty good stuff. We've got to do ever'thing we can to git this mob spirit quieted down. If we git the country niggers all scared, they won't come to town to do their trading. All this mob talk will jist about spoil our Home Town Industry Jubilee if they ain't a stop put to it."

Hattie Butts rang the sheriff's office.

"All right, Sheriff Ferguson," she said in a dreary, nasal tone. "Ready on Okmulgee. Hal-lo, Okmulgee. Hal-lo. All right, sheriff. Here's your party. Go ahead, please."

She listened in with her mouth agape. When she had let the plug go wriggling down from the long-distance socket, she plugged in on the Danziger Pharmacy number.

"Hello, Doc. Say, have you seen papa around

there anywheres? Yes, if you see him, I wisht you tell him to come up here a minute."

She plugged in another number. "Hello. Passtime Pool Hall. Say, is papa in there? Yeah, this is Hattie. Well, you tell him to come up here a minute, will you? Tell him to hurry."

Presently footsteps drummed on the wooden stairway of the First National Bank building. They came thudding along the hall. The 'phone office door opened and C. R. Butts came breathlessly in.

Hattie jerked off her headset and went over to the wooden railing.

"Oh, papa," she said in an excited whisper. "I jist listened to Sheriff Ferguson talking to the sheriff of Okmulgee County and he aims to move the nigger that killed Spike Callahan over there tomorrow night when ever'body's at the celebration. That means they'll head south out of town. You all could stop 'em easy at the Arkansas River bridge. . . ."

To state that the story of the catalogue is probably without parallel in the history of publishing, could hardly be called an exaggeration. . . . It is a story of stupendous, incomparable growth—from a few thousand books a year to twelve million. . . . Each one of its more than a thousand pages does an annual business averaging $200,000,000 a year. . . . In its three pounds are crowded the wonders of the world's market places. . . .

THE COUNTRY people began arriving early. Their gray, mule-drawn wagons, with extra plank seats laid across the weathered sideboards, were lined with children, little girls in lye-bleached floursack smocks and tightly braided pigtails; bigger girls wearing starched gingham and stiff straw hats with elastic chin straps; grown girls dressed in georgette crêpe or tub silk; small boys in their Sunday overalls and youths in their first blue serge suits. The young men came on horseback or in buggies with their sweethearts sitting alongside. Not many came in automobiles, but those who did rode in aged flivvers, tattered folding tops fixed with baling wire. The alley hitching racks were crowded. The courthouse square, all but the block on Broadway that had been roped off, was black-fringed with parked cars.

There was a good time coming for all the other boys in town. As for Waldo Ledbetter, Jr., he did not expect to have a good time ever again.

September had come, another month to be added to his default. It was only a matter of days now until he must pay the penalty for his crime.

Wednesday morning he came to work later than usual. He leaned his bicycle up against the back of the building and went into the shop. He picked up the broom and got a scoopful of red floorsweep, getting ready to sweep out, to start the morning routine. His father called to him.

"You don't need to sweep out this morning, son. Just let the sweeping go today. Go on out and have a good time. Go join the celebration."

"What celebration?" Waldo asked dully.

"What celebration! You're working here at the *Democrat* and you ask me what celebration? Here, didn't you never read this?"

Waldo took the big pink handbill. He had seen it a week before, the day it was printed. He glanced at the large type again.

HOME TOWN INDUSTRY JUBILEE

The Conchartee Merchants listed below invite every man, woman and child in the Conchartee Trade Territory to join them in a mighty celebration of Conchartee Merchant's "Live & Let Live" policy, and be their guests on

CATALOGUE

WEDNESDAY, SEPTEMBER 5th

Come One!!! $$$$ In Prizes $$$$ Come All!!!

For Ladies:

Rolling Pin Throwing Contest;

Husband Calling Contest.

For Gents:

Calf-Roping Contest;

Hog Calling Contest.

For Girls to Age 12:

Rag Chewing Contest.

For Boys to Age 12:

Cracker Eating Contest.

For Everybody: (Winner Take All)

Potato Race & Sack Race

Come Early!!!   Stay Late!!!

Free Shade & Ice Water

Band Concert by DeMolay Silver Cornet Band

Special Attraction:

At 12 Noon Wednesday $100 in GOLD, silver and copper coins will be thrown off the top of Pollack Bros.' Bargain Bazaar.

Waldo walked disconsolately through the crowd that had already begun to gather around the court-house square. There was nothing for him to celebrate. The DeMolay Band was tuning up in the bandstand over on the southwest corner of the square. A thin squeal from a clarinet followed by an *um▪pah* from the bass horn made the crowd laugh. Waldo walked

264

along under the heat-wilted trees, kicking at dried catalpa beans. He saw grizzled old Herman Gutterman kicking up his heels, already hilarious on his own wares. The peanut roaster was whistling in front of the White Front Grocery. Cripple Lund, the newsagent, sat in his little wagon on the corner holding a large gay cluster of toy balloons. Watermelon wagons were backed up to the curb, and their owners were bawling,

> Nice big watermelons,
> Fresh from the vine;
> Good erns fer a nickel,
> Better'ns fer a dime.

Two or three enterprising small boys with their iced tubs set on the sidewalk had started shrilling,

> Ice cold sody pop!
> Freeze yer teeth,
> And curl yer hair,
> And make you walk
> Like a millionaire.

When noon came Waldo, still skeptical about Pollack Brothers' throwing away money, stood with the crowd that had gathered in the street out in front of the store. Sure enough, the Pollack brothers' two swart faces appeared above the brick false story. They set a canvas money bag up on the ornamental sheet iron cornice for all to see and plunged their

265

hands in. Two handfuls of copper and nickel coins glinted in the blinding sunlight. There was a great shouting scramble in the dusty street. Waldo saw a dime fall and he went sprawling after it. A big farmer stepped on his fingers, barking them until they bled, but Waldo felt no pain. It was over all too quickly. The Pollack brothers shook out the coin bag to show that all the money had been scattered. They disappeared down the roof. The crowd milled about, laughing and comparing catches. Waldo saw some boys he knew.

"I got eighteen cents," he said proudly. "What did you guys get?"

"Aw, you didn't get that much. Nobody got that much without it was that guy that caught the $20 gold piece in the air."

"Let's see it, Waldo," Bill Huggins said.

Waldo held out his open palm, showing a grimy dime and a nickel and three cents. Bill Huggins slapped the coins out of his hand. The boys all scrambled for the money. Waldo stood there almost ready to cry. Bill Huggins walked off laughing. Two or three of the boys handed him back his nickel and two of his coppers, but his dime was gone.

"You wait, Bill Huggins!" Waldo called. "I'll get even with you!"

Up the street the potato race had started. There was a long row of potatoes for each contestant. Each row had twenty mounds, about a yard apart, twenty

266

potatoes in the final pile, nineteen in the next, until there was only one potato near the basket at the starting point. Men and boys raced stooping, each running to pick up potatoes in one of his piles, back to his basket to toss them in, back again to another pile. The first who finished his twenty trips with all his potatoes in his basket would be the winner. Waldo stood on the sidelines musing, trying to think of a way to win without having to make all those trips.

He noticed that several of the farmers looking on carried tow sacks tucked under their arms. Back of the crowded sidelines he saw Bill Huggins walking in a bran sack, holding the top of it clutched at his waist. He was inching along cautiously, trying to keep from stumbling. Bill looked odd with his beefy bottom stuffed tightly in a gunny sack.

"What're you doing in that tow sack, Bill?" Waldo asked.

"Practicing up for the sack race, what'd you think? I'm going to win me that five dollar gold piece prize. You watch me."

"Could I get in the sack race, Bill?"

"I guess you could. They ain't nobody holdin' you, are they? You cain't be in a sack race without no sack, though."

Waldo ran as fast as he could to the printing office. He got his bicycle and pedaled hard for home. When he got back to Broadway, panting and out of breath, they were already lined up for the sack race. Men and boys hobbled with gunny sacks stood in a line that reached from one side of Broadway to the other. Down at the crossing, half a block away, a crowd had gathered at the finish line. Waldo stepped quickly into line, pulled his gunny sack up over his legs and clutched it at his waist. Everyone was looking toward Al Kimball, who stood ready to fire the starting pistol.

The pistol cracked and the long, brown-hobbled line wavered and surged forward. One after another racers who tried to step out too quickly stumbled and went thudding down. Waldo could not see anything but the press of faces at the tape. Back of him he could hear the burly farmers striking the ground heavily, cursing and grunting. He did not look back. He took long steps, and every time he was about to stumble he would let out the big coffee sack a little more. A great shout of laughter went up from the crowd when they saw Waldo, up to his armpits in the huge gunny sack, his feet moving freely in its ample folds, striding out ahead. The only face Waldo could recognize in the white blur at the goal was Herman Gutterman's grizzled, red-nosed mug. Herman was cheering him.

"Whoopie! Come on thar, you, Waldo!" Herman kept shouting.

All along the course the racers who had fallen were getting to their feet again. Waldo took a back-

268

ward glance and saw that Bill Huggins was the only one close to him. Bill was coming on with a rapid twisting motion he had practiced. They were within a few feet of the finish when he reached out and clutched at Waldo. Bill lost his balance and went humping over on his face. Waldo stumbled against the tape and into the arms of Herman Gutterman, who let out another "Whuppy" that was a blast of whiskey breath in Waldo's face. He struggled free and the throng surged round him, laughing and shouting.

Mr. Lennox, the sack race judge, smiling his strained smile, held up the five dollar gold piece to present to the winner. Just as Waldo reached up to take it, Bill Huggins came hopping across the line, bawling angrily, "Hold on a minute there! He cheated! He had a great big sack whur the rest of us just had ordinary gunny sacks."

There was a murmur through the crowd. Opinion was divided. Some of the spectators were saying that when you came right down to it, using a big sack like that wasn't fair. A body could take full-length steps in a big sack. That Ledbetter boy was a town boy, too. The whole idea of a sack race was that you had your legs hobbled. Mr. Lennox hesitated, glancing timidly at the crowd.

A deep voice came rolling out over the heads of the people.

"Just a minute, Lennox!"

Banker Winston, the richest man in town, spoke, and the press gave way before his great paunch.

"There ought not be any difficulty in making a decision here," W. S. Winston bumbled, taking the gold piece from Mr. Lennox. "This lad here [putting his hand on Waldo's head] crossed the finish line first. Nothing was ever specified about the *size* of the gunny sacks to be used in this sack race. All the more praise to this lad for being slick enough to go get him an extra large sack. Any lad quick-witted enough to outsmart his competitors in the way this lad has done deserves *two* prizes. Here, my boy," W. S. Winston said, handing Waldo the five dollar gold piece.

"Amen, Double S! You shore spoke a mouthful," Herman Gutterman yelled, slamming his old black Stetson on the ground and stamping on it. "Any kid that smart deserves two prizes, and I'm a-goin' to reward the other'n to him right now."

Herman pulled a thin roll of currency out of his pocket, snapped off the rubber band, and handed Waldo a five dollar bill.

The throng laughed loud approbation. It was wonderful. It was a little too wonderful. Waldo did not linger. He squirmed through the thick stockade of legs and reached the sidewalk. He raced round the corner, down the quiet side-street toward the post office. Postmaster Shannon was standing at the

270

money order window. Waldo pushed the gold piece and the five dollar bill under the wicket.

"Mr. Shannon, would you look and tell me if this is real money?"

Sounds from the hog-calling contest came drifting into the quiet post office, "Sook-sook-sook, sooey, soo-oo-ey!"

"Why, yes, it looks like real money to me, Waldo. What's the matter? Did something make you think it was counterfeit?"

"No, sir. I *thought* it was real money. Then will you write me a money order for $9.40 to Montgomery Ward and Company?"

"Money order application blanks are right over there on the lobby desk, Waldo. You're a big enough boy now to be filling out your own blanks," said Postmaster Shannon.

All afternoon the sidewalks on all sides of the courthouse square were so thickly packed with people that anyone who was headed somewhere could scarcely get through. The DeMolay Band shivered the sultry air with brazen march tunes. After the hog-calling contest for men came the rolling-pin contest for women. This was followed by the husband-calling contest and the calf-roping contest. The white people kept to the west side of the square, but the Negroes stayed on the east side of Broadway, taking the full heat of the afternoon sun.

271

CATALOGUE

So the Home Town Industry Jubilee turned out to be a much bigger success than anyone had supposed it would be a few days before.

At first the catalogues had come in so slowly that the merchants had been apprehensive of the outcome. There were doleful predictions that the whole celebration was going to be an awful flop.

Up until a day or so before the date set hardly enough catalogues to kindle a fire had accumulated, much less enough to make a bonfire. But by the beginning of the week the farmers had begun bringing in their catalogues so steadily that the merchants thought they had the catalogues pretty well cleaned up before the final day. They were surprised to get almost as many catalogues on the day of the celebration as they had in all the week before.

There was also some unpleasantness when it was found, toward the end of the week, that Arley McIntosh, the grocer, and a few other non-progressive merchants, had been selling catalogues for fifty cents cash to be traded to competitors for one dollar in goods. This had to be ironed out by a committee from the Chamber of Commerce.

When all the catalogues were brought together and counted late Saturday afternoon it was discovered that more than a thousand had been brought in and traded for merchandise. This puzzled everyone until R. W. E. Ledbetter happened to think that there was nothing to prevent farmers who got their

272

mail at post offices ten, twelve, or even twenty miles away, from bringing in catalogues, or to keep farmers from ranging that far to collect them.

At any rate, they had the catalogues—a great sprawling mound of them—dumped on one corner of the circus lots south of Standpipe Hill. Little Muddy Creek goes dry every Summer, but it is swift enough in other seasons to have cut a long narrow gulley through the sandstone. Old brush had been piled into the deep dry creekbed.

After supper the crowd began gathering in the twilight.

R. W. E. Ledbetter, as master of ceremonies, struck a match and set it to the dry brush. As the flames crackled up, members of the Chamber of Commerce worked hard, dousing the catalogues with coal oil, tossing them on the fire. A few stood by with long poles, poking up the slow-burning blocks of paper. Others held dripping gunny sacks, ready to flout any blazing patch of grass.

The crowd had thinned out since afternoon. So many of the farmers had to get back to see about their stock before dark. But there were several hundred people there, nearly all town-dwellers, standing along the flaming ditch, their faces showing drawn and ghostly in the firelight.

The Negroes who had been on the streets in daylight had vanished into the night.

Little ember-spangled wisps of black floated up

into the darkness. Sometimes, when the goaded flames flared high, small boys would whoop, but only the bustling members of the Chamber of Commerce seemed to be having much fun. Few people seemed happy to see all the mail order catalogues destroyed.

"I reckon it's all over now," some people said, drifting away toward home. "Tomorra's another day."

"Yep, it was a big time while it lasted, but it's all over now."

"Yeow, I guess this is about the size of it."

"Well, I'll see you in the funny paper!"

"Between the sheets."

"Meet me at the pony show, boys. I got to be up early in the mornin' for the big race."

"What race is that they're havin' tomorrow mornin'?"

"Human race. Haw-haw-haw!"

"Better stick around awhile longer, boys. You ain't seen nothin' yet," others said mysteriously.

"Yeah, if you all go home now you're goin' to miss out on the biggest e-vent of the day."

"Don't leave yit awhile, or you'll be sorry to-morra mornin' when you find out what all you missed."

Long-drawn horn blasts from several motor cars came faintly from the country road south of town. Men and women began moving among the thinned-out crowd, whispering excitedly.

274

"Here they come! Here they come!"

"It's the nigger! They're bringing the nigger!"

The short line of automobiles came charging up the road and stopped with a great squealing of brakes. Men began piling out. Their faces were covered with black-stocking hoods, their eyes showing white behind the slits.

At the end of a rope behind the first car lay a misshapen, naked, human form, covered with blood-muddied dust.

"Come on, fellas! Grab holt here!" the leader shouted as he cut the rope. "We're goin' to heave him in the fahr."

They grasped the body and swung it and let it fall into the glowing ditch.

"Ain't it too bad Mrs. Callahan ain't here to see it," one of the women looking on said. "It would jist a done her heart good to see how they brung the nigger to justice."

"Yes, sir!" another woman said. "I don't think they done right, not tellin' Mrs. Callahan to make sure and be here."

C. R. Butts went slinking about the edge of the crowd. Bill Huggins came up to him.

"Mr. Butts," he said, wide-eyed. "How much would you take fer that there big toe you cut offen the nigger?"

"Oh, hell, son," C. R. Butts said importantly, "you ain't got enough money to buy that there nig-

275

ger's toe offen me. But I tell you what I will do—I'll sell you a piece of the clothesline rope we hung him with for four bits."

"Clothesline rope?" Bill Huggins gasped. "Did you hang him with a clothesline rope, Mr. Butts?"

"You're dang tootin', son. We hung that nigger with his own damn clothesline!"

We send it to you gladly without charge, confident that you will recognize its worth. . . .

T HURSDAY morning, before opening for business, Postmaster Shannon noticed that the stamp window needed some postal cards. He went over to the reserve stock in the big safe and took out four packs, adding one hundred postal cards to the stamp window supply. He did not say anything about it.

That noon, when the others had gone to dinner, Elvira Draper sold the last postal card at the stamp window. She got up and added a hundred more from the reserve stock.

Slemmons came in off his route earlier in the afternoon than the other carriers. He walked in at the back door, set his beveled tin stamp box down on his desk and hung up his big leather mail pouch. Pretty soon he came up front to check in his money orders and to replenish his stamp supplies.

"Give me fifty postal cards," he said, reading off the list of stamps he needed.

"Give you *fifty?*" Gladys Ferguson said in surprise.

"Yeah, fifty!" Slemmons said in a surly voice. "Sold ever' postal card I had and I could've sold fifty more if I'd a had 'em."

"Shucks, I'll have to git up and add some more

then," Gladys said, slipping down off her high chair at the stamp window. "We certainly have been having a run on postal cards today."

Postmaster Shannon overheard her say this, and he said, "No, there should be plenty of postal cards there. I added a hundred this morning. Maybe some have slipped down back of the drawer there."

Gladys Ferguson, bringing up four fresh packets from the reserve stock in the safe, said, "No, I guess not, Mr. Shannon. People have been running in here to buy postal cards all day. I'll bet I've sold a hundred myself. I don't know what's causin' it."

Slemmons, the R.F.D. carrier, standing there with his thick, quid-lumped face looking very glum, said, "Why, don't you all know what's going on? You'd ort to know what that derned Editor Ledbetter would do. Him and his bright ideas has jist doubled the work fer all of us. Jist go back to my desk there and see how many postal cards I picked up on my route today."

At that moment, Elvira Draper, who was getting ready to cancel and tie out the southbound mail, called out from the letter drop bin.

"Well, I wisht you'd lookie here! This letter drop is jist *stuffed!* Plumb *full* of mail!"

One by one the other R.F.D. carriers came straggling in, each bearing thick handfuls of outgoing mail.

Gladys and Elvira had to work hard to get all the

278

letters and postal cards canceled in time to catch the 5:45.

They did not have time to read *all* the postal cards, but those they read all said about the same thing. There were also a great many first-class letters enclosed in the brown, print-addressed envelopes of the mail order companies.

Postmaster Shannon and his clerks never knew what the letters said, but they guessed that these, too, like the postal cards, were scrawled,

GENTLEMEN: Would you all please send us another copy of your big Fall-and-Winter catalogue right away, as we want to order some things from you right away, and our other catalogue was made away with. . . .

This is the story behind this Catalogue . . . the expenditure of time and effort and millions of dollars. These labors have only one aim . . . to illustrate and describe our merchandise with absolute accuracy and truth, and by carrying this conviction to you, to win the privilege of serving you. . . . To serve you and satisfy you. . . .

279

Selected Bibliography

WORKS BY GEORGE MILBURN

BOOKS

Catalogue (New York: Harcourt, Brace and Co., Inc., 1936).
Flannigan's Folly (New York: Whittlesey House, McGraw-Hill Book Co., 1947).
Hoboes and Harlots (New York: Lion, 1954, paperback).
The Hobo's Hornbook (ed.) (New York: Ives Washburn, 1930).
Julie (New York: Lion Library, 1956).
No More Trumpets and Other Stories (New York: Harcourt, Brace and Co., Inc. 1933).
Oklahoma Town (New York: Harcourt, Brace and Co., Inc. 1931).

SHORT STORIES

"All My Love," *Esquire,* I (February, 1934), 42-43, 76.
"The Apostate," *New Yorker,* VIII (June 4, 1932), 15-16.
"Barbershop Blues," *Vanity Fair,* XXXIV (July, 1930), 38.
"Biography of a Prophet," *American Mercury,* XXVII (September, 1932), 83-91.
"By Moonlight," *Collier's,* XCV (June 15, 1935), 15.
"The Catalogues," *Harper's* CLXVII (August, 1933), 352-62.
"The Cowboy Sang Soprano," *Esquire,* XXII (April, 1944), 59.
"The Drummer's Shoes," *Story* III (June, 1933), 52-54.
"Fiddler's Choice," *Collier's* XCV (May 25, 1935), 24.
"The Fight at Hendryx's," *American Mercury,* XXV (February, 1932), 152-59.
"Fragments from Oklahoma," *Vanity Fair,* XXXIV (April, 1930) 78, 100. (Includes "Banker Brigham" and "Darling, Darling")
"From the Oklahoma Saga," *American Mercury,* XX (June, 1930), 185-91. (Includes "The Nigger Lover," "The Critic," "Earl

Abernathy," and "Hail and Farewell")
"A Hard Old Girl," *Vanity Fair*, XXXVI (March, 1931), 69.
"Heel, Toe, and a 1, 2, 3, 4," *American Mercury*, XXV (April,
    1932), 473-79.
"Honey Boy," *Collier's* XCIII (March 10, 1934), 24.
"How I Failed as a Farmer," *The Organic Farmer* (December,
    1950) 30, 59. Pseud. Ernest L. Forepaugh.
"Love Song," *Southwest Review*, XVII (October, 1931), 45-58.
"A Meeting of Minds," *Esquire*, XXIV (September, 1945), 39-41.
"Menace," *American Mercury*, XXV (March, 1932), 324-34.
"More from the Oklahoma Saga," *American Mercury* XX (July,
    1930), 345-52. (Includes "Those Seagrave Boys," "Soda-Water
    Green," "Mabel Barclay," and "Imogene Caraway")
"More Takes from Oklahoma," *American Mercury*, XVIII
    (December, 1929), 448-55. (Includes "Yellow Paint," "Looie
    McKindricks," "The Butcher, the Baker—" "Gerald Lee Cobb,"
    "Myrtle Birchett," and "The Baptist Christmas Tree")
"Mrs. Hopkins," *Vanity Fair*, XXXV (February, 1931), 47,90.
"Muncy Morgan," *Vanity Fair*, XXXV (January, 1931), 61,84.
"No More Trumpets," *American Mercury*, XXIV (December,
    1931), 421-29.
"Not on Speaking Terms," *Vanity Fair*, XXXV (September, 1930),
    67, 92.
"The Nude Waitress," *Vanity Fair*, XXXV (October, 1930),
    68, 110.
"Oklahoma Opera," *Folk-Say, A Regional Miscellaney* (The
    Oklahoma Folk-Lore Society, Norman 1929. Includes "The
    Taxi Talk" 108-112; "Pete Williams," "Beaulah Huber," and
    "The Holy Roller Elders" 115-119)
"Papa Was Foxy," *Collier's*, C (November 13, 1937), 43.
"Pilgrim's Progress," *American Mercury*, XXIX (August, 1933)
    488-98.
"Post Office Flag," *Esquire*, V (March, 1936), 90, 146, 149.
"A Pretty Cute Little Stunt," *American Mercury*, XXII (February,
    1931), 166-71.
"Revenge," *American Mercury*, XXVI (May, 1932), 105-13.
"The Road to Calamity," *Southern Review*, II (1936), 63-84.
"Sacrifice," *Esquire*, XXI (February, 1944), 73, 161.
"A Student in Economics," *Harper's*, CLXVI (February, 1933),
    265-78.
"Sugar Be Sweet!," *Harper's*, CLXVI (December, 1932), 11-19.

"Tales from Oklahoma," *American Mercury,* XVIII (November, 1929), 257-65. (Includes "The Contortionist's Wife," "Bill Hartshorn," The Nigger Doctor," "Hate," "Iron Filigree," "Willie Chalmers," and "Shorty Kilgore")
"Uneasy Payments," *Harper's,* CLXVIII (December, 1933), 26-37
"The Visit to Uncle Jake's," *Scribner's,* XCII (July, 1932), 19-24.
"White Meat," *American Mercury,* XXVIII (April, 1933), 401-07.
"The Wish Book," *Southern Review,* I (1935), 253-70.
"A Young Man's Chance," *Vanity Fair,* XXXIV (May, 1930), 56, 110.

ARTICLES

"The Appeal of Reason," *American Mercury,* XXIII (July, 1931), 359-71.
"Bolivia Bill," *Vanity Fair,* XXXVIII (May, 1932), 25,72.
"Catalogues and Culture," *Good Housekeeping,* CXXCII (April, 1946), 181-84.
"Circus Words," *American Mercury,* XXIV (November, 1931), 351-54.
"Convicts' Jargon," *American Speech,* VI (April, 1932), 436-42.
"A College Comic College in a Comic Opera State," *College Humor,* XXI (October, 1930) 66.
"Monroney of Oklahoma," *Nation,* CLXXVII (August 8, 1953). 110-12.
"Mr. Hoover's Stalking Horse," *American Mercury,* XXVI (July, 1932), 257-66.
"Murray, Possible but Not Likely," *Nation,* CXXXIV (April, 6 1932), 391-93.
"Oklahoma," *Yale Review,* XXXV (March, 1946), 515-26.
"Oklahoma, the OK State," *Vanity Fair,* XXXIX (January, 1933), 37, 56.
"Poesy in the Jungle," *American Literature,* XX (May, 1930), 80-86.
"Sage of Tishomingo," *American Mercury,* XXIII (May, 1931), 11-21.
"Sex, Sex, Sex and the World Crisis," *Nation,* CLXXVII (September 19, 1953), 230-31.
"Snakes: Guardians of the Granary," *The Organic Farmer* (July, 1951) 24, 50.

"Some Kind of Color: Notes on Being a Son," *Folk-Say,* IV
(Norman: University of Oklahoma Press, 1932), 29-42. (Among
these factural recollections and anecdotes Milburn includes
the story "Boy and Snake.")
"Statesmanship of Mr. Garner," *Harper's,* CLXVI (November,
1932), 669-82.

WORKS ABOUT GEORGE MILBURN

ANCOFF, CHARLES, *H. L. Mencken: A Portrait from Memory* (New
York: Thomas Yoseloff, Inc., 1956).
BASSO, HAMILTON, Review of *Catalogue, New Republic,*
LXXXVIII (October 7, 1936), 259.
BOTKIN, BEN A. *The Saga of George Milburn, unpublished
manuscript.*
CANTWELL, ROBERT, Review of *No More Trumpets and Other
Stories, New Republic,* LXXVI (October 18, 1933), 285.
Conquering Hobo - George Milburn, Vanity Fair XXXV No. 5,
(1931), p. 23.
FERCUSSON, HARVEY, Review of *Oklahoma Town, Books,* March 1,
1931, p.6.
GEHMAN RICHARD, "Hoping for a Revival," *Chicago Tribune
Books Today,* (October 23, 1966), p. 5.
*George Milburn, Writer, Dies; Best-Known for Short Stories,
New York Times,* (September 23, 1966), p. 37.
HERRON IMA HONAKER, *The Small Town in American Literature*
(Durham: Duke University Press, 1939).
JONES, HOWARD MUMFORD, Review of *Catalogue, Saturday
Review of Literature,* XIV, (September 12, 1936), 13.
LOWE R. L., Review of *No More Trumpets and Other Stories,
Nation,* CXXXVII (October 4, 1933), 386.
MARSH F. T., Review of *Catalogue, New York Times* (September
20, 1936), p. 6.
MCAFEE, HELEN, Review of *Catalogue, Yale Review* (Autumn 1936)
Oklahoma - A Guide to the Sooner State, WPA, (University of
Oklahoma Press, Norman, 1941), 85, 91.
Publisher Weekly, obituary, 190:43 (October 17, 1966).
SKILLEN, SAMUEL, Review of *Catalogue, Nation* (Oct. 17, 1936)
454.

SUGRUE, THOMAS, Review of *Flannigan's Folly, New York Herald Tribune Weekly Book Review.* (April 27, 1947), p. 16.

TURNER, STEVEN *George Milburn 1906-1966.* Southwest Writers Series 28, Steck-Vaughn Company, Austin, Texas, (1970), 42 pp.

UZZELL, THOMAS H., ed. *Short Story Hits— 1933* (New York: Harcourt, Brace and Company, Inc., 1934).

VAN DOREN, CARL, Review of *Catalogue, New York Herald Tribune* "Books" (Sept. 13, 1936)

VAN DOREN, MARK, Review of *Catalogue, Southern Review* (Jul 1937-Apr 1938) 171.

VESTAL, STANLEY, Review of *Oklahoma Town, Saturday Review of Literature,* VII (March 7, 1931), 643.

WINEBAUM B. V., Review of *Flannigan's Folly, New York Times,* (May 4, 1947), p. 14.

SHORT STORIES REPRINTED IN ANTHOLOGIES

"A Student in Economics" *(Harpers Magazine,* February, 1933)
Modern Short Stories, ed. Leonard Brown, Harcourt, Brace & Company (1937).

Here We Are, Dodd, Mead and Company (1941).

An English Reading Anthology, ed. William R. Wood, J. P. Lippincott (1949).

Stories for Youth, ed. A. H. Lass & Arnold Horowitz, Harper & Bros. (1950).

Twenty Grand Short Stories, ed. Ernestine Taggard, Bantam Books, (1st printing, Oct. 1947—32nd printing, Sept. 1984).

The College Years, ed. A. C. Spectorsky, Hawthorn Books, Inc. (1958).

Fifty Modern Short Stories, Row, Paterson & Co. - U.S. & Canada (1960).

The Writing Laboratory, ed. Burnham Carter, Dean Doner, Charles Green, Scott, Foresman & Company (1964).

Eighteen Stories, ed. Malcolm Ross and John Stevens, J. M. Dent and Sons, Ltd. Canada (1965).

20 Grand, Scholastic Book Services (1967).

Basic College Issues: Contemporary Stories and Essays, Random House (1969).

"The Apostate"   *(The New Yorker,* June 4, 1932)
    The Best Short Stories of 1933, ed. E. J. O'Brien, Houghton-
    Mifflin Co. (1933).
    Short Stories from The New Yorker, Simon and Schuster
    (1940).
    Modern Short Stories, ed. R. B. Heilman, Harcourt Brace &
    Co. (1950).
    50 Great Short Stories. ed. Milton Crane, Bantam Books
    (1952) —46th printing 1983.
    Short Stories from The New Yorker Victor Gollanz, London
    (1952).
    The American Century, ed. Maxim Lieber, Panther Books
    (Paul List edition Leipzig) - (1955).
    Ideas for Writing, Kenneth Knickerbocker, Henry Holt &
    Co. (1956).
    Readings for Communication, Western Michigan University
    (1959).
    Writing from Experience, ed. Richard A. Condon & Burton
    O. Kurth, Harper & Bros. (1960).
    Interpretation, Writer Reader Audience, ed. Wilma H.
    Grimes & Althea Smith Mattingly, Wadsworth Publishing
    Company (1961).
    The Family Tree Book, World Publishing Company (1967).
    People and Things, ed. James E. Heltsley, Wm. C. Brown
    Book Company (1968).
    Teaching the Universe of Discourse, ed. James Moffett,
    Houghton Mifflin Co. (1969).

"A Pretty Cute Little Stunt"   *(The American Mercury,* Feb. 1931)
    The Best Short Stories of 1931, ed. E. J. O'Brien, Dodd,
    Mead & Co. (1931).
    50 Best American Short Stories, ed. E. J. O'Brien.
    These Were Our Years, ed. Frank Brookhauser, Doubleday
    & Co. (1959).

"All My Love"   *(Esquire,* February, 1934)
    Stories for Men, ed. Charles Grayson, Garden City
    Publishing Co. (1944).

"American Joke Book"
    Folk-Say IV ed. B. A. Botkin, University of Oklahoma Press,
    (1932).

"Boy and Snake"
  Folk-Say, IV, ed. B. A. Botkin University of
    Oklahoma Press (1932).

"Captain Choate"   *(The American Mercury,* 1930)
  Southwesterners Write, ed. T. M. Pearce & A. P. Thomason,
    The University of New Mexico Press (1946).

"The Catalogues"   *(Harpers,* August, 1933)
  Short Story Hits, an International Anthology, ed. Thomas
    H. Uzzell, Harcourt, Brace & Co. (1934).
  Perspectives, ed. Leonard F. Dean, Harcourt, Brace & Co.
    (1954).

"The Cowboy Sang Soprano"   *(Esquire,* April, 1944)
  A Caravan of Music Stories, ed. Noah Fabricant & Heinz
    Werner, Frederick Fell, Inc. (1947).

"Fiddler's Choice"   *(Collier's,* May 25, 1935)
  The Best Short Stories from Collier's, ed. Barthold Fles,
    World Publishing Co. (1948).

"Heel, Toe, and a 1,2,3,4," *(The American Mercury,* April 1932)
  The Best Short Stories of 1932, ed. E. J. O'Brien, Dodd,
    Mead & Co. (1932)
  This Is Chicago, ed. Albert Halper, Henry Hall & Co. (1952).

"Honey Boy"   *(Collier's,* March 10, 1934)
  An Ozark Anthology, ed. Vance Randolph, The Caxton
    Printers, Ltd. (1940).

"Imogene Caraway"   *(The American Mercury,* July 1930)
  Roundup Time, ed. George Sessions Perry, Whittlesey
    House (1943).
  Southwest Writers Anthology, ed. Martin Shockley,
    Steck-Vaughn Co. (1967).

"Oklahoma Opera"
  Folk-Say, ed. B. A. Botkin, University of Oklahoma Press,
    (1929)

"Some Kinds of Color: Notes on Being a Son"
  Folk-Say IV, ed. B. A. Botkin, University of Oklahoma Press,
    (1932).

"Tales from Oklahoma:"
"Iron Filigree" *(The American Mercury,* 1930).
"Yellow Paint" *(The American Mercury,* December, 1929).
"Those Seagrave Boys" *(The American Mercury,* July, 1930)
    The American Mercury Reader, ed. Lawrence E.
    Spivak & Charles Angoff, The Blakiston Company (1944).
"The Taxi Talk"
    Folk-Say, ed. B. A. Botkin, University of Oklahoma Press,
    (1929).
"Uneasy Payments"   (Harpers, December, 1933)
    Literature and Life, ed. Miles, Stratton Pooley, Greenlaw,
    Scott, Foresman & Co. (1936).
    Our Reading Heritage, ed. Wagenheim, Brattig, Dolkey,
    Henry Holt & Co. (1956).

"The Wish Book   *(The Southern Review,* Autumn, 1935)
    Approach to Literature, ed. Cleanth Brooks, Jr., John Purser,
    Robert Penn Warren, F. S. Crofts & Co. (1946 14th ed.)
    Stories from The Southern Review, ed. Cleanth Brooks, Jr. &
    Robert Penn Warren, Louisiana State University Press
    (1953).
    Short Story Anthology Louisiana State University Press, U.S.
    & Canada (1953).
    Short Stories: University of Texas at Arlington, Wadsworth,
    Publishing Co. (1967).

A Treasury of American Anecdotes, ed. B. A. Botkin, Random
    House, (1957).
    Anecdotes from: "Wishes & Horses," "Mule Egg," "The
    Biggest Liar in McDonald Country," "The Smart
    Sow," "The Talking Heifer," "Grandpa & the Benzine,"
    "Figuring Relationships."